People Like You

Yurell Benítez Borrego

Edited by Theo Parsonson

Layout by : Amparo Alegre Calpe

ISBN: 9798852299352

DEDICATION

Every person that comes into our lives, whether they stay or leave, is there for a reason. And sometimes, those reasons are hard to understand or accept. But there's always a lesson to be learned, and this book is a beautiful expression of self-love that can help us find that lesson. If you're going through a difficult time, know that you're not alone. This story is for you, and it's a reminder that you are deserving of love and compassion – both from yourself and from others. So take a deep breath, and know that you can get through this. And remember, every person that comes into your life is there for a reason – even if that reason is just to remind you of your own strength and resilience.

Contenido

ACKNOWLEDGMENTS

I just wanted to take a moment to express my heartfelt gratitude for your unwavering support and encouragement throughout my book writing journey. Theo, your feedback and guidance have been invaluable in giving my book the structure and direction it needed. Your friendship has been a beacon of light in my life, and I am truly grateful for all that you've done.

Aunty, your calls and tarot readings have kept me going during the tough times. Your love and support mean the world to me, and I will forever cherish your kindness.

To all the people of my past who inspired me to write this amazing story, I am grateful for your influence and inspiration. Your impact on my life will always be remembered.

Thank you all from the bottom of my heart!

CHAPTER 1

´I can't believe in two days my life is going to change,´ I thought while I tried to find the last pieces of my stuff to put in the suitcase. Amsterdam; I've never been, but we decided to go there for a particular reason. We were in Poland, and I was finishing my internship for my hospitality high school course. In the beginning, it sounded like fun, but as soon as I got there, I felt sad and anxious, so I asked my boyfriend Ernesto to stay with me for a couple of weeks. I didn't believe I could deal with it by myself.

A couple of weeks ended up being three months living together and sharing a house: it was nice to have him there. I wasn't feeling so alone: he was there, supporting me and being away from his family to stay with me. Such a romantic thing to do for someone.

As soon as we met, he knew that I didn't want to live in Spain, so the conversation about where we were going to live was on the table, waiting to be taken. The first option for me was the UK: ´No, I don't like the UK,´ Ernesto said, with very determined words.

´But why? I lived there when I was eighteen for three months, and it was a fantastic experience that changed my life!´ I said, trying to convince him.

´It's too big, too busy. I don't want to go there,´ He said, looking at me with that serious face (which meant that we were going to do precisely what he said, with no chance to talk about it further). I still remember a fight we had in the middle of Krakow because it was a really cool city, and I thought it could be great to give it a chance and live there. It was HILARIOUS, the way that we had a fight before visiting St. Mary's Basilica because his decision was already made.

´We're not going to live here. I don't like Poland; I don't like the people, and I don't speak the language. And to be honest, I have no intention of learning it, either,´ he said, cutting off all possibilities and my emotions at that moment, even though I wasn't really thinking seriously about living there. It was just how his voice sounded when those words came out of his mouth.

So a very empathetic argument, like always. But getting back to why we chose Amsterdam. It was silly: we had a couple of options and Amsterdam was one of them. We just decided to move there because Amsterdam won Eurovision that year: the universe was moving our lives there. And so that where I found myself. Preparing everything to start my new life with Ernesto in the Netherlands.

We'd been together for a year, and even if we´d had a lot of fights and breakups, we always ended up together again. But I was always clear with him that staying in Cádiz was not an option, so if he didn't want to leave the country and move away together, the relationship would be done.

Ernesto had a skinny body, with brown hair and eyes. He was six years older than me, but sometimes he didn't act his age, and he could be really childish.

I went to the kitchen because I fancied some chat with my Mum to take my mind off the mess of the suitcases. ´I'm scared´ I told her while she was preparing some croquetas and fried mushrooms that tasted similar to fried chicken. She stopped what she was doing to give her attention to me.

´Of course you are. You´re taking a really a big step, and I've always wanted to have as many adventures as you´ve already had, and you're only nineteen! But I was stuck here; you were a child, and there were so many things going on. I tried to do my best to survive and keep food on the table for us. You were always my priority. But you've already done it, my beautiful boy. Remember the summer of 2018, when you went by yourself to London with 800€ and two huge suitcases. You were so happy, and it was the best summer of your life,´ my Mum said, touching my face with her soft right hand.

´Now it's a bit different, though; I'm not alone this time,´ I said. ´Aiden, I was also scared when your father and I married. I wanted to do it because I was in love with him, even though we had a huge fight the night before our wedding. And look how that all ended. Adults don't know anything; we just pretend that we do. For that reason, many relationships go wrong; in my case, it ended in divorce. Whatever you do, you're young, and you have time to make mistakes,´ she said, choosing her words carefully, trying not to stir up the shit from the past.

´Well, Mom, I'm not sure if this is helping or making me want to run away!´ I said. We both started to laugh until we realised the food was burning. Mum sprinted to turn the stove off, but the food was utterly ruined. All because we've been discussing the success of being in a relationship and getting married. Funny.

My phone started to buzz. I had a message from Ernesto. We messaged back and forth for a while:

Ernesto: Hey baby, how are you doing? Did you finish packing your things already?'

Aiden: Hey darling, I'm a bit stressed. I have so many clothes, and I want to take them all, but they won´t all fit. My Mum was cooking lunch, but we got distracted chatting, and everything burned 😊

Ernesto: Oh! Haha, that's a shame, I had the same problem with my clothes, but I decided to pack the basics, and if I need something, I'll get it when we're there.

Aiden: Yeah, you're right. Maybe I shouldn't worry that much about it... it's just that I'm not sure when we'll come back again.

Ernesto: I bet it'll be very soon. You know I love my family and friends. Even though they may visit us, I always want to be able to come back, the sooner the better for me.

Aiden: Yeah, I guessed so.

Ernesto: Are you coming for dinner later with my family? You know how much they like you and they want to spend some time with you before we go.

Aiden: Yeah, sounds good to me. I'll buy a nice bottle of wine. I know your mom loves it!

Ernesto: You know how to make them happy ;)

Aiden: See you later, baby.

I went back to my room to recheck everything in case I forgot something. I looked inside the closet for my Fenty Creepers shoes; they´re black with the blue suede. I found a shoe box, but it was covered in tape, like it didn't want to be opened. Intrigued, I grabbed the scissors and made a cut to open the mysterious box.

Old pictures, old letters. Presents from my ex-boyfriend Marcos.

I rifled through the pictures. We looked very cute together, but unfortunately, it ended in the most dramatic and chaotic way. Still looking through the box, I found a Nirvana CD, 'Smells like Teen Spirit', that he gave me for my 16th birthday.

Suddenly I started to feel a rush of memories; my heart started to pound faster, and the anxiety began to rise, filling up my whole self. I closed the box with all my anxious energy and put it back where it was, at the back of the closet.

´I'm so stupid; why did I open it?´ I thought. I guess I hadn't left the past behind, and I must have wanted to remember still all the pain and suffering I had with Marcos.

´Aiden! Lunch is finally ready! And it's not burned!´ Mum called from the kitchen, raising her voice so she didn't have to move from there.

Breathe in, breathe out. It's not worth it. This is the present, and he's part of the past. He's not coming back.

I went to the bathroom and washed my face in the sink with cold water to chill out all the demons of my toxic love with him, remembering my sad youth.

´Aiden! The food is going to get cold! Come on. Bring some wine as well, darling.´ She approached the table, placing the plates like a waitress, holding as many things simultaneously as she could.

I went to the kitchen to get the bottle opener, uncorked the bottle of red wine and poured some for my Mum first.

The food tasted amazing; she's just so great. I don't know how she can deal with doing so many things at the same time. Sometimes, she looks like a robot, but she's happy with her routine.

´Thank you for making lunch, Mum, it's delicious. You know how much I love your food,´ I babbled. ´Of course, darling. I'll not be there to prepare this every day, so now you'll need to do it yourself until I come to visit you,´ she smiles at me. ´Yeah, well, you know that I have a good hand in the kitchen, even though I'm a bit lazy,´ I said, wiping my mouth with the white napkin next to the plate. ´I'm sure you're going to be great, Aiden, but I know you, and something is telling me that your mind is somewhere else at the moment,´ she replied.

´I found a box with pictures and memories inside,´ I said, looking melancholic.

´Let me guess, it's about Marcos?´ Detective Emma had arrived. She always picks up every single detail, and of course, she was there during those painful years of the relationship, so as soon as Marco's name was mentioned, there was an uncomfortable feeling around the table. ´Yes, I got anxious as soon as I opened it, so I left it where it was. I don't want to know any more about it´.

´It's been two years already, and you need to let that go. The past is dead, Aiden, and now you're with Ernesto, and you can tell he's in love with you. Just think how nice he was to stay in Poland, spending those months with you,´ she said.

´Well, it's not like he had something more interesting to do: he was watching tv or hanging out with his friends. He wasn't working. But I did appreciate it, and not many people would do the same for me,´ I said, realising that what she was saying was true.

´Be gentle with him; you know he's not my cup of tea, but you decided to be with him, and you need to appreciate the good things´ She took my hand to reassure me. ´Yes, you're right,´ I replied.

I finished cleaning the dishes and tidying up the table; I needed a nap. It was an intense conversation with my Mum.

CHAPTER 2

I fastened the silver button of my tight black jeans and put my pink t-shirt on. I sprayed some 'One Million' fragrance on my neck, and I made my way to Ernesto´s.

It was fifteen degrees and a bit windy: the weather was annoying me and the road was uphill. I reached the town feeling sweaty and flustered. Passing by Sacramento Park, I found myself in the centre of San Fernando. I turned right and went straight to the supermarket that was seven minutes away from his house.

It was freezing in the supermarket, and I found my body immediately cooled from all the heat and sweating as soon as I stepped inside. There were so many different varieties of wine and I checked all the different ones on the shelves, loving their distinctive colours and shapes. I decided to pick up one called 'Judas' Blood'. Of course, I didn't forget to get some black pepper and lemon crisps. Some people might think that sounds disgusting, but I find them tasty and sour.

'It´s 5.95€ please,´ said the cashier, clearly just waiting for it to be 10 P.M. to finish her shift. Probably to go to her house, wake up and repeat the same routine. I paid with some spare coins that I had.

It was time to get ready for dinner and for some reason, I was feeling a bit anxious. Maybe I was still upset about the shoebox. 'It's going to be okay,´ I reassured myself. My mother-in-law Carmen had always been super friendly and close to me;

I had to say that I liked her a lot, and I felt very comfortable with her.

I finally reached the building where Ernesto and his family lived. I pressed the button for number 19.

´Who´s this?´ asked Carmen from the other side. ´Meeeee Mummy in-law!´ I shouted, making some funny noises. ´You silly cow, come upstairs,´ she laughed with her sweet voice, opening the door.

I went to the elevator, feeling too lazy to take the stairs; I couldn't be assed.

Floor 9.

I waited patiently in the small lift, feeling the gravity of each floor passing by.

The doors opened, and Ernesto was waiting for me out in the corridor with a smile. ´Hello baby!´ he said, kissing me on the lips, tasting like Marlboro. ´Hey!´ I replied. ´You´re all right?´. ´Not bad, It was dull today, waiting for you, coming late as always´ Ernesto said, reproaching my lateness, while his eyes went straight to the wine. ´You know me, I do my best´ I laughed. ´Let´s go inside; they´re excited to see you,´ he said, inviting me to come in with a slight movement of his hand.

I closed the door and went to the kitchen where Carmen and Rosario were.

They both turned and hugged me. ´Finally here! So lovely to see you,´ Rosario said, wearing her soft, green pyjamas, looking like she had a lazy one. Well, it's not like she did a lot in general. ´Yes, honestly, I thought I would melt down in the street. It´s so humid out there´ I said, drinking a glass of water straight down.

´Well, shall we open that beautiful wine that I saw you brought and maybe have a cigarette?´ Carmen asked, gesturing for me to open the wine and pour some for her and Ernesto.

They both smoked heavily, and Rosario hated it, but she wanted to be part of the conversation. She had an opinion on everything, so she stayed.

There was a mix of smells in the kitchen: first, fried potatoes with eggs; second, the cheese in the middle of the table; third, the cigarettes and last but not least, the sweet wine. It´s one of my favourites: a Spanish red wine but sweet, so it´s effortless to drink and get drunk on as well.

´So, Aiden, did you look for any jobs in Amsterdam yet?´ said Carmen inhaling the smoke from her cigarette. ´Yes, I´ve been sending my CVs, and this morning I received a call from a big-name hotel. They want to interview me as soon as I get there!´ I got excited just thinking about it. ´That´s amazing! Sounds exciting! What about you, son?´ She was looking for a connection with him, looking desperately for nice words from her son. Sometimes it felt like he'd forgotten how to be a son. Instead, he had the attitude of someone's husband from the ´70s when he was in the house: always expecting to be in control. ´I´ve been looking, but I haven´t seen anything interesting,´ Ernesto said, with the cigarette in his right hand. ´Darling, you know I´ll help you with that!´ I said to him, holding his hand from the other side of the table, reassuring him. ´I know, let´s enjoy the food at the moment.´ He cut the conversation there. I guessed he didn't want to talk more about looking for a job in Amsterdam, and that seemed fair enough to me. Maybe he was very used to living a comfortable life and not working.

We started to eat the fried potatoes with the fried egg. The extra virgin olive oil makes a real difference in the food. It's the perfect flavour. I ate some small pieces of cheese and drank the last drops of wine.

´Thank you for the food Mom, it was nice,´ Rosario said, touching her hair and looking at Instagram at all times. ´Yes, Carmen. It was lovely, thank you!´ I said as well.

´My pleasure, it´s our last dinner together until Christmas! But now you know what´s next. Ernesto, Rosario, time to clean everything.

Aiden, you stay here with me for a chat,´ she said with a cheeky smile and winked her left eye at me, opening the cigarette box to offer me one. I lit it up and relaxed.

´Do you know that girl that was in my class?´ Ernesto asked while he was placing the plates inside the dishwasher. ´The one that was a bit crazy?´replied Rosario.

´Yes, today I´ve been talking with my friends, and they can´t deal with her anymore. They said she´s reaching a point where she wants attention and will try to kill herself, so she can see how worried we all will be in hospital for her but they think no one will go,´ he said, smirking. Ernesto´s friends were all about drama and gossiping; you can tell they were lovely people to have around. ´That´s awful! How can they say something like that? ´said Carmen, looking confused because of her son's friends. But in the end, whatever she said, Ernesto would not let her have an opinion. If he wanted to bring them over, her opinion didn't matter.

´I know but it is not my business at all. I don´t care, you know, sometimes they say that kind of thing,´ he said, trying to excuse his friends disgusting words. ´Poor girl, you know, I've known her for years, and it´s so sad to hear this from her. Maybe she needs someone to help her with her mental health problems.´ Carmen was trying to have empathy with the situation. Still, in that house she was the only one with any knowledge of that simple but significant word. ´We´re leaving in two days, so it will be easier to have her far away. All this drama is draining me a bit, and I don´t care about her so...,´ he said. Such kind and respectful words, proving what a nice person he was.

Ernesto and Rosario finished cleaning the kitchen, and we all moved to the living room. The air-conditioning was on, and it was very cool in there. ´Aiden, I´m happy you´re taking this next step together. You know I´m going to miss my baby boy a lot, but it´s the best decision for his future,´ Carmen said, touching Ernesto´s face. He looked disgusted, quickly getting away from her hands, avoiding any physical touch. ´Yeah, I´m excited as well, and my Mum feels the same. She´s going to miss me a lot, but it´s not my first time moving to a different country so it´ll be alright,´ I said, confident in my decision. ´Since Ernesto met you, he's changed. Before, he wasn´t nice to us and spent more time in his room. Now he´s less unfriendly.´ Carmen was trying to show me her gratitude with those words, looking at me with bright eyes. Behind them, there seemed to be a massive weight of sadness.´Mom, can you stop? I don´t want you to be talking about my shit,´ Ernesto said, looking at her with a nasty face. I could feel how he started to get pissed about it but I didn´t under why he reacted in that way, it seemed so unnecessary. ´It´s okay, baby, she's not saying anything wrong about you,´ I said, trying to calm him down. ´I don´t care. I don´t want to have this conversation,´ he said, already annoyed but without much reason.

I looked at Carmen: her brows were knitted together in a frown. I could feel her disappointment, but she was so used to it that nothing could hurt her. People get used to being treated like that and think they deserve it or that nothing could change.

´Shall we watch a movie?´ Rosario said, trying to defuse the tension. ´Sounds good, but I think I might go home. I want to spend some time with my Mum as well´ I had the perfect but real excuse to get the fuck out of there.

I gave everyone a hug, and I left the house as soon as I could. Too much: I had fun but preferred not to be in the way when Ernesto started with that attitude.

PEOPLE LIKE YOU

.

CHAPTER 3

It's 10 P.M. when I left Ernesto's flat; I put my headphones on, feeling like I needed to listen to something. I scrolled through the list and found the perfect song, ´Ocean Eyes´ by Billie Eilish. The song's melody started to invade the space of my whole body as I made my way home. I could feel the breeze on my naked arms, but it was not that bad; actually, it helped because I tend to walk fast, so I get sweaty. I had a strange feeling, like a pressure in my chest, like a bad vibe; I didn't know what it was, so I tried to focus on the music to help me to disconnect. It's a beautiful song with a bit of sadness, but the remix had something that I felt connected to. Here I am again, talking to myself and focusing on the music's lyrics and melody to ignore my thoughts and feelings, nothing new. Why is Ernesto like that with his family? I keep walking down the street, pretty dead, but there are still some young lads. It wasn´t the first time he has had a strange attitude toward his family.

Maybe I was just feeling anxious, but I started to remember when Rosario had a boyfriend, and Ernesto had has cards marked from day one; the guy was indeed useless, and she deserved more, but Ernesto didn't even hide his feelings and ignored him, was rude to him, and tried to tell Rosario to leave the relationship. She got annoyed about it, but they finally broke up. I know that when Ernesto came back from

Poland, just a couple of weeks before me, to be there for Rosario's graduation, he realised that she failed most of the subjects and needed to do like five exams in September or she would not get her high school diploma. He was so, so angry with her. He went for a week without even looking at her, disapproving of her actions and trying not to let her out of the house. I tried to speak with him because I knew how tense it feels to have his anger and disappointment directed towards you. He was outraged, but I said to him, ´you're her brother, not the father. That's not your position, and even though she failed, it's her problem. You need to support her to try to get it done for September. But if you control her actions, she will hold that against you.´ At least that helped a bit, but his face was a poem, even with that.

How long have I been overthinking? I'm already at my house.

I went inside, and Luna, my Mums Yorkshire terrier started to bark more and more; as always, she's a little bitch that loves attention, but at the same time, I tolerated her.

´How was the dinner? ´ Mum said, laying on the sofa with the T.V. on in her pyjamas, with natural flavour crisp in a bowl, next to a small glass of wine. ´Was all right, I was feeling a bit tired, and I wanted to spend a bit more time with you, so I didn't sleep over there,´ I said, taking my shoes off. She smiles at me and starts to spread cream for cellulitis on her legs, it has a powerful eucalyptus smell. It's just her thing to do before going to sleep. ´What are we up to then?´ She said, while the cream reaches every single part of her thighs. ´Shall we watch something on T.V?´ I said. ´Whatever you like, son, but nothing horror; you know I'm not too fond of it,´ she said, begging with her eyes not to see anything gory or scary. It's funny because when I was a child, and it was me and her, she spent time with me, and one thing I will never forget is when we played horror games on the PlayStation 2 and went to the cinema together to watch that kind of genre. With time this has changed, and now she hates it, but it was a good memory. We spent the rest of the evening watching this gossip tv program about celebrities' secrets; it was total crap, but very entertaining. ´It's midnight already, darling. I can't deal with my soul. I'm going to sleep.´ She cames close to me, hugged me, and kissed me on the cheek. Luna started barking again; jealous bitch. ´I love you´ My Mum said with a tender voice. ´Love you, Mom, goodnight.´ I filled my bottle of water, lay down on the bed, and hid under the thin sheets.

The tossing and turning started: one round, another round. What's going on? Am I nervous because I'm moving away again? I didn't have this kind of feeling before. Is this the right decision? Why has Ernesto got that attitude sometimes? After too much thinking for the day, I went into the kitchen and swallowed a 5mg tranxilium that I found in the cupboard, hoping that would help me sleep.

PEOPLE LIKE YOU

CHAPTER 4

After having some issues with sleep the night before, it felt cosy in bed; I could have slept for ages. Suddenly I heard something, "buk, buk, buk, ba´gawk!!" Oh my fucking god, my neighbour´s fucking chickens again. Every single damn day was the same; it´s so odd to have chickens in such a small place and annoying to others. I checked the phone—7:00 A.M. Oh lord. I woke up from bed a bit sleepy and went straight to the toilet. I washed my face with cold water to feel alive but I was still anxious.

I opened the kitchen door in silence, so Luna didn´t start barking, trying not to wake up my Mum. ´What are you doing awake so early, Aiden?´ My Mum said behind me with messy hair, taking my heart to the edge (and not of glory). ´Fucking Jesus!´ I jumped and accidentally gave a small scream. ´Mom! How often have I told you not to come up behind me in silence like that?´ I say with my right hand touching my chest, feeling my heartbeat racing. ´Sorry, it wasn´t my intention, I just heard the door, and I didn´t have my contact lenses in,´ she said, still a bit sleepy with half of her head in the clouds.

Luna started to scratch the door; of course, she wanted to go to the backyard to have a shit; I´d do the same if I was her. My Mum opened the door, and Luna ran so fast outside. ´Would you like something for breakfast?´ asked my Mum, starting to clean last night's dirty dishes. How come she always does that as soon as she wakes up, without even having a coffee? It´s so noisy. ´I´ll prepare the coffee and you do the breakfast,´ I replied, trying to avoid making much effort in the very early morning.

After some preparation, we sat at the round wooden table in the living room. I always hated those chairs; they were pretty uncomfortable but expensive. ´I forgot to bring the napkins and the sugar with me. Do you mind?´ she asked with a sweet voice after the first sip of the coffee. ´Of course not.´ It´s so funny, she always forgets it.

Smells so nice, just having toasted bread with extra virgin olive oil, smashed avocados and sliced tomatoes, an orange juice from the bottle and a watery coffee. ´I´m going to miss this, Mom,´ I say, looking at her while I chew all the food. ´I know, but you can always prepare it for yourself, my darling.´ Those simple words made me realise that someday I´d need to, and although leaving is good for my freedom, it´s sad for my inner child. ´I know, but you know how much I do like it when I feel taken care of.´ I think I expected to have this feeling forever, of being unique, of being someone´s priority. ´I´m always going to be here for you to prepare as much food as you want, beautiful,´ my Mum said, holding my hand next to me, followed by the last sip of the watery coffee. ´By the way, don´t forget that we´re meeting your grandma and your aunt at 2:00 p.m., so we will need to leave here around 1:30 p.m., you know that sometimes there´s traffic and I don´t want to be late´. She knew what she was doing and knew me well enough too: I can be slow and late.´Okay, Mum.´ After finishing breakfast and tidying up, I decided to go for a walk by myself.

I put my trackies on and started my playlist, a bit moody this time. Songs of "La oreja de van goh" begin to play; there´s nothing more typical of Spanish pop culture than that band. I was walking through Barrero park and listening to those songs. I stopped in front of a seat surrounded by trees and grass. My first kiss with Marcos was there; I was 15 and he was 16: he was terrified, as apparently, he was straight, but when I checked his profile on Instagram, he was a massive fan of Rihanna, so after a couple of weeks texting each other, he told me that he wanted to try it, he watched Orange is the New Black and felt inspired by the lesbians. So after a couple of times meeting him, it was one evening in July when we kissed, and we fell in love.

Oh fuck, again. Not again. I decided to leave that park and have a walk somewhere else. Honestly, one part of myself was happy to leave San Fernando as I had a difficult time there in high school, being depressed, and then with Marcos. After the walk, I went to the bathroom and took a shower. I put the speaker on with loud reggaeton music to cheer up my vibe and danced a bit; god, I hope I do not break my face in the shower. I put some cream on my face to get hydrated and checked my outfit: black jeans with a blue shirt that had some white birds on it. ´Aiden, time to go!´ called my Mum from the other side of the house; I guess she is starting to get nervous because we were not already in the car. ´Coming!´

.

CHAPTER 5

My Mum drove us to visit my Grandma; I sat beside her in the car. One thing I love about being in the car is the fact that I can choose the music; this time, I chose the soundtrack of ´Mamma Mia. It's one of my favourite movies. I stared out the window, taking in the surrounding busy environment. Almost there, my Mum turned to the left. The road was in terrible condition, and the car was jumping all over the place. ´BEEP BEEP!´ She pressed the horn so my Grandma could open the door. My Grandma locked the dogs in the backyard, and the door slid to the left.

Once we were inside, I got out of the car. My Grandma was waiting at the patio door in a comfortable outfit for hanging around the house. ´Hello, handsome! You look lovely,´ said my Grandma, coming closer to hug me. My Grandma is the kind of woman that you can tell is peculiar. She was 65 at the time, but honestly, still so pretty. Blonde, with a ponytail and blue/green eyes. When I was a child, I remember brushing her hair a lot; she always had long hair like Rapunzel. ´Thanks, you as well, Granny,´ I said back to her. My Mum got closer and gave her a kiss on the cheek. ´You're on time!´ my Granny said. My Grandma believed in punctuality: my Mum believed in keeping my Grandma happy and being the perfect daughter. ´Where's my sister?´ Mum asked, knowing the answer already. ´Late, you know,´ she said back to her. They laughed together, with a bitchy edge. You can tell they're mother and daughter. Still, at the same time, my Mum is a bit different to her. My Grandma tends to judge more and analyse every single action in the surrounding conversation, so she can get information later to ask questions, like if we were being interrogated by the FBI. ´C'mon let's get inside; the food is almost done.´ Grandma went inside and moved quickly to the kitchen to check that nothing was burning. We stepped inside the corridor, and a heavy and delicious smell impacted my nose. I bet she had been working all morning in the kitchen preparing food. It´s her passion: she was a chef in a care home for many years, and also she's vegetarian, so she taught my mother different recipes to cook for me. ´Smells amazing!´ I exclaimed, getting excited about the lunch. ´Prepare yourself because I prepared a lot of food.´ If she's said that, it means that I'm about to put on another five kilos, like always. She doesn't stop feeding until you can't take any more. ´Mum, do you need help with anything?´ asked my Mum, trying to give a hand. ´Start taking the plates and the cutlery to the living room; Aiden, you can take the glasses and the lemonade I´ve prepared.´ We took everything to the table when suddenly we heard something from the outside. A car horn sounded ´BEEP BEEP!´ followed by a familiar voice: ´MUUUUUUM! I´M HEEERE!´ And there she was, Aunty Mimi making her remarkable entrance. We all jumped, as no one expected such a piercing loud shout. My grandma pressed the button, and the doors opened automatically. Aunty parked the car and got out. She was wearing a black coat with a red shirt, oversized trousers and high boots. ´Hi, everyone!´ Aunty said, dropping her cigarette outside of the house. She stepped inside, smelling of exotic perfume and cigarettes. ´Hello, daughter. You were really loud outside; you almost gave me a heart attack.´ my Grandma said coldly. ´I was calling and texting, but no one replied, so for that reason, I had to use this fantastic strong voice that is the gift of this family,´ my Aunty shot back. ´Please, next time, wait because I don't want the neighbours to think that we're a crazy, low-class family here,´ sniffed my Grandma in response. Of course, I forgot to mention that my grandma is a bit classist. She's not a bad person. Still, I found it best not to get into any political discussions with her: her views on things are very different to mine, as I found out when she told me that she didn´t think transgendered people should have surgery that was paid for with taxpayer´s money. But let´s not get into that. ´Anyway, Aideeeeen! Come here, my beautiful nephew!´ She gave me two kisses on the cheeks and a big hug. ´Alright! Food is ready. Help me with this. Aiden, you can wait in the living room.´ After one minute, they all started bringing the food to the table. Literally, she hadn´t lied about the huge amount of food. They started placing different bowls and pans on the table. My Grandma uncovered all the rest of the food. ´Okay, so everyone takes some of everything; I've been busy all morning preparing this, and no one leaves until it's done,´ Grandma said, with a commanding tone. So: we had some couscous with almonds, chickpeas, the essence of curry and cumin, and some raisins. There was also a zucchini lasagna with cheddar, parmesan, tomato sauce, bechamel and basil from her garden in another bowl. And last but not least, marinated tofu with seaweed and Morrocan spices. ´So Emma, how are you doing? Is everything with Ricardo alright?´ Aunty Mimi asked my Mum, trying to get some conversation going with her and, of course, wanting to know if something was going on. My Mum took a big sip of the homemade lemonade that my Granny had prepared. ´Yes, thanks for asking. Everything is well, like always. What about your husband?´ my Mum replied, trying to move the question back to her. ´He's alright. You know, working and playing the console. It sounds like I'm talking about my son; unfortunately, I´m not,´ Aunty Mimi replied. I could see how my Grandma was trying hard to look like she was only focussed on devouring the food but I knew that she was actually listening hard to every detail, desperate to get the gossip – that woman has the ears of a bat. ´Oh my god, Grandma, this is delicious,´ I said, tasting every single flavour of the food.

´It tastes incredible, Mum; I can't eat a lot though I'm on my diet,´ Aunty Mimi said.

´Oh, no way: here, you have some more.´ She started to serve even more portions to everyone while we looked across the table at each other, knowing that we would be sick of eating that much.

´So, Aiden, do you already have a place to stay when you get to Amsterdam?´ Aunty Mimi asked. ´Yes, we´ve rented an Airbnb room for a week; I think that will be enough time to find something,´ I said, sipping the lemonade. ´Only a week? But isn´t Amsterdam a difficult city to rent in?´ Grandma asked me while she still had food in her mouth. ´Yes, but I trust we'll find something soon, as I also have my interview in the hotel, so if everything goes well, we shouldn't have any problem,´ I said, more confidently than I felt. ´Has Ernesto arranged any interviews as well?´ my Mum asked, curious about it. ´Not really, but I'm crossing my fingers that he will get something soon.´ ´Well, you know, you have that money that you saved from when you lived in London, and the rest we're going to help you out between the three of us,´ Mum said, sending me love from the other side of the table. They all looked at each other, smiled and agreed. ´Anything for you, Aiden, we don't have much money, but if you need a bit of help, we'll do as much as we can.´ Aunty Mimi said. ´Honestly, I don't have words. I feel very grateful for this. I couldn't do it if it wasn't because of you all,´ I said. ´You deserve it, Aiden. And we will always be here to support you. We love you,´ my Mum said. ´Always, you know that but don't say anything to any of your other aunts. We don't want to create unnecessary drama. You know how they are,´ Grandma said, almost like taking a vow of silence at that square table full of plates. And this was the truth; they were always the part of the family I've been more connected to. The rest of the family is a bit peculiar. ´I love you all.´ I said to them.

After 20 minutes of letting the food go down, I picked up all the plates while my mother and my aunty took the rest to the kitchen. ´Alright, now the dessert,´ Grandma said, knowing what she was doing. We were going to end up in the hospital; this amount of food was insane. She made an Arabic tea with brown sugar, green tea and mint. It´s my favourite. ´I prepared a Red Velvet cake as well; it took me ages, but I'm pleased with the result,´ she said, looking at us, compelling us with her eyes to eat more. ´Mum, it looks really great!´ Aunty said. ´I know, that was the intention,´ Grandma answered back, touching her ponytail with a cheeky smile. Grandma brought the Red Velvet cake to the table and served everyone a portion. It was delicious; I would love to have as much talent as her. After the delicious dessert, we all chilled out for a while on the sofa. I literally couldn´t move. ´Aiden, I'm going for a fag; you wanna come with me?´ Aunty Mimi asked me, looking for the cigarettes in her massive bag. ´Sure.´ We stepped outside and sat in the yard, trying to get far from the window, as my grandma hates the smell of tobacco. She offered me a cigarette. ´Thanks.´ She lit up hers and then mine. ´You know I love you like a son, and I know you have made the right decision, but if anything happens, you know you can contact me,´ she said to me. ´Thank you, Aunty. You know I will.´ She is my confidant: literally, the only person who would never judge me, that's sexually open-minded to talking about anything, even if she has her own things going on. She´s cared for me like a son. ´Do you think this is going to work? I'm just not sure at all,´ I asked her. She exhaled the smoke from her cigarette out from her lungs. ´No one knows, Aiden. I've been married three times. You never know until you try, but life is about deciding and getting it wrong. If not, you´ll end up like me,´ she said, pointing at her chubby belly, and we both laughed. After a short chat, we went back inside. ´Aiden, it's time to go. You still need to check your luggage and rest. We have to leave early tomorrow.´ My Mum knew that if we didn't leave soon, we would be there for ages. ´My beautiful grandchild, I wish you the best in this new chapter, and I'm going to miss you so much,´ Grandma said to me, giving me a hug. ´Come here and give me a hug, you slutty bitch!´ Aunty Mimi said with a naughty voice. My Grandma looked at her, quickly disapproving of that language. I waved my hand to both of them while we were leaving. ´No more plans. Now time to chill and get ready,´ Mum said while driving the car. ´Don't worry, Mum, I feel tired and full.´ She drove home, and we both sat quietly, chilling and enjoying the silence.

.

PEOPLE LIKE YOU

CHAPTER 6

October 17th: the day had finally come. We were already at the airport, looking for a spot in the parking to leave the car. I had packed two big black suitcases and one handbag: it felt like they would break at some point, they were so full. I hoped they would survive the trip, at least until we got there. I had planned to meet Ernesto inside the airport, so I could spend the last minutes with my Mum.

´Well, are you ready?´ asked my Mum. ´Yes, I think so. I'm very nervous, though,´ I said as I stepped out of the car. ´Just take things as they come, and if you need anything, you just need to give me a call,´ she said, smiling at me, trying not to cry. ´I know, Mummy, thank you.´ She locked the car and took hold of one of the cases to help me.

We stepped inside of the airport, which was not as busy as I thought it would be; it was early, though. My Mum is the kind of person that needs to go to the airport four hours before a flight, otherwise she gets very nervous. We walked to the reception of Transavia Airline, flight number 12. I showed my ID, and the check-in clerk reviewed the information about the flight. ´Okay, so it says you can check in one suitcase and take the other on the plane. But as the flight is not full, you can give me both and just keep your handbag,´ she said. ´That's fantastic! That would be great, thank you.´

´Keep this number with you. Have a good flight,´ said the clerk, handing me a piece of paper with the number for my luggage.

'Thanks!' I moved towards my Mum. She was texting Ricardo to say that we had made it here safely. 'Where is Ernesto?' she asked, looking at the time. I checked my phone and dropped a message to him.

A: Darling, where are you?

E: Sorry baby, I forgot to tell you I was a bit late, almost there.

'He's coming now,' I said to my Mum, putting the phone away in my trackies. 'Shall we go for a coffee while he's coming?' suggested my Mum, wanting to spend the last few minutes with me. We grabbed a table and had a look at the different coffees that they had on the menu. 'Are you hungry as well? I can buy you a pastry if you want.' She's adorable and is always looking after me. 'I'm fine. I think I'll just get a Café Bombón'

'Sure, treasure,' she said, getting her credit card out of her wallet. After 20 minutes of chatting and having our coffees, Ernesto finally arrived! He was wearing his camel coat, yellow jumper, and backpack, but he didn't have his case; he must have already checked in. He took his black sunglasses off. 'Hey baby, I'm sorry I'm late, my Mum just dropped me off, she had an appointment with the doctor so she couldn't stay. I checked the bags already, so whenever you're ready, we can go!' Ernesto said, smelling like Marlboro even from a distance. He got closer to me, hugged me, and kissed my lips. He had one more hug for my Mum. We walked together to the airport control doors. 'Please let me know as soon as you get there,' said my Mum to both of us. 'We will, Mum, don't worry.' She hugged Ernesto and touched his face with tenderness. 'Please, Ernesto, take care of each other and of him,' she said this a bit bossily, but I knew she was just worrying about me, knowing inside herself how I felt about this decision. 'You don't even need to tell me that, Emma; since I've met him, I've just taken care of and loved him,' said Ernesto, trying to sound confident of himself, as if he really were. 'Well, enough, Mum, I love you so much, I'm going to miss you a lot,' I said to her, knowing that it was him and me from that moment on. 'Me too, but I'll see you soon. I love you.' She got closer and gave me a kiss on my cheeks and a strong hug.

We passed the security without any problems and looked for the gate on the big screen. 'Amsterdam gate 26, 10:20 am,' Ernesto said. After 5 minutes of walking, we found the gate and sat down to wait.

´Did you have a good time with your family and friends last night?´ I asked Ernesto to get some information about what happened after I left. ´Yes, baby, they were sad because you couldn't make it. I met my friends to say goodbye. I went with my Mum and Rosario for dinner to ´La Tagliatella´, and had a fantastic carbonara pasta,´ he said, smiling at me. Convincing me how important I was supposed to be to his friends with his words, when actually, I didn't like them. They've never treated me badly (most of them), but I always had this kind of feeling that I didn't fit into the group, and again, I can't be surrounded by fake bitches. ´That sounds lovely, baby. I'm happy that you had a good time with them! I needed to chill for the rest of the evening: lunch with my family got me very tired, and I was a bit nervous, so there was nothing better than disconnecting my mind.´ I said. ´Nice. Are you excited to start this new adventure with me?´ Ernesto asked, holding my hand and looking into my eyes. ´Of course! I love you, and we've been talking about this moment for ages. So you know, I'm happy that you've decided to come with me and start from the beginning, where no one knows us,´ I said, but the reality was that I wasn't really sure about the change that was about to come: was this a new adventure or a prison sentence for my own freedom? ´Just you and me now. We have to look out for each other.´ Ernesto said.

´We will.

.

CHAPTER 7

'Ladies and Gentlemen, we will be landing in Amsterdam Schiphol in 15 minutes. It's 12:30 p.m. and 10 degrees. Again, thank you for trusting in Transavia, and we hope to see you again.'

'Baby, we're arriving,' said Ernesto, tapping my left leg and trying to wake me up. I cuddled his arm, moaning because I´d just woken up; it was very uncomfortable to sleep on the plane, but I felt cosy with him. 'Already? Oh, that's quick. I thought it would be impossible to get some sleep, but there´s nothing like listening to 'Cigarettes After Sex' and feeling relaxed and out of the world,' I yawned. 'Yeah, you were even snoring! Hahaha. C'mon, wake yourself up; we need to get organized now,' Ernesto said, looking around the seats. The plane had already landed: we got out of the plane after 5 minutes of standing, waiting until they opened the doors. It´s so annoying. I hate to wait. We found ourselves carrying a massive amount of luggage and pushing our way through the crowd to the train station inside the airport. 'What's the address of the Airbnb?' asked Ernesto looking at the different screens. 'Okay, so first we need to get a train to Almere and then take a bus.' I said to Ernesto with the address on my phone, trying to orientate myself. 'Right, let's buy the tickets.' We found the machine, and Ernesto tried to figure out how to pay for the tickets while I checked which bus we had to take later. 'Almere, you said, right? There´s so many strange names here.' I have to say that Ernesto's English is not the best, even though he had a basic qualification, but after that, he didn't use it much - just when we were in Poland and when we had our first threesome in Oslo. ´Yes, darling,´ I said to him, getting impatient, already tired because of the flight. ´Bloody hell, 25€!! For both tickets. Ridiculously expensive!´ Ernesto said, with his hands on his face, complaining. ´Fuck me! Well, it's not like we're going to rent a bike and go there riding, right? I said, laughing. ´I guess so,´ he said. ´I'll transfer you the money once we're on the train,´ I said to him, as we were always sharing everything and splitting the bills. ´It´s Intercity 1843 Leeuwarden, Platform 1/2.´ We rushed to get on to the train and take a seat. It was going to be 25 minutes. The sky looked grey and rainy. All I could see was grass, lakes, and the highway. We held hands on the way there. ´So, here it says that we need to get off in Almere Centrum, and the Street is J.J Slauerhoffstraat 23,´ said Ernesto, double checking the details. ´Shall we just get a taxi?´ I said, exhausted and really wanting to arrive. ´Whatever you want, my baby, we can take a taxi,´ Ernesto said, trying to please me. After an old guy checked our tickets and dropped us off in Almere Centrum, we took a taxi to the house.

The owner of the house was a Polish woman with short blue hair and white skin in her 30´s. She looked friendly, and after arriving, she showed us everything in the house and the space we had in the fridge for that week. The house was quite extensive. It had the main floor and two more beyond that, with a yard as well. Pretty cool.

We decided to go to the supermarket that was 15 minutes away walking, as we didn't have anything to eat, just the omelette and cheese sandwiches that my Mum had prepared, and we´d eaten them already. It was pretty strange how different they called things there: whatever, after taking everything we needed to survive for at least a week and stacking everything in the fridge, we went to the bedroom. ´Finally, honestly, I'm just so tired! Do you want to have a nap with me, baby?´ I said, falling on the bed and feeling super lazy. ´Of course, I'm feeling quite tired too,´ Ernesto said, leaving his phone on the small table. We got undressed and got into the double bed with soft, warm sheets and memory foam pillows. This looked promising! I snuggled close to Ernesto to spoon him; I could feel his body heat and his own sweet smell. Time for a nap.

After two hours in the clouds, the alarm started buzzing. It was 6 p.m. already, the perfect time to start preparing dinner. ´Did you sleep well? I feel a bit grumpy,´ Ernesto said, rubbing his eyes. ´Yeah, I wonder if we will be able to sleep later on, two hours is quite a lot,´ I replied. ´It's not like we have many options,´ he said, winking at me. ´Honestly, I'm feeling lazy. I don't want to be cooking for ages, and I bet that you don´t either, so shall we just drop the four cheese pizza in the oven,´ said Ernesto, trying to be practical. ´That completely works for me,´ I said. I checked my phone, and there were a couple of messages from my Aunty Mimi, Grandma, and of course, my Mum.

Mum: Did you wake up from the nap already? How are you doing?

A: Hey Mum. Yeah, we're fine, thanks. Ernesto is preparing some pizzas, and we're just going to relax for today. The travel took ages.

M: Fair enough; I'm glad you slept well, my baby. We can speak at another time if you want.

A: Sounds good to me. I love you, Mum.

M: I love you too.

She sends a lot of hearts and emojis. So cute.

Ernesto came back into the room. ´10 minutes and it will be ready. Are you texting your Mum?´ He came closer and took a quick look at my phone. ´Yes, nosey.´ Then suddenly, he ran to the other side of the room and lay on the floor, face down.

´Baby, what are you doing?´ I said, confused, and I don't know why, but I started filming it with my phone. I liked to have these moments when he had a funny scene. It didn't happen often, so I took my chance when I got it. He started crawling slowly towards me, but without looking at me. ´Baby, you alright?´ Strange noises comes from his throat, and he was getting closer. ´You're being creepy!´ I said, shitting myself. He jumped quickly onto me, making me jump and kissed my lips. I stopped recording. ´Did I scare you?´ he asked, with a mysterious face. ´Was a bit strange, but I liked it,´ I laughed. ´Pizza should be ready, why you don't you go it?´ he said to me.

After having that cheap four cheese pizza and taking an incredible shower that was very relaxing, we watched 'It: Chapter 2'. It was rubbish, if I'm honest, but at least I had Ernesto's company.

.

CHAPTER 8

It had been a long day. We´d woken up at 6:30 am for an appointment in Utrecht to get the BSN (Insurance Number) and then another in Amsterdam to register at the Spanish embassy. We'd been busy doing paperwork all morning and part of the afternoon. To be honest, I hated it. ´It's a bit rainy and cold. Shall we go to a coffee shop?´ I suggested to Ernesto, as I hadn't had any joints since I arrived, and after that messy day, I really fancied one. ´A coffee shop? Can we not do it another time?´ Ernesto sighed, trying to escape from that option. ´C'mon, baby! I fancy going to one, and it's been a long day for us. You don't need to smoke, maybe just have a coffee or hot chocolate? We have yet to see much of Amsterdam. Even just a coffee shop to relax in would be great.´ I said, trying to convince him with my persuasive words. ´Alright, as you wish.´ He rolled his eyes and breathed out heavily. I stopped one moment to look at Google to see the closest one in the area. ´Katsu coffee shop, it's only 12 minute´s walk, pretty close!´ I said, with an excited voice. ´Okay, that sounds alright. Let's go, baby.´ Ernesto made an effort and tried not to complain much for the moment.

We walked towards there, holding arms under the umbrella. As soon as we were closer, we realized we found ourselves in The Pijp, which is a bit of a bohemian posh suburb in Amsterdam, with a cute market in the street where you can find everything, from cheese to socks. Many restaurants, bars, trees and buildings with grass on the facade. You can really smell the environment. It's a mix of weed with fast food and then moist. ´Katsu, here it is.´ We stepped inside, and I went to order for us at the counter while Ernesto found a table. A charming guy with long hair and a lot of tattoos waved at me. ´Hello! Welcome; what can I do for you?´ he said with a beautiful, friendly smile. ´Well, I'd like to order two hot chocolates, one with oat milk, please. And also, I'm wondering which weed I should smoke. I don't want to get too high.´ I said to him, trying not to get stoned, visiting my first coffee shop. ´So, we have a new one that is getting popular; it's called Blue Dream, with some fruity, fresh flavour, and perfect for chilling but without getting too spaced out,´ said the handsome guy, placing the weed on the counter. ´Sounds good to me! You sell it well! I'll get two grams, then,´ I said, smiling back at him, feeling attracted, but of course, he's heterosexual. At least he was friendly. ´Fantastic, here you have some papers and filters. It will be 26.50€.´ God, it looked like I was going to get poor; it was so expensive there. I tapped the card machine without taking my eyes off him, but not being too intense. Some people need to be observed patiently to see every single detail of the perfection of their faces, like an art piece. ´Nice! Here you have your weed, and I'll bring the hot chocolates to your table,´ he said, turning to the coffee machine and preparing the drinks.

I looked around the small room and spotted Ernesto at the end, at a table in the corner. ´Look what I have, baby´ I said, waving the bag with weed and winking my eye at him. ´Nice, you can't say now that we didn't come or that I'm not flexible with you.´ Already moaning at me. ´C'mon, why you don't chill a bit with me?´ I took his hand. ´Smells really strong in here, though,´ he huffed. I hoped all the smoke in the shop would get him a little high at least. Perhaps that would make him a bit mellow and he would be nicer. The chap from the counter walked towards the table, just in time. ´Here you are, guys, two hot chocolates, one with oat milk,´ carrying the black tray between his arms. ´Thanks!´ I said, wanting him not to go and sit with me instead of Ernesto. ´Enjoy!´

´This chocolate is tasty. It was a good idea to come here; at least we've done something different today.´ Ernesto tried to chill out. He knew his mood was a bit annoying. ´You see? It's not all that bad, darling.´ I started inhaling my beautiful joint, which was huge. I loved it.

The taste was fresh, and it didn´t even take 10 minutes for me to feel a bit high. But I was still present enough to have a conversation. ´Your eyes are completely red; you have your interview in the hotel tomorrow, so you shouldn't smoke more.´ Ernesto came back again to his everyday bossy mood. ´Darling, I'm fine. The interview will be okay. Just let me chill, please.´ I exhaled the smoke from the joint as soon as I finished that sentence. ´Alright, I'm not going to get on your back,´ he said, looking to his right side. ´I appreciate it.´ I'm still impressed by the fact that we could be there, sitting in a ´coffee shop´ and drinking hot chocolate and smoking weed. Unbelievable. Many different tourists were coming inside, buying pre-rolled joints and leaving. The environment was chill, and the atmosphere friendly. ´I've been looking for apartments in Amsterdam central or nearby, it´s going to cost us around 2500€ per month, without bills,´ Ernesto said, sipping the hot chocolate and showing me a couple of screen shots he had taken of the apartments. ´That´s impossible, we can´t afford that. What about if we look for a room?´ My face started to sweat just thinking about paying that much money. ´Well, here's the thing, I found a couple of doubles room where we can share a house with more people, and that would be around 700€ for both of us, so it would be 350€ each.´ He kept scrolling through the pictures. It looked like he had spent a lot of time trying to find us a place. ´That's good; it sounds a more reasonable price.´ That made me feel a bit calmer. ´It's a reasonable price, but if I'm honest, I don't want to share a house with anyone else. I just want to be with you.´ I knew it was too good to be true. Ernesto was not that easy to convince. If he wanted something, he thought it should be done as he said. ´Yeah, baby, I know, and I would love to be able to afford it, but we don't have enough money.´ I tried to make him understand the situation. ´What if we looked outside of Amsterdam? We can always take the train.´ That was not a bad point. ´Have a look if you want, but we don't have much money.´ I felt nervous already. That sort of stuff stresses me out a lot. ´Do you trust me? Everything is going to be okay. I promise.´ That's the typical phrase that should be a warning, as in my experience, every time someone says it, something terrible has happened.

He held my hand, smiling at me. Sharing a house with more people can indeed be annoying. Still, I was worried about the money and living alone with him. ´Look, I found one studio in Almere for 1000€ without the bills, and it's next to the centrum and the train station. Shall I send an email to see if we can have a look soon?´ Ernesto was really confident about what he was doing. ´Yeah, all right, we can try. We're already staying there.´ I tried not to think much about it and to leave it to him. ´Trust me. You have to believe more in me. I know what I'm doing,´ he said, very determined. I found it very annoying sometimes when he was like this, but I loved him, even if I wanted to kill him at some points.

´Could I borrow an outfit for tomorrow? I don't have anything posh for the interview,´ I asked him, knowing already the answer. ´Of course, you know I'm fashionable, and I have something for you. I was a bit worried about it, to be honest. Because your clothing is not as appropriate and elegant as mine for an interview. I'm here to help you, so it doesn't matter,´ Ernesto said, feeling glorious for doing me a favour. Maybe he believed he was the incarnation of Donatella Versace. ´Thanks, baby,´ I said. ´I'll help you in the morning to choose something,´ he said, touching the end of his thin, bearded chin. ´I'm starting to get tired. Shall we take the train back? We still have to prepare some dinner.´ I wanted to get the fuck out of there. We left the coffee shop; it had stopped raining. My body felt chill, and my mind. I needed it. I had a stupid look on my face and red eyes as Ernesto looked at me and laughed. But whatever, I just wanted to get home and sleep. I was done with walking that day. ´Thank you for coming to the shop with me. I really wanted to go,´ I said to him. ´Anything for you, my boy.´ He came in closer and kissed my lips.

.

CHAPTER 9

The alarm started to buzz, making me jump, and my heart race. Holy shit, I didn't expect it. I swear, the alarm from the iPhone is going to kill me one day. ´Good morning, baby, come here. Did you sleep well?´ The first words of the day from Ernesto were cute. I snuggled my head into his chest. ´Not really, I had weird dreams, but now I can't remember them,´ I said, trying to recover from that loud unexpected noise. ´Now it's gone, you should focus on your interview today, and it will be all right.´ Ernesto said, snuggling me back. ´I hope so.´

We both got up from the bed and went to the kitchen to prepare an omelette with coffee for breakfast; Ernesto decided just to have a coffee, as he was not a breakfast person. After devouring all the breakfast, feeling energetic enough to carry on with the day, I realised I stank. ´I need to shower. Do you want to come with me?´ Ernesto gave me a cheeky smile and didn't even think about it. We locked the door in the bathroom upstairs in case the Polish girl tried to come inside. We smiled at each other and got undressed, leaving all our clothing on the floor. The water started running. It was warm, the perfect temperature. We were both naked, letting our bodies get closer to each other. ´You're getting me horny,´ Ernesto said, realising that his penis was erect. Of course, I couldn't resist touching it. My cock felt hard too; I didn't even think at the time, I just got on my knees, and started to suck him off. ´ I need to feel it deeper.´ I said while he took my head and started fucking my throat more deeply and quickly.

I couldn´t breathe that much, but I was feeling really wet. The steam of the shower made the things in the room barely visible. ´Fuck yeah, that's how I like it, suck it more. You know that's what I want from you,´ Ernesto said, aggressive pleasure written all over his face. I started wanking myself while I felt the quick rhythm of his movements and the girth of dick in my throat. I stood up, and we kissed, rolling our tongues in each other´s mouths. I bit his lip. ´Calm down with biting! It hurts! Now suck me off,´ he said again; I followed his orders and got on my knees again. The water was still running, and my body felt hot, but I didn't care. All I wanted was his spunk. He moaned whenever I took his erect penis into my throat for a few seconds. I loved to deepthroat him. I just wanted to give him pleasure. ´I'm fucking close. Open your mouth; now I'm going to feed you,´ he said dominantly, a look of triumph on his face. I touched my penis quicker, getting harder. Ernesto gave a loud moan, filling my mouth, I couldn't hold it anymore, and I felt the release as I came as well. ´That was so hot, babe.´ He took my hand to help me up, and kissed me tenderly. ´I really enjoyed it,´ I said to him, cleaning my mouth with the running water from the shower. ´It's been a couple of days, and I missed it,´ Ernesto said to me. ´Yeah, me too. Wait, what time is it? We should rush. I have the interview at 12 p.m.,´ I said, trying to wash my body as quickly as possible.

´So what should I wear for today? I'm feeling a bit indecisive,´ I said, looking at myself in the mirror and annoyed. ´What would you do without me? Look at these,´ Ernesto proudly said, giving me three shirts; one is pink, the next is basic white, and the other is pink with some red squares. Also, one pair of trousers, not skinny but very formal. I hated them, but I needed to give a good impression. I decided to take the third one and wear it. ´You look amazing, my clothes really suit you. You should buy more things like this,´ Ernesto said, looking at himself smile in the mirror on the other side of the room. ´Thanks, but I look a bit weird; what about the shoes?´ I tried to convince myself that I felt comfortable in that outfit. ´Here you have it. They´re the only ones that I have for you.´ Ernesto took a pair of black shoes from his giant suitcase, very formal, and I realised I looked like I'm part of a wedding. I hated them. ´Nice, thanks, baby.´

´Wait a moment; I just received an email from Empari. They want to invite me to a group interview today at 1:00 p.m. in Amsterdam

Central,´ Ernesto exclaimed, excited about the news. ´Ernesto! That's amazing, so you should get something posh and fancy for them. You know how they are there, but you're gay, skinny and handsome. I'm sure you'll get this,´ I said, joking with him. ´You silly boy! Yes, give me some time. I need to focus. Could we meet after the interviews for some lunch?´

´Yeah! Sounds good to me,´ I replied, feeling quite nervous but happy for both of us. I looked in the mirror; I really didn't like the outfit, I felt out of my usual style, and it made me look older. But as it was only for the interview, I thought it should be fine. I styled my hair with some hairspray and put One Million on my neck. Teeth brushed, hair done, outfit done. Wait: I couldn´t find the folder with the documents for my hospitality course. I had a quick look around the room, looked inside my bag and there it was. Ernesto got ready very quickly. He'd been looking at himself in the mirror for at least 10 minutes, checking that he had every detail of his face right. ´Babe, maybe it will be nice if I get there a bit early, so they see that I'm on time and can relax a bit. I'm feeling nervous.´ I said to him, walking the room in circles. ´Well, my interview is at 1 p.m., so I could go with you to the hotel, stay a bit and then leave so you don't feel alone. I want to support you,´ Ernesto said, looking at his eyebrows in the mirror. I needed to be alone. I wanted to clear my mind. I don't know how to explain it. He was very intense. ´That's fair, and I appreciate it, but I think I might need some time alone before-hand.´ Ernesto looked at me through the mirror and exhaled. ´Aiden, please, I insist, let me go with you, I'm here to support you, and this is an important moment. I don't want you to feel anxious and alone.´ He said it very assertively; I guessed I didn't have another choice. I didn't want to start an argument. I needed to focus on the interview. He was not going to stay longer, so fuck off. ´Alright, babe, whatever is fine.´ I said to him, evading any shit face. I started to get even more nervous. I needed that time for myself, but I couldn't have it. Ernesto finished getting ready. I sat there waiting, lying on the bed, checking Twitter. Not much interesting going on, oh wait, Lady Gaga was recording a new album: sounds exciting! ´Nesto, we should leave now. I don't want to get late, if not I can go alone. I don't mind.´ I said, trying to see if there was a slight chance to get that precious time alone. ´I'm ready! C'mon, let's go.´

We headed to the train station and bought the tickets. It was a bit busy but not crazy. Actually, I was starting to feel that having a house there was not that bad. Maybe living with him was not as bad as I thought. ´Amsterdam Zuid is the stop,´ I said, checking the screen to see which platform was the one. ´It´s platform 2.´ We walked upstairs and waited five minutes on the platform before the train arrived.

We were sitting next to each other. He was holding my hand and laying his head on my shoulder. ´Everything is going to be all right, Aiden. I love you,´ Ernesto said. I had a strange sensation inside myself. It's difficult to explain. ´Yes, I guess so. I love you too, baby,´ I replied, trying to sound confident about my answer. It was 30 minutes on the train, so I had enough time to appreciate the green, wet views outside. It was a bit sunny that day, I still couldn't believe we were there and that we had moved all that way together. I'm not gonna lie, I didn't know how things would be, but I agreed to go there with Ernesto, so I guessed I just needed to go with the flow and see what happened. ´Aiden, I just received an email from the real estate agent from the house in Almere Centrum that I told you about yesterday. They said it is still available, and we can arrange a viewing tomorrow at 10:30 a.m.,´ he said. ´That's fantastic! Okay, no problem at all. Send them an email saying that we will be there at that time.´ I realised that the moment was getting closer. ´I'm very excited, baby. Can you imagine living just you and me together? I can't wait to say it to my mom and friends.´ Well, we hadn't even seen the place. Maybe he should chill out a bit before telling everyone. I'm not surprised, though; he loves to be recognised by others. ´Shall we wait a bit? Until we have made a decision,´ I said, trying not to compromise myself that quickly. He stopped smiling and rolled his eyes up. ´Whatever, like always, baby,´ looking upset.

´C'mon, I'm excited as well. I just want to ensure that we have everything under control before telling everyone. After some minutes, we heard the speaker, "Volgende halte Amsterdam Zuid" We both got off the train. The station was more extensive and busier. ´Which way is it?´ Ernesto asked, looking to each exit in the station. I checked on the maps. It was 10 minutes walk. ´This way, c'mon.´

Outside the train station, the area was surrounded by a lot of significant buildings and looked like it was a business area. There were some cafés and shops close to the station. Some people were sitting next to the grass. I guessed they were enjoying their break. We crossed a square next to a hotel. We needed to follow a small bridge that connected to the other street. I could see houses and flats; I wondered how much it would cost to live there. Suddenly I saw from the other side of the street the big blue letters of the hotel. I still had 20 minutes left, but I needed to send Ernesto on his way, so I could be by myself. ´Here it is! I might pop in now to focus on what I will say in the interview.´ He looked at his phone, checking the time and had a moment of thinking. ´Okay, it's fine. At least I know you're safe. Text me when you finish, and I'll meet you at Empari's entrance,´ he said. ´Yes, darling, good luck! I'm sure you'll get it´ He grabbed my hips and gave me a hug and a quick kiss. ´Good luck to you too! See you then.´ Ernesto started to walk on his way to the stop while he looked behind and waved at me. God, I couldn't believe it. I wondered why he had to come with me if he needed to go in another direction. He was very demanding sometimes. But never mind, I needed to focus on this interview.

I stepped inside the hotel. There was a light brown carpet, with three sofas in a U shape, a table in the middle and in each corner, some magazines, and a lamp.

Looked like a fancy place. I walked into the reception, and this beautiful blond girl attended me. I explained to her that I had an interview at 12 p.m. She took the phone and contacted Helen from HR, and invited me to have a seat while I waited for her. I had a couple of WhatsApps, but I couldn't be bothered to reply. I doubled checked all the documents in my folders again and took some slow breaths in and out. ´Aiden? I'm Helen. We spoke on the phone a week ago. I'm the HR Manager for the hotel. Please come with me to the bar and we can have a chat.´ Helen said. She was wearing a dark blue skirt, white shirt and a black blazer with the hotel's logo. ´Nice to meet you, Helen.´ I gently shook her hand, making eye contact and smiling. I followed her to the restaurant. She found a high table in a corner, and we sat there. ´This is a lovely spot. Would you like something to drink?´ She put her notebook on the table and made herself comfortable. ´Oh, that's very nice of you, thanks. I'd like a mint tea please, with some honey.´ After ordering, she returned to the table, and I showed her my documents. ´This is my Hospitality diploma. I studied for 2 years in the sector and I know how to serve properly, attend a table and prepare drinks and coffee,´ I said to her; I tried to make sure my body language was relaxed and confident and that I made good eye contact with her, like I´d been taught. ´That's fantastic, so what does this paper mean then?´ she asked, putting on her glasses. ´So here is a reference from the owner of the restaurant that I worked in during my internship in Poland, who said that I'm capable of working in a restaurant. You have his telephone number and all the information about it.´ She looked interestedly at the papers. I quickly took in my surroundings for a couple of seconds. The restaurant looked pretty, had a chilled atmosphere, and was not big at all. ´So, let me explain a bit about the position. We're looking for a Food & Beverage assistant, full time, 40 hours a week, the break is actually paid, you can have 50€ less on your payslip to have the option of eating the staff food, if not you will need to sign a paper. It is for evenings in the beginning, but there's a chance you'll also be doing some mornings. If you live further than 2 kilometres away, we also give you an amount of money on your payslip, so it helps with the transport cost.´ Helen said, reading off a document that she had on the table. ´That sounds amazing! I'd like to be part of the team!´ I exclaimed. ´That's fantastic. I need you to give me all your information, and I'll process everything in the system. Hopefully, soon, you'll be starting. So the position is all yours!´ she said. ´Oh, Helen! Thank you, I'm grateful for this opportunity.´ I said to her, feeling great as it was one thing less to worry about. ´It's our pleasure. We like to have a strong team: people who are willing to learn and hard workers. I know you don't speak Dutch, but it shouldn't be a problem. This is a business hotel, so you'll get more foreign customers, and 90% of the staff doesn't speak Dutch.´ she replied. ´That's helpful! I would like to learn it, though. I just need a bit of time,´ I said. ´No worries at all. I'll contact you soon and send you the contract´ We shook hands again, and she guided me back through reception and out of the hotel.

I felt delighted. I couldn't believe it was that easy. I hoped this time it would work out; I got very anxious in Poland because of the language, and I didn't enjoy being around the restaurant, even though they treated me well. I made my way to Amsterdam city centre. While I was waiting at the cable car to get to the stop, I finally replied to messages that I had, and I called my Mum.

I jumped off close to Empari, fuck! I just remembered that I needed to text Ernesto.

A: Hey baby, I'm here waiting. Hope is going well. Let me know when you finish!

He didn´t reply, so I took myself to the closest coffee shop. I fancied a spliff. A small one was not going to hurt anyone. I sat inside and took some pre-rolled ones, as they were less potent. Oh yes. I felt much better. I started to cool down and feel a bit mellow. My phone started to ring. It was Ernesto calling.

E: Baby, I'm outside. Where are you?

A: Hey baby! I'm close. Give me 5 minutes.

I hung up and went back to Empari. Ernesto was there, waiting in his fancy posh outfit and black sunglasses. ´Hello! Guess who got a Sales Assistant position?´ He yelled very intensely and with emotion. ´That's fantastic, baby! I'm very proud of you. Guess who got a F&B assistant position in the hotel?´ We both cuddled each other with the emotion of the moment. ´Have you been smoking? You smell like weed.´ He stopped the cuddle to smell me. ´Oops! You caught me, I was just killing some time, so I went to the coffee shop until you called me.´ That's fine. I hope you're not too high, though,´ he sighed. ´Shall we have lunch? I'm starving,´ I suggested.

We took medium size fries with cheese sauce and hot spices on top. We sat on the bank of the canal, watching the boats and the people walking. The fries were delicious. ´We should go somewhere to celebrate this!´ I said. ´That sounds good to me. I fancy a drink. Where shall we go?´ Ernesto said, eating the last chips. ´Well, I haven't been to the queer area here. I would like to know if we can go there and look. There's a place called Bar Blend that had good reviews.´ I was hoping to go somewhere nice and not listen to Ernesto give me any complaints. ´Sure, let's go there then.´ He said, this one was easier than I thought. As soon as we both finished eating, we walked 10 minutes through the city centre. It was busy, and the buildings had quite exciting structures. Also, they're quite short, and there were many bikes cycling around. It was incredible.

We entered the queer area, and I saw many rainbow flags. You could tell where we were.

So Bar Blend had two floors, and the toilet is on the third. What about disabled people? Never mind: we found a table outside on the street. Ernesto came back from the bar with two pints of beer. ´Cheers, baby, for us, for our future together.´ We tapped our glasses together. ´And for our new jobs!´ This country was very expensive, 6€ for a pint, bloody hell! ´I've been thinking, and I believe that it will be great if we both try to meet friends, like not having the same ones here, and you know if there's a chance for you to hang out with people, do it, I'll be very happy for you,´ I said, smiling at him. ´What? Why are you saying that? That's so selfish.´ His face changed immediately and his attitude became very stern. ´It's not selfish, Ernesto. I just thought that it's healthy for us to have our own space, just that,´ I explained, trying to have a sip of the pint. ´Well, that's not fair, and if we came to this country together, we're gonna be together in everything, darling. That is what we have to do.´ I drank a quarter of the beer straight away. I didn't understand the situation. Why was he saying that? Was it fair? We should have our own space. Why did he think that it's selfish to have our own group of friends? My head was confused, and my heart started to race. ´I don't know, Nesto. I guess so.´ I said, lying to myself. ´I love you, and I'm very excited about living together and sharing our lives together. This is just the beginning, darling.´

"This is just the beginning" is the only thing I could hear in my head.

I had a terrible feeling. I didn't know what it was. But something was wrong.

.

CHAPTER 10

What a fantastic way to start our day. We took the bus to Almere Centrum to view the studio apartment and decided not to buy a ticket, thinking no one would check it. To our surprise, a bus conductor entered every door of the bus at the following stop. We looked at each other, knowing that we had screwed it. There was no escape.

Yes, they knew it, and we needed to pay a 50€ fine, but at least they gave us a travel card with 10 trips included. Ernesto looked pissed, but there was not much to do about it, we risked it, and they caught us. ´I can´t believe that happened. Honestly, it´s so annoying, and now we´re late. What a shit,´ Ernesto said angrily. ´I know, darling, but it´s already done, let´s now focus on the viewing.´ I took his hand, trying to calm him down. I felt a bit uncomfortable when he has that kind of reaction, but I wanted to help him. I knew that I was not perfect, either. We reached the address, Dichterhof 17. Wow, literally, it was two minutes away from the station. Everything was so close.

Ernesto buzzed the doorbell, and the real-estate agent came downstairs to meet us. She was a tall skinny blonde girl with subtle make-up, and wearing in a black and grey dress. Formal but not too much. ´Goedemorgen! Mijn naam is Susana, ik zal je het huis laten zien.´ The real-estate agent said, in Dutch. ´Oh, good morning! Sorry, Susana, I´m Aiden, and this is Ernesto. Sorry, we don´t speak Dutch. Is it alright for you if we speak in English?´ I apologised to her, knowing we were not the first foreigners coming to that country and not speaking the language. 'Of course, not a problem at all, please follow me and I'll show you the apartment,' she said, inviting us to come inside the building. We took the stairs, it was just one floor and there was a lift as well. That looked very useful. There were two doors between the stairs and the apartment which opened with a button on the right side. The apartment was the first one on the left. Number 17.

'So this is the apartment. The building it's pretty new, and no one has lived here before, so everything is brand new. It's 25 meters squared and equipped for the winter, so you just need to turn the heater on, and you will not want to leave the house!' Susana said, trying to be friendly to get that juicy commission. 'I see. That's amazing. Look at these, baby!' Ernesto was discovering each corner of the house. He looked excited. So the place has no separate rooms, basically just a wall dividing the living room to create a sleeping area, but there was no door, just the toilet and a shower with a bath at the left. And a small room for the washing machine. It also has a small terrace, big enough for a table and a couple of chairs. I found it very cute, if I'm honest. 'So, please could you explain the contract and everything to us, Susana.' I ask her. Following that, she opened a folder and looked through the papers. 'The rent is 1000€ per month, but the bills are not included, so I say total costs would be around 1250€. It's a two years contract, and we will need two months in advance, and the month you're already paying to live in.' She said this with the folder in her arms. 'All right, just give us 5 minutes to discuss something.' I took Ernesto to the terrace and closed the door behind me. 'This place is amazing, Aiden. We need to take this chance, we have seen a couple of places already, and this one is perfect,' Nesto said, sounding like he had already made the decision. 'Darling, I really like it too, but first of all, we don't have 3000€, and second, it's two years contract, do you think we'll be living here that long? We could try to look for a room that will be cheaper and save money.' Ernesto looked at me with disapproval, but he reached for my hands and looked into my eyes. 'Baby, I don't want to live with anyone else that's not you. I don't want to share; I told you already I moved here to be with you, not with a group of people in a house.' He was begging for a "yes" with his eyes. 'Ok, and what about the money?'

'Well, we can always ask your Mum for it, mine doesn't have much and complained a lot when she gave me the money to come here, so it's impossible for her to help more, but I know yours will do anything for you.´ Ernesto went straight away to my Mum´s business without even talking more deeply about it. ´I need to ask her, Ernesto, I´m not sure.´ I was starting to feel already a bit pressured. ´Believe me, everything will be fine, just you and me, looking after each other.´ Those words sounded like dealing with the devil. He returned to Susana and told her we were interested in taking the apartment but that we needed to sort out some things with the bank. He told her that we wanted to receive all the documents and move as soon as possible. She didn´t raise any problems at all, just asked for our work documents as we needed to prove that we were working. We didn´t yet have contracts for our jobs but Ernesto knew how to lie convincingly, so he told her he would send everything as soon as we got the house contract from her.

Later that day and I was lying on the bed, feeling stressed and not understanding why. We had found the perfect place for us, in a charming location. But why did he have to rush me to make a decision now? And why did he think it was OK to count on my Mum´s money? It felt like there was no other way than his. Equally, he felt thrilled and excited. He wanted to live with me, just with me. I wondered if maybe I was judging him unfairly: was I? I spoke with my Mum about it, and we agreed to give her the money back as soon as we started to work. She sounded a bit confused as she also suggested a room would be a better idea to start with. Still, as I said, Ernesto wanted to bring all the family together for Christmas, and he wanted everyone to stay at our place. My Mum sometimes said a lot without saying anything. At least we would have our own home. A two-year contract. It felt like a long time, though. Why did I feel so confused? I was the one behind Ernesto moving in somewhere together, maybe I was just being too sensitive, and it was a normal feeling. ´Baby, I just signed my contract for Empari. They sent me everything by email. I´m starting tomorrow!´ Nesto said, smiling broadly. ´That´s exciting! I´m very happy for you, honey.´ I cuddle him for a while, feeling his body heat and the sweet smell of his neck. ´Did you hear anything from the hotel?´ I unlocked my phone and checked my email. Oh, here we had it!

´Dear Aiden, thank you again for meeting me last Thursday. This email follow our interview and I´m delighted to tell you that you nailed it! Please feel free to come this following Monday; we will give you the uniform and everything you need. We´re pleased to have you joining our team. Please find attached the contract of employment: please send it back to me signed as soon as you can.

Looking forward to seeing you on Monday.

Kind regards,

Met vriendelijke groet

Helen Mijn

Human Resources Director.

Amsterdam.´

´I got it, Nesto! I got the contract. I start on Monday!´ I jumped from the bed, excited for my new start. ´That´s fantastic! We can send our contracts to Susana then. It´s a perfect chance for us, baby. You will see, everything is going to be all right,´ he said again. Those fucking words.

CHAPTER 11

It had been two weeks since we moved into the studio. I won't lie, it had been chaotic as we didn't have any furniture because the apartment was completely unfurnished. We just had the fridge, oven and cooking area. We went to Ikea (far from where we lived) to buy the cheapest, basic things we needed to survive. We spent all of my savings plus the money that my Mum lent us. So it was a bit difficult, but my Grandma and Aunty Mimi sent me some money as well for some cutlery and pans. The sofas and bed were out of our budget, and the cheaper one was a metal one, which was really small and uncomfortable. So basically we went to Ikea to buy a couple of things.

We ended up buying a second-hand mattress that was very thin, not the most comfortable thing, but it was just 40€. It was the best we could do; we were not going to sleep on the floor, so at least for that moment, it seemed like it could work for us. Surprisingly, we went behind the building, and there was a sofa, a bit old but still perfect for at least a month. It was a bit broken in the bottom, but after an intense cleaning, we "fixed it" by adding a piece of wood: Ernesto was a bit disgusted by the idea but it was that or sitting on the floor. Our neighbour told us he was giving away a table, which was the perfect solution for us. The funny thing was that he didn't have the chairs. Still, one night after finishing my shift in the hotel at 11:00 p.m. and getting to the train station, I found 4 white leather chairs on the street, which were a bit heavy to carry all the way through. But at least our place was mostly furnished, and most things were free! It looks like I'm stingy with money, but sometimes it's better to save and survive with other things rather than have nothing.

Also, Ernesto and I started working, and it had been good. He felt happy with it, even though he was still learning to speak English properly, but as he was in the warehouse of Empari at the bottom of the store, it didn´t matter too much. But he showed his confidence to the others. Ernesto was very sassy, so he wouldn't have any problem. I mean typical cliché from Empari workers: White, skinny, good-looking, superb homosexual.

I found it quite interesting working in a hotel with six floors and 450 rooms: it's a lot. I felt lost the first few days, but I was beginning to get used to it. It was not a difficult job. I mainly served coffee, wine, beers, or anything else, but not cocktails. And the menu in the restaurant was ´Spanish´ food (fucking expensive, two croquetas 10€! I would prefer to be stabbed in my kidneys!) and even though I hadn't talked with many people at all, I had some conversations with my F&B colleges, one of whom was an Italian guy, in his mid-20´s or, Lucciano. He was short but taller than me, ginger with big hands and caramel eyes, he was very handsome. God. I was still 19, but why did my eyes always go to straight people? I would have loved to shag him, though: Italian guys are very cheeky, and I felt horny sometimes thinking that I could even have a chance to have sex with him. But I felt bad like I shouldn't be thinking like that. I knew I was with Ernesto. I thought I enjoyed sex with him, so the best thing was not to think about it and focus on my monogamous relationship with him.

Aiden! Our stuff from Spain just arrived.´ Ernesto sounded excited. I jumped from the bed quickly to reach him. ´We need to go downstairs. They have quite a few things.´ I left the door open, and we started taking the boxes upstairs. God, I was so happy that at least we had a lift. ´Careful with that, let me take it.´ I told the delivery guy, as it was my 37" 3D TV that my Mum sent from Spain, she's an expert on these things, so I was sure she could make it safe all the way through. She's amazing.

A couple more boxes, and it was all already done. ´I can't believe it! Finally, we have a TV and my Playstation 4!´ I started moving from one side to the other and I couldn't control my emotions. ´Baby, please stop moving and help me with the boxes. It is not like I'm going to do all this by myself!´ He looked at me, a bit moody. ´Darling, I'm just excited. We have all the day to do it. I want to place the tv and the ps4 and connect it to the internet.´I replied. ´Yeah, whatever. Can you come with me for the groceries? We need to do the shopping for the week. We barely have anything,´ Ernesto said, looking inside the fridge. ´That sounds fair enough; c'mon, let's go.´ It was pretty good living in the centre where we just needed to walk three minutes, and Aldi was there. After 25 minutes of wandering around the supermarket and taking our food, Ernesto put three bottles of red wine and a six-pack of beers in the basket: the cheap ones, but they tasted good. Since we got together, I tried to make him vegetarian, or at least not eat as much meat. Because when I met him, he was eating something with meat every day at every mealtime. Until I suggested doing a blood test to check his health, he didn't care that much, and it had been ages since the last one, and again I was right. He needed to have a more balanced diet and reduce the amount of meat he was eating. So it was easier to go to get the groceries together as we shared the bill. We shared everything. Sometimes he wanted to treat me to dinner somewhere, but if not, we split the bill, or I paid the next time. Now that we didn't have that much money, it was the perfect way to manage things. But we had our own savings, and no one would touch that. My money and my savings were mine.

´Nesto, since we both started working, we barely share time. I get here at midnight most of the time because of my shift in the hotel, and when I'm off, you're working.´ I said while we entered our studio and started putting away the groceries. ´I know, baby, but there's not much I can do now. I'm new here and still getting used to everyone and when I can ask favours and when not. My manager is a Portuguese girl who's very sassy and shady but has a lovely perception of me so far. She likes to work with me, so I could try speaking with her. But now we both need to work to get the money.´ He looked at me, giving half a smile, convinced of what he was saying. ´I know, even though I want to change my shifts. I can't be assed to get home at midnight every day. It's crap, but it's what it is,´ Ernesto simply accepted things as if fighting for something was not within his capability. ´For now, I´m not going to do anything about it,´ he finished. ´I'm going to prepare some rice with tomato sauce. What do you think?´ I asked Ernesto, trying not to think about the conversation. I got close to him, and we hugged each other, feeling our bodies and the bulge of our genitals. ´Well, let's stop because I need to focus now, cheeky bastard. ´He laughs at me and touched my bum. ´Shall I open the wine?´ Nesto offered, showing me the bottle that we just bought. ´You don't even need to ask that. Go ahead.´ After serving the wine and raising our glasses to each other to ´cheers´, I prepared everything, chopping the garlic and the onions with the extra virgin olive oil. It smelled amazing. I put all the ingredients in the pan to make the tomato sauce and left it on low heat when it was done, while the rice was still boiling. I love to cook, honestly. I took a sip from my glass. I felt like a 45-year-old lady sitting in a corner reading a book at night with a glass of red wine. ´By the way, baby, yesterday some of my colleagues from Empari told me that today they have a house party, and I've been invited,´ Ernesto said to me while he was preparing the table. ´Nesto! That's amazing, where is it?´ I was excited for him. ´It's in the house of one of the girls working with me downstairs, but I said we were not going.´ He looked at the floor while holding the wine glass. ´Well, I didn't know I was invited, but why don't you go? Honestly, darling, it will be excellent for you to go there, have some fun, have a few drinks and socialize with new people!´ I exclaimed to him, hoping he would take the chance to get out and open his mind. ´I said no because I prefer to stay with you. You're more important to me than that stupid party.´ Nesto was trying to convince me that he was doing it for me. ´But baby! I'll be fine here, you should 100% go, don't worry about me, I'll be very happy for you.´ I really wanted him to go, as I hadn't seen him socialize out of his ´beautiful´ group of friends. ´I told you I came here to be with you, and I don't need anyone else to have fun with rather than you´. Why was he doing that? It was a perfect chance to go out and socialise with more people. That party sounded cool. Usually, we had fun together, but it was not like he was up for going out or doing something new – he would only do a certain limited number of things that he was really into. Sometimes he confused me. If he declined the invitation, why did he tell me about it?

After a while, the food was ready, and Ernesto smoked a cigarette on the balcony.

I plated up the food and called him in. ´Smells really good. Thanks, baby. Do you want more wine?´ he said, coming back into the room.

´Thanks, yes, please.´ I put the plates on the table and flicked the control to choose something to watch on Netflix. I found a reality show called "Selling Sunset": it's basically about white blonde bitches from LA who are Real Estate agents, and they gossip about each other and blah blah. It was enough to keep us entertained for a while. ´Oh wait, let me change the language. It´s in Spanish.´ I swapped it to English (VO). Ernesto took the remote from my hands before I finished the sentence. ´What are you doing? I wanna watch it in Spanish.´ Ernesto was being bossy. ´Baby, if we watch everything in Spanish, we can't learn more English, and it's not like you're at your best with it. And I'd love to go to the cinema someday, can you imagine paying 10€ for a film that you don't understand?´ Ernesto raised his right eyebrow. I could see from his face that he was upset. ´Like always, we do what you want, don't you see?´ he said, already angry. ´The food is getting cold. Please eat; what do you think if I only put Spanish subtitles on?´ He broke the egg yolk, and spread the tomato sauce with the rice, and raised the spoon to his mouth. ´Fine, the food is good, by the way.´ He was chewing the food. Looked like he was hungry. ´Thanks, yes, it is indeed!´

It took us 30 minutes to watch the show and finish the food, and we barely spoke to each other during that time. Ernesto took the dishes and started to wash them.

I lay down on the sofa and lit my spliff. My head needed to chill; this was my new home with Ernesto, but there was something that I didn´t understand. I was feeling a bit out of everything, and even though I was happy working in the hotel and deciding to move there, my head was confused again, and I didn´t know why. When Ernesto finished the dishes, he came to the sofa, and I put my legs across him once he was seated. ´That smells awful! I hate it.´ Nesto hated the smell of weed. ´Well darling, I´m sorry, but I fancy having a spliff now, and I don´t like the smell of the cigarettes, even though I smoke, but I think this smells better.´ He looked at me sideways; clearly, he disagreed. I started to feel mellow and chill: just what I needed. ´Ernesto, I want to do something with my hair.´ I suddenly felt like I needed a change. ´What do you mean by something?´ He had that disgusted look on his face again that he had every time I asked him to do something for me. ´Shave it all off. Can you help me to shave my hair with your trimmer? ´I said, smiling at him, waiting for a kind answer. ´Me? But why do you not go to the hairdresser, like I do?´ Another thing that he does, comparing me to the things that he does. ´Darling, you spend 12€ every week and a half for the hairdresser, so you spend around 45€ a month: that´s more than 500€ a year! But I can get it for free and save that money.´ I said, a valid argument. I don´t want to spend lots of money, especially if I can do something myself. ´I´m not a hairdresser. Do you really want me to do your hair? What if it looks terrible?´ Ernesto was trying to avoid helping me by being negative with all his body and soul. ´Nesto, it´s not the first time you cut my hair, darling. I´m not asking for much. I want to shave all. But if not, give me the shaver, and I´ll do it myself.´ He sighed deeply. ´Yes, Aiden, all right, I´ll cut your hair. Can you leave me to chill after that? I´m on my day off, I´m tired, and I have washed the dishes already.´ I didn´t feel too good about how he was talking to me. It felt a bit arrogant, but feeling mellow helped me to stay calm, so I preferred not to take it seriously, even though I was not feeling okay at all. ´I appreciate it. Thank you, darling; it will just be a moment.´ I sat on the white leather chair that I found next to the bin; I was glad the floor was easy to clean. I got almost naked, wearing my ugly underwear to be comfy in the house. ´So you want it all shaved off?´ he said, looking pretty annoyed, but I didn´t care. It is not difficult to help your partner for 10 minutes, and he had nothing better to do.

I stepped into the bathroom. Welcome back again, bald Aiden. Looked pretty sexy. ´Thanks, baby, I love it. Do you like it?´ I looked at him in the mirror. ´Well, you are handsome, but I prefer you with your normal hair.´ Whatever: I went to him and kissed him on the cheek. ´Now I´m going to chill on the sofa. You clean the messy hair on the floor because I´m not doing anything more. I´ve done enough,´ he said, making his way back to the sofa. I quickly brushed the floor and cleaned up the rest of the hair on the chair.

I locked myself in the bathroom, exhaled and turned on the shower tap. I tried to find a temperature that was hot but not burning, and I moved the tap a bit to the left cold side. I looked at myself again in the mirror, wondering whether he was right and I looked better with hair? Was it a mistake to shave it off? I look good… do I? The room started to get steamed up, and it was the perfect moment to get into the shower.

Lovely temperature, the water started running on all my naked body, oh yes, after a spliff having a shower is a fantastic feeling. I washed my head to get rid of the rest of the hair. And I started to spread the lavender shower gel all over myself. I started with my shoulders moving my hands in circles to the arms, hairy belly, penis and legs.

I could feel myself clean and refreshed. And suddenly, I wasn´t alone. I felt a lip kissing my back slowly, close to my neck. His left hand squeezed my left nipple piercing. It felt so nice. His right hand started to move up and down my cock, getting me harder. I look behind me, and it was him, Lucciano, naked with hair everywhere and a strong body. He started biting my neck and moving faster. The room was full of steam, and it was tough to see anything through it. Oh, fuck this is so good. He moved his hand with a rhythm. I felt like, oh yeah, I´m fucking coming. I let a loud unintentional noise of pleasure come out of me. All the cum washed away down the plughole in the shower.

KNOCK KNOCK! ´Aiden? What was that noise? What´s going on?´ Ernesto tried to open the door, but it was locked. I looked behind me, and there was no one there. Oh my god, I just had a wank thinking that I was having sex with my workmate Lucciano. ´Everything is good, baby! I opened the cold water, and it was too cold. I almost fell out. ´Oh, alright. Come on, don´t get too much longer. I want to shower.´ I could hear Ernesto saying that from the other side of the door. I was so glad that I locked that door. What would it happen if he saw me having a wank in there? Maybe he would join me. Or would he ask why I was having a wank in the shower without him? Either way, I felt released now and more chilled. I looked again in the mirror, and my face was more relaxed.

Breath in, Breath out.

CHAPTER 12

It was Thursday, and I was doing the late shift again. What a long day: God, I couldn't wait to go home. There were a couple of customers at different tables. The environment was chill, with the candles on, and the light was not bright. It was relaxing and romantic, with Spanish flamenco music playing on the restaurant's radio. Suddenly, a couple came inside the restaurant. They sat at a table next to the entrance, hanging their coats on the chair and waved at me.

´Goedenavond, we willen graag twee glazen rode wijn alstublieft,´ said the Dutch guy who had just taken a seat at the table. I went quiet for a second, looking at them a bit confused. ´Good evening. I'm sorry, I'm afraid I don't speak Dutch yet. Is it okay for you to speak in English?´ The gentleman in his 50s looked at me from the top to bottom and looked at his wife. ´This is incredible; you're living in the Netherlands. Why do I have to speak English? In the Netherlands, you speak Dutch.´ What a cunt, honestly. Did they know this was a Spanish restaurant? Did I expect them to speak in Spanish? So fucking rude. I hated my job. ´I understand, sir, but I just arrived a month ago and didn't have enough time to start learning the language. If you're happy to speak in English, I'll be pleased to serve you,' I said, holding my tongue. ´Don't worry.´

He looked at his wife again, and they both took their coats and stood up. ´Wat jammer dat er elke dag meer immigranten komen zonder de taal te kennen!´ exclaimed the Dutch gentleman loudly, taking his wife's hand, and leaving the restaurant. ´Bye! Thank you for coming!' Stupid cunts, what racist bitches. I wondered why I had to deal with these things.

I went back to the bar, and I started to take the last orders as we were about to close. Suddenly a girl from housekeeping appeared from the door that connected to the kitchen and the elevator. ´Hola! You're Aiden, right?´ She looked very friendly: a very short and skinny girl, with dark blonde hair. She was wearing a white shirt and blue jeans. ´Hey! Yes, I'm Aiden, I've seen you around, but we never spoke much; what's your name again?´ I asked, very friendly. ´I'm Vanesa! Lovely to meet you!'

She smiled at me, very happy and energetic. This girl had a good vibe. ´Is lovely to meet you too! I'm from Cádiz; I moved with my partner Ernesto a month ago, and I'm still getting settling in.´ She came closer and lay on the glass counter. ´Do you have any friends yet? I didn't see you speaking with a lot of people.´ Vanesa said. It sounded as if she's been analysing me for a while. ´Not really. I haven't had any time for anything. I just work and try to get the things for the house done. It's been a bit of a messy time, not gonna lie. I just have time with Ernesto, and that's it at the moment.´ I laughed about it. ´Oh! Well, I was wondering if you fancy coming tomorrow for a couple of drinks in the city centre? The girls from housekeeping will hang out together, so feel free to join us.´ She looked at me kindly and excited, touching her hair. ´Actually, I'd love to! I'm off tomorrow, so that's amazing. Do you have Instagram?´ The common thing that someone from the new generation said. ´Of course, I have! I may be 37, but I am still modern!´ Vanesa said. ´What? C'mon, you're lying. You look like 30!´ I was really surprised by that fact. She looked proud of looking that young. ´I'm afraid it's the truth, darling. But I have this young face, so I can't complain!´ She said, lifting her face with both hands. We swapped Instagram and followed each other. ´Okay, kiddo, I'll text you tomorrow with the address. Let's say 18:30.´ Vanesa confirmed our little plan for the following day. ´That's perfect, darling. Thank you!´ I said to her, excited to have a bit of social life finally; that didn't involve Ernesto. ´My pleasure, now excuse me, but I have to finish room 214. A fucking bitch left a lot of shit there, and you can't believe how filthy the room is. Unbelievable!´ Vanesa took her bucket and notebook with her. ´Bless you, darling. I hope it's not too horrible for you. See you tomorrow!´ She waved at me and ran away to the back door. What a lovely girl.

I took all the payments, cleaned the tables and did the counting. I put all the money in the office's safe box and went to the train. I was exhausted. As soon as I sat down on the train, I lay my head back against the hard seat. It was not very comfortable, but I couldn't be assed to stay still. I was feeling quite happy about meeting Vanesa the following day with the other girls. Actually, I really felt that I needed some space for myself and to create new connections. I was just spending time with Ernesto, and I loved it, but I thought that it would also be nice for me to make other friends.

After 30 minutes on the train, I finally arrived in Almere. Home "sweet" home. It was freezing outside, so I sprinted back to the studio. I opened the door, and Ernesto was on the sofa, watching Youtube and having a glass of red wine. ´Baby! I missed you! You're finally here.´ Ernesto jumped from the sofa and gave me a big cuddle. I could smell him. He took a shower, I could tell. He kept cuddling and kissing me. ´How are you, baby? How was your day?´ I asked while he went to serve me a glass of wine. ´Here you go. You deserve it. My day was great; I was doing customer service today as someone called sick, and the Portuguese manager was delighted with me. You know someone was trying to get a refund for a black shirt. Before that, the manager told me that we don't accept refunds so I needed to break one of the shirt's buttons so they couldn't have the money back!´ Nesto said with a cheeky smile. ´Wow, that's very shady. Is it legal? What happened with that woman, then?´ I asked, intrigued by the idea of breaking an item to make it nonrefundable. ´I don't know, but I can tell the lady was confused and slightly disappointed. We laughed a lot about it later in the lunch break. Empari is so shady, so I enjoy the scene. What about yours?´ We both sat on the old sofa we found on the Street. I drank a bit of wine. I needed it. ´Well, it was long, and at the end, I had a couple walk in who were a bit racist with me because I didn't speak the language, and they just left. It was hilarious, to be honest. But the rest was fine; it wasn't hectic, and a girl from housekeeping invited me tomorrow to hang out and go for a couple of drinks. So I'm very excited about that!´ I said, laying my feet on Ernesto's legs. ´First of all, fuck that couple. Honestly, I don't understand why people are like that. And then I'm happy that you have plans for tomorrow, baby! I will work until very late, so I can't join you. But you can go and enjoy yourself. Perhaps I can meet you when I finish my shift and we could go home together?´ Ernesto was expecting to meet me at a certain point. I appreciated that he wanted to come home with me, but why could he not just go home and leave me to enjoy myself until I wanted to come back? ´Thanks, yeah was a bit of an uncomfortable situation, but whatever, this job is not forever, so fuck it. And I'm not sure, I will see as I don't know when we will finish. Are you sure you don't mind?´ I asked again, in case he forgot the permission that he was giving me. ´Don't worry, baby. You go and have fun, just keep me updated, please. I don't want anything bad to happen to you. You know there are a lot of drug addicts in the streets of the city centre at night.´ I thought he was pretending to be my Dad. ´Baby, I'll be fine. Don't worry, I'll text you, and no one will hurt me.´ He moved in closer, kissed my cheek and lay his head on my legs.

We had a lovely sleep together. He cuddled me all night. When his alarm sounded in the morning, he kissed me and tried not to make any noise. He never had breakfast, so he prepared himself a coffee, and that was it. That day, Ernesto had to work 12 hours shift, so I knew he would be tired after work. ´Love you, handsome,´ he whispered in my ear. ´Love you too.´ I said, sleepy and turning myself over, looking the opposite way. I felt sluggish. He left the house, and I stayed in bed for a few more hours.

I loved to spend time with him, but when I was home alone, I felt free, like I needed that peace sometimes, even if it was just because I wanted to play music or sing. It's just being with myself.

I put the kettle on to boil washed my face and drew back the curtains. The day looked grey and chilly outside. I poured some hot water onto my instant coffee with 2 spoons of sugar, and when the cup was less than half full, I stopped and poured a dash of Almond milk. I decided to make some tomato toast: a typical Spanish breakfast.

At that moment, my Mum sent me a message:

Mum: Good morning, Aiden, my darling. Just to let you know, I have already confirmed my holidays so I can come to you for Christmas. I've booked my flight for the 18th of December, so I'll be there for your Birthday on the 19th!

A: Hey Mum, that sounds lovely! I can't wait to see you. I miss you a lot. We'll pick you up at the airport, don't worry about we still have a month. It's cool because we have four days for us and then on the 22nd Carmen and Rosario are coming.

Mum: Lovely, I'm very excited. I miss you very much! Is anything that you need me to bring? Like cheese?

A: Don't worry about it, Mum. I'll let you know more when the time comes. We'll speak soon. I have plans for today. I love you.

Mum: Okay, Aiden, I love you too. But please don't leave everything to the last moment because I need to organise myself. Have fun!

She can be a bit intense sometimes and needs to have everything under control all the time, but I'm not like that, so I needed to not think about it at that point. I spent the rest of the afternoon cleaning the house and getting some groceries in. I had a shower, and I got ready. I decided to wear a green /grey jumper, with my black coat, black jeans and my white Adidas Superstars, which didn't look that white anymore. I sprayed some One Million fragrance on my neck and wrists. I thought that I looked good for the evening. I took some weed with me and left the house.

While on the train to Amsterdam central, I text Vanesa.

A: Hey, gurl! I'm on my way on the train, can you send me the address of the place?

After 5 minutes, she replied:

Vanesa: Hey! Yes, we're already here, so the address is Korte Leidsedwarsstraat 49, 1017 PW, The Waterhole.

A: Fantastic! See you soon.

I arrived in Amsterdam Central at 6:00 P.M. It was 8 degrees outside and already dark. There was a strange smell in the air, somewhere between rainy weather and weed. I made my way to the pub, crossing the city centre. It was just 15 minutes away from the station. It was Friday night, so the centre was busy, with many tourists everywhere. I checked my map, and realised that I'd arrived!

The Waterhole: I could hear the music from the outside. There were round tables that were held up by a barrel. I opened the door, and there was a good atmosphere. It was a small place but had enough space to hold the crowds when things got busy. There was a seating area with some tables and a long bar counter that ran from one corner, taking up almost half the total length of the room. There was a live show in progress, I thought it sounded kind of like rock music. Doesn't matter. Even though it was full of straight people, I kinda liked it.

`Aiden!´ I turned back, and there she was, sitting with more people at a table. I ordered a pint of lager from the bar and went over to the table, feeling slightly nervous. `Guys! This is Aiden. He's the new F&B waiter in the restaurant.´ Vanesa said out loud. And everyone started to introduce themselves.

So, we had Jenna, a Colombian girl in her 30s with black hair and a bit wide. With a very sassy attitude. She was married, but her husband was not with her that night. Oh my god, I was meeting someone in their 30s who was married. Then we had Fernanda, a Black girl with pink braids, very smiley. She was from the Dominican Republic, and she was the youngest one in the group for sure. Ignacio is a handsome guy from Argentina with dreadlocks and blue eyes. Very friendly and chatty. And last but not least, Jacobo. He was in charge of the accounts and marketing of the hotel. He was half Spanish and half Dutch. Blonde short hair, blue eyes, always wearing a suit and more serious. `Well, guys, it's my pleasure to meet you all! I'm very excited, thank you for inviting me.´ I said, a bit shy, looking at all of them. `C'mon, my friend, now you have people to hang out with! We don't bite!´ Ignacio was trying to make me feel part of the group, which felt good. `Of course, Marica, we love to meet new people.´ Jenna was having her pint at a rapid pace. It looked like everyone from South America used the word "Marica" for everything. `Oh, guys, that's so kind. Thank you.´ I felt a bit strange, as I'm a social person, but it's not like I had many groups of friends in the past. In fact, I was a bit alone. So, how long have you been here, then?´ asked Fernanda, while the pub started to get busier. `Let's say around a month. It was a bit complicated, just finding somewhere to live, a job and everything. I'm still trying to find my place here.´ I tried to calm myself and be open with them. `Did you come alone, Aiden?´ Jacobo looked intrigued, so I swallowed the last bit of the beer in the pint before answering. `No, I haven't. I came with my partner Ernesto, we live together in Almere. `Where does he work?´ They were all keeping their attention on me. `So now he's working in Empari, but honestly, he's not getting much money,' I said. `That's shit! I'm happy for him because he has a job at least. Still, Empari is not well known for their excellent salary.´ Fernanda was happy being a housekeeper. She didn't know either Dutch or English. She just needed to clean. `I don't want to look nosey, but how long have you been together? I know we are asking you so many questions. It is just that we want to know you better.´ Everyone agreed, nodding their heads and kept drinking while Vanesa waited for an answer. `It's okay. I'd be curious too. So basically, we've been together for a year.´ They all looked at each other. `So you have just been with him a year and decided to move to another country together?´ The girls look at each other, impressed by Jacobo's question. `Jacobo, they're young, and having that experience is cool.´ Jacobo looked at Ignacio, disagreement written across his face. `Thank you for your point of view, Ignacio. I didn't know that was that relevant,´ Jacobo replied. Oh my god, I'd just known them for an hour, and there was drama already. `Maricas, you both stop. This is not to see who has the biggest cock, is it?´ We all laughed simultaneously at Jenna's observation, and Vanesa winked an eye at me. `I know what you mean, Jacobo, but sometimes you must take risks. I knew that I didn't want to live in Cádiz, so it's better to try, and if things don't work, at least I tried.´ I was trying to justify myself in the face of an unexpected and arrogant point of view. `Yas Marica! Jacobo, please don't be a dick. Keep that for the office.´ He looked at Fernanda a bit angrily. `Whatever, Aiden, it's your decision, and you're still very young, so you can do whatever you want.´ Jacobo tried to sound more friendly, even though it seemed more likely that he was quite a severe person.

After a couple of hours of talking and drinking more pints, I went home, a bit tipsy. I was just listening to some music until I arrived home. I opened the door, and Ernesto was sitting on the chair next to the main door. `Hey, baby! How was your day? I've been looking forward to seeing you!´ I said to him, quite loudly, because of the drinks. Ernesto moved his head slowly towards me. `Hello baby? I've called you 15 times, but you didn't reply to any of my messages.´ He looked at me with a disgusted face. I needed clarification, unsure if it was the pints of beer or if I needed help understanding the situation. `Oh my god, Ernesto. I'm sorry, I completely forgot about it. I had a lovely time with my workmates and didn't check my phone,' I explained. `I was waiting for an hour at the main door of Empari, thinking that you were coming. It was freezing, and now I feel sick. Honestly, why are you so selfish? Are your "new friends" more important than me?´ Ernesto was playing the victim and blaming me for something stupid. `Darling, I apologised already. I don't understand why you're reacting like this. I told you I would see about picking you up and coming together, but I confirm that I was going to do that or give you a time to meet,´ I said, while trying to take my jeans off. `Don't change the subject, Aiden, you told me. Do you remember the conversation? I'm feeling very angry with you right now.´ He stood up from the chair and walked to the sofa without looking at me. `Please, I don't want a fight, Ernesto. I just remembered that I had to text you.´ He kept his eyes on his phone. `Are you going to ignore me?´ I didn't get any answer. I was feeling baffled. I put on some comfy clothes and put the ones that I wore out back in the drawer. I sat next to Ernesto and took his hand `I don't want to talk to you. This is really rude of you and selfish. You could have just texted me.´ He was stabbing me with his eyes. You could tell he was furious. `Nesto, please, you know it wasn't my intention, I got a bit tipsy, and I forgot, you know, sometimes I have my head in the clouds,' I said, trying to defuse the situation `Honestly, don't talk to me.´ Those were the only words that Ernesto had to say.

CHAPTER 13

It was Saturday. I opened my eyes and turned over in bed; Ernesto had already left for work. I yawned, and I stretched my body. I went into the kitchen and prepared a strong coffee with 2 spoons of sugar. I'd woken up hungry so I quickly ate a banana. I put the coffee down on the chair next to the sofa, as we didn´t have a small table. I drew the curtain from the corner to the right end of the room. It was raining; I had a day off that day, so I thought I would spend it resting and maybe preparing some food. I sipped my coffee and started rolling a spliff. Yes, it was 10:30 a.m.: I don´t know. I didn´t want to think much. I just needed to zone out. I opened the balcony window so it didn't get to smelly inside. My phone started to buzz. It was my Mum.

´Hey Mum, what´s up?' I said as I answered the phone. 'Aiden! How are you, darling? We've not called each other for a while so I thought I'd ring you,' she replied. ´Yes, I know. Sorry, I have just been busy, Mum, and tired. How are you?' I said. 'It´s okay, I just missed you, and even if you´re busy, I´d like to know you´re doing alright.

Even though I know you will be fine, you´re there with Ernesto, so at least I know nothing bad will happen. I´m all right, feel a bit tired, you know I´ve been working all week in the office, and now I´m going to clean the house and do some jogging. I need to prepare the food for the week. Busy as always, darling. But I want to know how you are.' Yes, she was always busy. 'That sounds good, Mum. For sure, you´re pretty much more productive than me! Well, I´m not sure what to say, Mum...' I tailed off. 'Why are you saying that? What´s wrong?' She sounded a bit worried and intrigued to know what was going on. I had another couple of draws from my spliffs and held it for a few seconds. And exhaled. I started to feel more chilled. 'It´s just that I don´t really know if I want to be here, Mum. I have a strange feeling and… I don´t know.' It was hard to explain. 'Wait, Aiden, but you just moved a month ago! I´m a bit confused, isn't it what you wanted? To move there with Ernesto and have the apartment?' she asked. I was quiet for a couple of seconds. 'I don´t really know why I feel like this, Ernesto has some attitudes toward me that I don´t understand, and I feel sad. I think I should come back.' As I said it, I knew that was how I felt. 'Aiden. Darling, you know you can come here whenever you need it. This is your home. Remember that. But just keep in mind, I just literally sent you all your stuff. You need to think about what you really want; things are difficult. And also, you just signed the contract for the house. I´m okay with the money because I´ll always help you in any way I can, and I know you both will give me the money back. But you´re 19, you made that decision, and you were happy about being there,' she rationalised. I exhaled deeply. 'I´m not sure anymore about anything. I just know that I don´t know how to deal with this situation,' I sighed. 'Look, Aiden, I´ll be there soon, in a month, and we´ll spend time together. Why you don´t give yourself a bit of time? And if things don´t work, you can move to a room elsewhere. But try to fix things with him; you both need to take care of each other, you´re in another country, and these things are better if you talk about them. And you can always speak to me whenever you know that,' she finished. 'I guess you´re right, Mum, you know that I´m very impulsive. Can´t wait to see you,' I replied. 'Of course darling, things will get better. Can I ask you something?' she said after a moment. 'Yes, go ahead, Mum.' I knew what was coming. 'How much are you smoking?' she asked. 'Why are you saying that? I have my own job, Mum, and my own house. It´s not like you can sniff around if I´m smoking weed,' I snapped back, annoyed. I started to feel nervous, and my right leg started to swing. 'Please, darling, I don´t want to fight. I´m just worried about you, smoking weed can look fun, and you can say that you feel relaxed but can´t escape your problems,' she said. 'Thank you for caring, but I don´t want to talk more about it, Mum. I need to hang up. I love you.' I needed to get off the call. 'Don´t get angry at me,' she replied 'I understand you may need some space now. I love you, Aiden.' She hung up. I smoked the rest of the spliff and lay on the sofa. I closed my eyes, feeling a bit sleepy.

'Aiden? Are you all right, darling?´ I opened my eyes, sleepy and confused, looking around the room. Ernesto had just arrived home. 'Hey, why? What time is it?´ I said, still sleepy. 'It´s 3 p.m., baby.´ He removed the dark grey Empari jacket and hung it on the chair. Ernesto moved closer and sat on the sofa to cuddle me. 'What? I must have fallen asleep on the sofa. Very weird.´ I move myself as I felt uncomfortable laying there for hours. 'I missed you today. It was a long day, and I only wanted to be here with you, the best company.´ I cuddled him back, and we kissed again. 'I´m sorry, I didn´t prepare any food. I've just woken up. I don´t know what happened.´ He looked into my eyes and touched his hair. 'Have you been smoking?´ Ernesto tries to smell me, to know if I'd even had a shower. 'Yes.´ I didn´t need to lie about something obvious. 'Maybe you should try to smoke less, or not in the morning. You know, I get that you fancy it and all of that. I don´t mind the fact. It would just be nice if we could organize it better so if I come home you can have lunch ready or the housework done if you know what I mean.' I knew what he meant 'I know, Nesto, I just needed to chill; I felt sad about last night.´ I replied, hanging my head, a sign of weakness. 'What about last night?´ It looked like Ernesto wholly deleted from his mind the argument we had. Or that he had towards me. 'Darling, you were completely angry at me because I forgot to text you,´ I said, refreshing his memory. 'Oh! I see. Well, baby, that was yesterday. Today it´s a new day. It´s not worth it to be talking about these things. Today we´re fine, aren´t we?´ He tried to smile at me, but it didn't feel true to me. His eyes were entirely still; no wrinkles in the corners. ' I guess so, darling, was your shift long, then?´ I said, moving on. Ernesto stood up and went to the fridge to open a can of beer. 'Yes, downstairs was pretty messy, and we had a new delivery, and one of the new girls messed up and changed the labels, so you can imagine. Also, we had more work because a couple of colleagues were sick. But now I´m feeling better. I´m with you, so I can´t ask for more.´ He took a drink of the beer and stripped naked, showing his hairless body. I couldn´t resist taking a look at all of him, even though I like men with more hair and a bit more weight. ´I need a shower. I´m feeling filthy. Why you don´t prepare something quick to eat?´ Ernesto said, winking an eye at me. ´Sure, what about some pasta?´ That was the fastest option. ´Sounds good.´ He shut the door, and I started boiling the water. I have a spiced tomato sauce, so I will get that ready and grate some cheese. The food didn´t take long as preparing the pasta is very quick. It smelled really nice. What a simple plate but very useful. I sprinkled the grated cheese on it, and I started to mix it properly. Some salt and lots of black pepper, I loved it.

The bathroom door opened up, and a lot of steam came out. Ernesto was drying his hair and had already dried his body. He was wearing black boxers, which looked good on him. His ass looked impressive, even though he didn´t have much. What miracle boxers. I felt him cuddling up to me from behind. ´That smells amazing. Have you put some basil in it?´ he said, kissing my neck. ´Of course, always! Get your comfy clothes on, and let´s have lunch.´ He pulled on his grey trackies, and we sat at the table in front of each other. He still had the beer, and I was drinking a glass of water. ´I´ve been thinking, maybe I could go with you next time you meet with those friends? They sound like friendly people to hang out with!´ Ernesto was looking at me, like always and blowing the hot pasta to take it into his mouth. ´But how do you know that? I couldn´t tell you much last night, darling, but yes, they would love to meet you.´ I said, although unsure about my answer, as I didn´t mean it. ´That´s amazing, we will have friends together, sounds really fun!´ He smiled at me while I returned my attention to the pasta. ´I guess so, by the way. I know we did it a couple of months ago when we were in Oslo, and you told me that you didn´t want to talk about it again until next year, but I´d like another threesome.´ Ernesto stopped eating and puts his full attention on me, swallowing the rest of his food. ´Well, yes, we did it, but it´s not like there´s a rush to do it again, right?´ I started to move the pasta around the plate with the spoon. ´It´s not like I´m in a rush. It´s more that I really liked that experience and sharing it with you. I don´t know, it was very hot, and I´d love to discover more things with you.´ I felt like a child again, asking for permission to do something. ´I´m not saying we´re not going to do it again. But we´re going to do it together. And now there are other things to focus on. It´s not time for that. I don´t fancy it. I just fancy you.´ Ernesto said. Analyzing my words and body language. ´I fancy you as well, baby, but I just wanted to tell you how I felt.´

I remember when we did our first threesome together, I´d always wanted to do it. Still, he wasn´t ready, and the most that we did was have sex in Chatroulette in front of more people, wanking, watching us. So when we were in Oslo, I tried to convince him. That was a difficult day because we had a huge fight. After all, he yelled at me, and I needed to be like an hour explaining to him why I was feeling sad and really uncomfortable with the way he'd spoken to me, as my past experiences weren't the best. Now I was thinking, do I really need to spend one hour speaking to someone that is my partner to make him understand that if he yelled at me, I would feel despondent and anxious? Whatever, he agreed to it, and we met a Norwegian guy who came to the Airbnb where we were staying in, and I fucked him. Ernesto didn´t want to, so the guy sucked him off. It was a very horny situation, and I came quickly as I'd wanted that moment to happen for so long, so I got too excited. After that, I mostly spoke for an hour with him all naked in the bed, and Ernesto was quieter, but sometimes he joined in the conversation. Until the guy left. I remember he followed us on Instagram. Ernesto got annoyed because he replied to one of the pictures I posted. It was not like I didn´t want Ernesto. Still, since I was younger, I´d been intrigued by being with more people and sharing sex together as I find more people attractive, and I´d fuck them for sure. But I never tried it before Ernesto, as my other relationship was very toxic. I was, and he was. We both were in a challenging situation, and I cheated on him after one day of breaking up to then get back together the next day. Until he cheated on me. Wait, why I´m thinking again about Marcos? I WAS JUST THINKING ABOUT THE THREESOME, NOT HIM!

PEOPLE LIKE YOU

CHAPTER 14

I was late again! For fuck sake! I sprinted to catch the train towards Amsterdam Zuid. I was doing the morning shift, and I started at 6:30 a.m. I'd spoken with the manager about my rota, as I'd been doing closing since I began, and I barely spent time with Ernesto. Equally, I was just going from home to work and vice versa. So now I was going to be doing mornings most of the time. It was a bit hard to wake up so early as I had to be there on time and the train was half an hour away. Hence, it was just my awful time management. Since I was a teenager, I had gotten messy talking about being on time and that kind of thing. It is not like I was really desperately late, but even if I woke up on time, I ended up having to rush myself not to miss the train and not be late.

But at least with the new hours, I'd finish between 3 and 4 p.m. and have the rest of the evening for myself, and hopefully, I'd have some time alone with Ernesto. They treated me very well in the hotel. The only issue was that the morning team were basically two old ladies who wanted to be gossiping and talking with the customers all the time, asking me to do most of their duties. Who the fuck did they think they were? What bitches, but honestly, I couldn't be bothered. It was just for a couple of hours. Later, I'd have to be by myself downstairs, opening the bar and serving coffee and lunch.

It had been busy that morning with the breakfast. Still, actually, I liked it because it was more straightforward than working in the restaurant. It didn't mean that being downstairs was difficult, but when it was a buffet service, you didn't need to worry much about anything other than having to restock everything and fill up the orange, apple, and cranberry juice and the black filter coffee. It was quiet. Just a couple of customers were using their laptops and drinking mint tea with honey. I guessed they were business people staying in the hotel and were doing "important things". For that reason, they were wearing suits and black office shoes. I went around the corner cleaning a few things as they didn't want me to stay still, not doing anything. So I was very focused on it when suddenly I heard very close to my ear: ´DON'T BE SCARED!´ I jumped, and I turned around. It was Ignacio recording me. ´ You bitch, you scared me!´ I said, my hand on my chest. ´Why? I have a smooth voice.´ Ignacio was very cheeky, and we both started laughing. ´Oh god, I'm going to kill you! Do you want something to drink, darling?´ I offered him, as he was a lovely guy, and I liked to give small treats like that to the people I liked and who were nice to me. ´Yes, Aiden, that would be beautiful. I just escaped for a bit. I have to hoover the stairs, it's so annoying.´ We both went to the bar. He was sitting in the high chair while I prepared a coffee in a takeaway cup. Suddenly Vanesa and Jenna made a big entrance from the door next to the hotel's reception with the task folder and a blue pencil. ´Well, Marica, it looks like you're both having fun, right?´ Jenna said, being sassy and embracing a bitch character. ´C'mon Jenna, you know I'm doing a great job. I just came to have a quick coffee and chat with this handsome Spanish boy.´ Jenna wasn't the only sassy one, as Ignacio knew how to answer and get away with it. ´I see. In that case, Aiden, can you prepare two more lattes for us?´ Vanesa asked, looking at me with a cheeky smile and then at Ignacio. They held it for a couple of seconds. Until they realised, we were still there and got back to a normal position. ´Is my pleasure, darling.´ The three of them sat beside each other, drinking their coffee quickly. But Vanesa and Jenna were the supervisors for Housekeeping, so they had things under control. ´Where's Fernanda?´ I was intrigued, as she was very noticeable with that fancy hair. ´She's not working today. The bitch called in sick. So today we need to do a bit more, but the hotel is not as busy as it will be at Christmas, so it will be all right.´ Vanesa replied, checking all the tasks in the folder again. ´Are we meeting soon, right? I'd love to have some pints in the Waterhole,´ Ignacio proposed, as the Spanish language was keeping us, foreigners, together. Jenna and Vanesa agreed by nodding their heads. ´Yes! The sooner, the better. I'll let everyone know, and by the way, Aiden, if you want to bring your boyfriend, you're more than welcome. It would be lovely to meet him.´ I hid my hands under the counter and started moving my fingers quickly, touching them. Was this normal? Vanesa was just inviting Ernesto to hang out with us. ´Yes, sure! That will be nice. I'll tell him later on.´ I gasped quietly, pretending that I loved that proposal when my body told me I was in danger. ´Fantastic, thank you for the coffee, Marica. Ignacio, the hotel is not going to clean itself.´ Vane laughed at Jenna's sassy answer. ´Look at her. She's feeling the power of being a supervisor. Yes, boss Aiden, thank you for the coffee. I will see you around!´ They all left, and I went to pick up a couple of dirty cups on the table. ´Buongiorno! ´ Lucciano came from the back door. He looked very handsome in his uniform. I knew he was straight, but seeing him getting close to me made me melt. ´Morning! How are you doing? Nice to see you.´ I saw he was wearing this dark blue tight t-shirt, so I could see a bit of hair coming out from his chest, very close to his neck. ´I'm doing all right, feeling ready for today. All good so far?´ Lucciano went to the coffee machine, took the smaller cup, and made an espresso. He drank it immediately, with no milk, sugar, or anything. So Italian. ´Yes, I was a bit busy with the breakfast, and you know, they're a bit lazy, but I came here as soon as it was time. But there are not many customers here.' Lucciano looked around the restaurant to check how many people there were. There was a blonde lady in a corner, reading a book with a glass of white wine. She was wearing a black semi-short jacket with some transparent and black-lined stockings. ´Santa Madonna, have you seen that girl? She's so attractive. Look at her legs with those heels. Looks like she's going to get naked as soon as you get close to her.´ You could tell he had the common observation of a cis straight man, but I looked at him spying at her, biting his lip and looking at me for some approbation. I thought I'd love to have sex with him. I was thinking about that again, I don't want to sound annoying, but what could I do? My body was speaking to me and asking me for it. ´She's very hot, you're right. What a shame that I'm not into women.´ I said back to him, trying to fit in the kind of conversation that straight men have. ´C'mon, Aiden! You never slept with a girl?´ He asked, curious. ´I'm afraid not, haha. I'm not into it, but who knows, maybe someday. I really doubt Ernesto is even going to get close to panties.´ We left the conversation there and decided who would cut the ham. I told him to do it, as I found it very disgusting, and cleaning the machine was a nightmare.

After finishing my shift and finally getting back to Almere Centrum, I found Ernesto coming out of the off-license on the corner of the street. ´Hey baby, what a surprise!´ Surprise? I told him that I was on my way, but whatever. ´Hey, darling.´ I got closer, and I kissed his lips. ´What are you doing here?´ I asked Ernesto as if I didn't already know the answer. ´Just came for some cigarettes, I was running out, and you didn't have more either, so I got you some as well.´ He placed one Marlboro on his lips to smoke it on the way home. ´That's all right, thanks, baby. I'll transfer you the money now.´ We got back to the flat, and while I took a quick shower, he filled up two glasses of red wine. This time it was more smooth and a bit fruity but strong. I loved it. The heater was on, so I stayed in my underwear. ´Cheers to us, baby. I love you.´ Ernesto said, smiling at me, showing his crooked teeth. Sometimes I didn't know if it was a lovely smile or if he was smelling a piece of shit. I couldn't tell the difference on that face. ´Cheers, I love you too.´ I said back, and Ernesto took my hand to bring me closer. He smelled like cigarettes. ´I thought we could go today to the cinema to watch Maleficent: Mistress of Evil,' he suggested. ´Oh yeah, that sounds cool. It's in the original version?. I hope it is not in Dutch because if it is, I'm not paying for that,´ I said. ´Yes, it is in English, with Dutch subtitles, and in 3D. What do you think?´ Ernesto was looking at the cigarette box, tempted to get another one. ´I'm up for it. What time is it on?´ I felt a bit lazy, but making a plan with him could be nice. ´7:00 p.m., so we still have time. I've been thinking about planning the week,´ he said, opening the agenda on his phone. ´Oh yeah? My workmates say you can come next time, by the way, they want to meet you.´ I said, also intrigued to know what he's been thinking. ´That sounds fantastic! They look lovely. ´He took a sip of wine and carried on talking. ´Today: Cinema and chill in the house. Tuesday: We stay at home and rest together for the evening. Wednesday: Celebrating our anniversary here, so you cook something (and get some wine as well, please). Thursday: Reserve a table in the Italian restaurant for dinner there. Friday: You pick me up from Empari at 5 p.m., and we go to Bar Blend to have a couple of drinks and try to look for someone for a threesome. Saturday and Sunday: we stay together at home and, if we fancy it, we could do something in Almere.´ Wow, I didn't know I had my own manager, literally with a rota for the week. ´Do you want to do a threesome with me? I thought you said yesterday that you needed more time.´ I said to him, feeling a bit confused and excited at the same time. ´I'm ready and want to have fun with you, darling.´ Ernesto gave me a cuddle and touched my left cheek quickly. ´Shall we download Grindr, then?´ It's the easier way to meet someone to have sex with. Unfortunately, socialising is difficult these days if it's not on the internet. ´You can have it on your phone for that day. After that, you delete it, okay?´ Why did he only want to keep it for one day? It is not like I would cheat on him, but at least he agreed, so we would try to find someone to have fun with on Friday.

PEOPLE LIKE YOU

CHAPTER 15

It was a sunny day but I couldn't tell if it was warm or cold. I found myself in the middle of the hallway of my huge old house, it was all blurry, and I felt alone. 'Mom? Dad? Where are you?' I thought inside of my little head until I realized they were outside, in the open yard where everyone from the street could see everything. I needed them. I felt myself shaking; they were just shouting at each other, I called out to them, but they raised their voices even more. I couldn't stop crying desperately, feeling alone. Chucky (my 10 years old Chow-Chow) sat next to me; tears were the only thing I could see. It was bright and blurry, with the awful sound of my parents throwing shit at each other. I cuddled Chucky and held him; he was protecting me and knew I felt sad. 'Mom? Dad?' No one answered me.

Suddenly I woke up covered in sweat, my heart racing fast. It was a nightmare, but who could say it was when it happened? Why was I dreaming this? Ernesto was half asleep but tried to cuddle me. I escaped from the bed and went straight to the balcony. Breathe in, breathe out. I told myself it wasn't real anymore, it was a very long time ago, it was part of the past. It was cold outside, but at least it wasn't raining. Sometimes I felt like my head was going to explode. Why was I having these feelings? I couldn't resist this damp cold. I went back inside and shut the door slowly trying not to make any noise.

I locked myself in the bathroom, but I didn't want to shower this time. I needed a bath. I hardly opened the hot water, and it started to pour out. I added a good amount of lavender shower gel to make foam. While waiting, I stared for 10 minutes in the mirror while it started to steam up, my reflection becoming barely visible. I shouldn't have shaved off all my hair, my hair was fragile, and now I looked hideous with such a short amount. I was not feeling comfortable with myself anymore. Maybe I was lucky to be with someone like Ernesto. He could be better, but I made many mistakes and look at me. I was a walking mess. The bath was full, so I closed the tap and drowned myself inside. It was hot and burning, but it didn't matter to me. I held my breath and soaked in the bath. I felt the pressure in my chest getting weaker, feeling the world's weight. I just wanted to be happy. But I was not happy. 'Why did I move here?' I wondered. I was stuck in my mind, I wanted to tell Ernesto, but he wouldn't understand. I couldn't hold my breath anymore. I lifted my head out and took a huge breath. How long had I been? It didn't matter. I was still breathing, I was okay. I felt how the vapour soaked in through my pores. I washed my body slowly. I lay inside the bath for a while in silence: my mind was racing, but at least there wasn't any noise.

Today was going to be a shit day, I thought, while I dried my hairy body with the cheap towel from Primark. Again, I realized that I was going to be late for work, so I quickly pulled my uniform on and threw an outfit for later into my backpack. Yes, I was going out with Ernesto.

As soon as I entered the hotel and I left my stuff in the locker room, I made my way upstairs, where the breakfast area was. I had managed to get there five minutes early, so I prepared a strong espresso and put some honey in it. If Lucciano were there, I'm sure he would have been panicking. Italian people quickly get offended when you add random things to coffee. I took a breath: Okay, let's fuck this shit.

It was a hectic day, and I didn't stop running from one side to the other, cleaning tables and taking the dirty plates to the Kitchen Porter area. I only stopped during my break, which was at 12 p.m. I needed it. I was starving. I walked to the canteen, and I served myself some rice with chips and mushrooms on the side in a bowl. Honestly, at least I had some pepper to fix it.

Fernanda and Vanesa came into the canteen and sat down in front of me after they collected their lunch. 'Hey, girls!' I said, waving my hand at them. 'Hey, Marica! How are you doing?' Fernanda was looking happy, at least she always does. 'Honestly? Now it's better, but I haven't stopped. I don't know what's happening, but it's been bustling.' I said while shoving a spoonful full of rice into my mouth. 'It's because Christmas is coming, and there are a lot of tourists and business people here as well.' Vanesa sat down as soon as she added salad and some chicken pieces to her plate. 'Fair enough, it does make sense. What about you guys?' They both looked at each other and sighed. 'Awful, honestly, these bitches are so filthy, and they leave the room like a complete mess.' Vanesa said, with the same face as someone who works in hospitality. 'I had to do 10 rooms in less than an hour, and you can't believe how bad it was. Sometimes it is impossible to do that many rooms in that short time,' Fernanda's complained, and it seemed to me that she was actually right about it. 'You know that is not up to me, darling. I have the supervisor position, but the managers are the ones that have control over everything.' Vanesa replied to Fernanda, trying to make her feel empathy from the other side, as Vanesa did start like that and knew the challenges of the job. 'I'm sorry to hear that. Sounds crap like this food.' They both laughed. 'Are you doing something later, Aiden?' Vanesa asked. 'Well, I was supposed to meet my boyfriend Ernesto at 5 p.m., we thought of going out for some drinks.' I told them, trying to look happy about it; one part of myself was, but the other was feeling blue. 'Why don't you come with us? We would love to meet him!' Vanesa exclaimed, trying to be friendly with me. 'Sounds good, but I need to ask him first.' I replied. 'Well, we will go to The Waterhole. It's the happy hour until 7 p.m.' Fernanda added, convincing me with the cheap drinks. 'All right, I'll text him. I have already brought some clothing with me.' I said to them, feeling actually more excited about that plan. 'We will shower in the changing room, so let us know if you need a towel,' said Vanesa, drinking some water from her glass. 'Thanks, girls. I'll come to the office later and let you know.´ I went into the smoking area and felt a bit nervous, but I was glad I brought a couple of cigarettes. It was cold, icy outside and wet. I messaged Ernesto.

A: Hey darling! How's your day going? Do you remember the girls from housekeeping that I told you about? They invited us to hang out with them later. We said to go alone today because we wanted to have some fun with someone else. Let's stay for a bit and then go to the Blend bar.

After 2 minutes, he answered.

E: Hey baby, I'm a bit tired. It's a long day but exciting for later. Yes, 100% we could do that. We are both off tomorrow, so we don't need to worry about the time or being hungover. I'm excited to meet your friends!

A: Okay, baby, I'll send you the location later and meet you there.

E: No worries, see you there. Let me know when you get there. Love you

A: Love you too!

Did I really want this to happen? Was it selfish to feel weird about introducing my boyfriend to my "workmates"? They were not my friends, but it was the only time I had to socialize and talk about any shit outside work without him. Did I really want to share that with Ernesto? I wanted to have my own space. But he said it was selfish, and we that we came together. Whatever, that night he'd agreed to meet someone else to have some fun, so I thought that I shouldn't be complaining. I went back to the housekeeping office and couldn't see them, but Jenna appeared suddenly behind me: ´Marica, what's up? What are you looking for here?´ Jenna was looking bossy but kinda funny. ´Hey darling, I was looking for the girls to tell them that we're all going out, my boyfriend Ernesto agreed.´ I said to her. ´Is your boyfriend coming? Oh, that's exciting.´ She touched her black hair and waved it from side to side to show her excitement.

My break was already finished, and so I went back downstairs again. I worked by myself until another colleague joined me at 3 p.m. The morning team were there while I was having my break. The rest of the day went by quickly (a thing I really appreciated after that morning.), and I got a towel from the office. I'd never had a shower in the changing room, but it seemed and smelled very clean, so I was okay with it.

I set out my clean clothes and just took my clean underwear and the towel with me.

I had a shower, not too quick, but not the longest. No one was waiting to enter; I wished it, but it wouldn't happen. I finished, and I dried myself. Put on my tight blue slips. Looked very sexy on me. And I left the shower, sat on the bench, and looked at the bag to get dressed in order and put some One Million fragrance on myself. Lucciano came inside the locker room while I was dressing. ´Ciao! How are you doing, Aiden?´ Oh, he looked adorable in his black coat. He dressed like my dad, but you could forgive him because it was very cute. ´Hey, Lucciano! I'm good, finally done, I just had a shower, and today was busy. Hopefully, the evening will be pretty easy for you.´ I said to him while I found my socks to wear. ´Yeah, I hope so. Are you going out?´

He said while he took a quick look at me. Wait, was he looking at me? ´Yes, I'm hanging out with housekeeping girls and my boyfriend.´ His locker was a half meter from mine. He opened it and took off his shirt and trousers, standing just in his white boxers and long black socks. ´That sounds fun. Well, you have the weekend off, right? I guess you'll have a nice time with them, the girls are very nice.´ I observed his body while he was looking for the uniform in the locker. I could see he was a hairy man as well, not chubby and not skinny, very sexy. And oh my god, can we just talk about the perfect shape of his bum in those white boxers? I could see through them a bit. He put his T-shirt on. 'I'm unsure how it will be, but it sounds exciting. Can't wait.´ I got distracted looking at his bulge, it wasn't big, but it still kept my attention. I needed to stop looking at it. I didn't want to make him feel uncomfortable. Did he notice me looking? He finished getting his uniform on and left the room, waving at me. 'Have a nice one!´ I exclaimed to him, not too excited. I didn't want to show any strange interest in him. ´Thanks! Ciao!´ I realized that I had gotten erect while we were talking. I checked, and a bit of precum had leaked out of me, just a little bit, but enough to lubricate to start something I wasn't going to. I pulled on my red tartan trousers: I was in love with them. I pulled on my black t-shirt with my pair of black Puma Fenty shoes with blue soles. I also grabbed a black jumper and put on my black coat.

I waited for the girls in the bar, and Lucciano offered me a drink, so I got a small San Miguel beer, sitting in a high chair at the bar. I was just scrolling Instagram and Twitter while waiting. I sent Ernesto the pub's location, but he didn't reply. He was about to finish. Half an hour later, the girls were all ready, and we got in the tramcar together.

We finally arrived at The Waterhole. It was raining so we went inside as soon as we could. It was Friday and very crowded everywhere. There was a specific smell: It was a mix of beer, cigarettes and smoke from the stage. We grabbed a big table inside the smoking area, on the other side of the bar on the right. I got myself a pint after waiting 5 minutes in the queue. It was happy hour, so for only 3.50€, I could start the night well. Suddenly I felt someone touching my back: I turned around, and there he was. Ernesto. With his stylish hair (honestly, I didn't know how he'd managed to keep his hair perfect with that crazy rain outside) wearing a beige sweater with a white shirt with blue stripes underneath and basic blue trousers. ´Hey baby, I'm finally here!´ He gave me a hug, I squeezed him quickly, and I moved back into my space as soon as possible. ´I'm all right, it was exhausting today, fucking Christmas is coming, and there were a lot of customers, what about you?´ He touched my face with his left hand and kissed me. ´I'm pleased, I had a good day, and it went quickly. Very excited about tonight.´ I waited another 5 minutes at the bar while Ernesto ordered another pint, and I took him to the smoking room where we were sitting.

All the girls were talking when suddenly, they looked at the same time at us as they noticed Ernesto's presence. ´Hello! So lovely to meet you!´ they all said at the same time. They all had the typical Spanish two kisses, one on each cheek, and Ernesto sat next to me. ´So, Ernesto, Aiden told us you're working at Empari, right? How's it working there?´ Vanesa broke the ice straight away. ´It's alright, I mainly work in the warehouse downstairs, but sometimes they bring me upstairs to be on the till. But there are a lot of Karens and rich people, you can't believe how much money they spend there. The salary is not that good,´ Ernesto said honestly to Vanesa. ´Yes, I agree.

I'm earning 500€ more than him, working the same hours.´ I added to the conversation. ´That's a shame, right? So do you spend time together, or are the shifts different?´ Fernanda asked, curious about it. ´Most of the time, I finish later than Aiden. And I'd like to spend more time with him, to be honest.´ Vanesa took a cigarette out and gave a quick look to Jenna, who returned the look to Ernesto. ´So, will you be interested in finding another job for a higher salary?´ Jenna asked. Ernesto lit a cigarette and looked at me with a thinking face. ´I mean, yeah. It's been a bit difficult to save money, so yes.´ He hadn't even talked to me about it. ´The reception at the hotel is looking for a receptionist, so we might be looking for someone soon. We need to talk with HR, but in case you're interested, do you have experience in the area?´ Jenna asked as if this evening was about being interviewed. ´No, actually (he said, straightening his back to look more confident), but I didn't in Empari either. I just studied level 3 Marketing. But maybe I'm interested, so I'd be closer to Aiden, and we would be in the same environment.´ Wait, what? Why was this conversation happening? They didn't even know him, and I didn't know if I wanted to have him around. I wanted my space. Yes, he would be getting more money if he got the position, but why couldn't I just have my own fucking space? It was so annoying. I took a big sip of the pint. ´Yeah! That sounds lovely! It will be so nice to have you there.´ Why had I just fucking said that? It was time to get more drinks. I went by myself to the bar, and I saw Jacobo and Ignacio. Ignacio hugged me and went to sit with everyone. ´Hey Jacobo, I didn't know you were coming. How was your day at the office?´ I asked him, lying across the bar to get the bartender's attention. ´It was tedious, just calls and emails. Honestly, I couldn't be bothered. But yes, nice to see you too. What are you having? Let's have a shot together.´ Jacobo looked at me and, without a smile, kept his eyes on me for a couple of seconds. ´Oh really? You don't need to.´ I said, surprised he wanted to buy me a shot. He gave me a half smile and ordered two shots. We both swallowed the shot at the same time. The taste of Jagger was delicious. I order a couple more pints and two shots of tequila. I was waiting at the bar while the bartender prepared the drinks. ´Is your boyfriend here, then?´ Jacobo asked the question while drinking a big sip from his pint of beer. ´Yes, why?´ He looked to each side as if he didn't want anyone to hear the conversation. ´No, no reason in particular. I was just curious about it. It's just I've never been with a guy before, and if that was going happen, it would be with you.´ Wow, that was so random, he was so straight in his suit, and I barely knew him, but it sounded like he was saying he wanted to try. ´That's normal. I mean, if you have never tried, you never know.´ I winked an eye at him and paid for the drinks. I piled all of them onto a black tray, and we went to the smoking room.

Should I say to Ernesto what Jacobo told me? I thought I might keep it to myself: even though he was not the most attractive guy and was a bit of an asshole, the idea of fucking with him turned me on. Actually, the idea of just being with someone who was not Ernesto made me even hornier. I placed the drinks on the table. Ernesto was explaining something. ´And that's how we met. You never expect that meeting someone from a bar on a random night could bring me here, right? Look at him.´ He was saying to everyone. The reality was he was lying. We didn't meet in a bar. We met on Grindr. Why was he lying? ´Oh my god, you two are super cute and in love. I know the feeling.´ Jenna said as I felt the attention of everyone looking at me. I looked down at the floor. I was feeling a bit over it. I didn't really like talking about how much in love we were. ´So, you might be working with us soon? That's exciting, mate.´ Ignacio placed the cherry on the top of the cake of my patience. I touched Ernesto's shoulder, and I gave him the tequila shot. All straight down the throat, licking the salt off my hand and biting the lime. I fucking loved it. ´What about you, Vanesa? How's your romantic life?´ She looked at me and exhaled the smoke from her cigarette. ´I'm almost 40, and I never got married. I wanted to, you know, be with someone to build a family and have children, but I just got myself into an abusive relationship, and here I am. Living like I'm in my 20's.´ There was a moment of silence at the table. You could just hear the loud conversations in Dutch in the background mixing with the band playing on the stage. ´Well, it's not like you need to be in a relationship or have a family to be someone. You're here already, with your own independence and your job. Of course, you might want to build something, but things happen for a reason.´ I said to Vanesa as if I were an expert.

So after several pints and many random conversations about our jobs, Ernesto and I decided to leave. It was time to be by ourselves. It had stopped raining outside, but it was cold though. All the street was wet and full of people, with a weed smell everywhere, like nothing new, right? 'They are lovely, it's so nice that they offered me the chance to work there; it will be great for us to be closer to each other,' Ernesto said, quite excited. 'Yes, I guess so.' He took my hand, and I moved in close to him. I wanted to get some warmth from him. We stopped in front of Bar Blend, but it was bustling, so we tried, this time, the next bar. Taboo. It looked similar, so it was okay. It was also packed, but we found space next to the bar. Pop hits were playing on the speakers, and there was a TV where you could see the music videos. The light was atmospheric and low, and there was like a neon blue light. We each got three shots and a half pint. 'I'm already drunk, hahaha,' I got closer to Ernesto. 'Me too.' We went upstairs, and I looked around to see if there was anyone interesting, but everyone was in their own bubble. We sat on the sofa, and we finished our drinks quite quickly. I put my hands on Ernesto's thigh and started licking his neck. He got turned on and kissed me back, and we exchanged a funny play in our mouths with our tongues. I moved my hand to his crotch, and I pulled his zipper down to put my hand inside, and I could feel how hard it was. 'I'm getting horny.' I said to him, melting inside of myself. 'Keep going,' he said with an authoritative voice. So, I played with my hand for a little bit inside his trousers. Yes, it was risky, and we were doing this on a sofa that was literally next to the stairs, but we were so drunk that we didn't care. 'Nesto, I want to suck off someone else. Honestly, I'm very horny,' I begged him with those words. He stood up and went to the toilet. I waited on the sofa, noticing that I got hard as well. He showed up and made a sign to me to follow him. I went inside the disabled toilets, and there was a tall guy inside. Ernesto found someone already. He was not very attractive, but to be honest, I was drunk and horny as fuck, so I didn't care. I locked the door and took my coat off. The floor was very nasty: I didn't care. We got on our knees, and this guy took his cock out. We looked at each other, and I sucked his cock, tasting it, playing with it, feeling it. Ernesto took it and swallowed all of it. He enjoyed it, he held it very hard and went deeper on it but didn't do anything else than that. 'Fuck yes, that's how I like it.´ The tall guy was moaning like a heterosexual beast. Ernesto kept going until I stopped him. Now it was my turn. What a selfish bitch. He just wanted all the cock for himself. I started to play again with it again, looking at this guy and enjoying the moment. I wished I could be doing this forever, sharing my sex, mouth, and tongue, and not just with Ernesto. I sucked it off, in and out, making this movement with my head, and then Ernesto took it back. He started to go deep and fast: not much longer until the guy moaned loudly. You could hear that Britney Spears was playing in the background. He came into Ernesto's mouth. He just said 'thank you' and left the toilet. ´Did you swallow it?´ I asked Ernesto, feeling jealous about it. ´Yes, it was very salty.´ He said, licking with his tongue the side of the lip. ´Okay, so now it's my turn. I got him again on his knees and made him suck me off. I took his head towards me, trying to get to the end of his throat, but he gagged. He kept going and started to wank himself as well. Everything was happening so fast, and the toilet smelled awful, but this was my moment. He was doing what I wanted. For once, that is fucking saying something. I was not going to stop. I took his mouth, and 1 took control of it, in and out, and deep. I accepted the rhythm, and I went more quickly. I couldn't hold it any longer. ´I'm fucking coming´ I said, getting to my drunken climax. ´Give me your milk. I want it.´ Ernesto begged, looking at me with a slutty face, and I came inside Ernesto's mouth. Now he had a double one. As soon as he felt my warm spunk in his throat, he moaned and came on the floor.

CHAPTER 16

The next day, I was feeling very hungover: coffee was taking the edge off things but I still felt a bit shit. 'Baby, do you want to go for a walk?' Ernesto asked, with a broken voice from smoking so many cigarettes the previous night. I guessed it might help with the awful hangover. I immediately drank a full glass of water and placed it in the sink. I pulled on my grey trackies and a warm wine-coloured hoodie. I couldn't be bothered to get dressed up posh: the day was going to be a lazy one, and I love to be in comfortable clothing. Not like Ernesto, he needed to get himself dressed as if he were about to be in fashion week, with a lot of hairspray and cream on his face, just for a walk at 11 a.m, but he was like that.

It was cold outside, but at least it wasn't raining. We made our way to the centre, where all the shops were. We were holding hands, but it felt pretty weird. It was busy, full of people of all ages, getting groceries or just sitting in a bar, whatever. It was alive and friendly to see everyone doing their own thing. 'Do you fancy sitting in here to have a drink?' Ernesto suggested, looking at me. 'Yeah, let's go.' "Le Baron" was a restaurant/bar/coffee place that was very fancy with 2 floors and light brown wooden tables in the same colour as the chairs. There were also a couple of tables at the left side of the room, facing the window with low fancy vintage chairs of different styles. There was atmospheric music playing in the background, and actually, it was pretty full of customers.

We had a seat, and the blond Dutch waiter brought us the menu a couple of minutes after. ´What are you drinking?´ Ernesto hesitated with his head thinking, looking at the drinks menu. ´I might get the hot chocolate. What about you?´ he said. ´Mint tea, I think it will help to cope with this feeling.´ We ordered, and the waiter took the menu. ´Did you have fun last night, baby?´ Ernesto was holding my hand and looking at me like he saw a piece of diamond in the sky. ´Yes, a lot. And actually, I found it very hot when we sucked off that guy at the toilet. I still can´t believe how quickly you found him.´ Ernesto smiled and let out a small laugh. It sounded a bit fake. ´I don´t know, I just saw him and asked him if he wanted me and my boyfriend to suck him off, and it worked, but I was very drunk. I have never done that kind of thing before. I´m not that kind of person.´ Ernesto added to the conversation as if being an ethical slut is a bad thing. We got our hot drinks at the table, with one caramel waffle cookie. It's very typical there to cover the hot drink with the cookie so it melts the caramel. It was boiling, so I needed to wait a bit. ´I know, but I was thinking, I really enjoyed it, but it´s like I want more. Sometimes I feel like I´d like to do it more often.´ Ernesto pulled his hands from me and looked hard and questioningly at me. ´What do you mean? Wasn´t it enough for you?´ He changed the tone of his voice from sweet Ernesto to an accusation. ´Well, I just feel like I need to discover more about myself sexually, and I like to have sex with you, but I´d like to try more things.´ He listened very carefully to me, his eyelids twitching. ´Like what, Aiden? I´m confused. You said you wanted a threesome, and again I agreed to do what you wanted to, and now you´re telling me that you want more?´ he reproached me while I took a few bites of the waffle and I blew on my mint tea, putting the cookie on the side. ´Ernesto, I just want to enjoy my sexuality more, and yes, I enjoyed last night. But it is not because it´s not enough. For example, I have been behind you to penetrate you for a long time because you always say that it hurts and doesn´t fit. I got you that small toy to try and help, and you didn´t even use it. I´m just feeling in a routine, darling.´ I said honestly to Ernesto, as I was feeling bored of the same thing. ´Aiden, if I don´t let you penetrate me is because I don´t want that, and I told you it doesn´t fit, and it hurts. Why you don´t respect that? And what do you want to say about enjoying your sexuality more? Do I have to remind you that we are together, we are a COUPLE!´ He makes the word couple sound like an intense statement of life or death. ´I just wanted to share how I´m feeling. This doesn´t mean that I don´t love you. It's just that I feel attracted to more people, and I´d like us to be in an open relationship. I´d like to have sex with more people and for you to do the same.´ The disgust on his face at that point was unbelievable. He needed to put down his hot chocolate on the table and breathe. ´Open relationship? Is it never enough for you, Aiden? You wanted to have a threesome, and you got it, and now you´re here, asking me to be in an open relationship because you want to fuck more guys? Don´t you have enough with me? And who else do you feel attracted to?´ I started to feel anxious, like a slight stabbing pain in my chest. ´Ernesto, I love you and want to be with you. I don´t understand why you make it look like I´m selfish and it´s never enough for me. It´s not fair; I´m just expressing how I´m feeling. If, for example, I´m feeling attracted to someone at my work and I want to shag them, it doesn´t mean I will leave you or not care about you.´ Ernesto looked surprised and angry simultaneously; there were not many nails for him to bite left, as in his nervousness, he'd already chewed them off. ´Here you go, so there´s someone in your work that you want to fuck, and for that reason, you want an open relationship? Have you lost your mind, Aiden? Do you think I want to be with someone like you? If we are together, we don´t share. The fact that we suck off one guy doesn´t mean that we are open or allow you to be feeling like a slut.´ He said, throwing hate towards me, just with the simple way that his face looked at me. ´Why are you just focusing the conversation in that way? Those are my feelings. It´s not wrong to feel attracted to more people. I don´t get why you´re talking like that to me. I have an awful headache, and you´re just making it worse. What can I do if you don´t give me what I need? It´s just so annoying.´ Ernesto stood up and took his camel coat from the brown chair. ´So we shouldn´t be together then.´ I didn´t even have time to say a word before he left the venue. I was feeling confused and down at the same time. I didn´t understand why he pretended to be alright and acted like nothing was happening when it was. I tried not to argue with him because it always ended up the same way.

I finished my mint tea and called the waiter to pay the bill. That was a brilliant point, he felt angry and lefts, so I had to pay for his fucking hot chocolate. I rolled a spliff while walking to the lake of Almere Centrum. I went straight away, walking around for five minutes and turning to the right. There was a modern black building with an interesting structure: it was not in perfect shape and looked a bit twisted, and it got my attention. I kept walking on that fabulous, cold wintery Saturday and found my place. There was a wooden pier behind the Merkur casino of Almere. It was beautiful just to see a quiet location surrounded by water and full of swans swimming around. I sat on one of the steps, and I lit my spliff. I didn´t know if it would help with my hangover, but I really need one then. I checked my phone, and I saw that I had a message from my Aunt Mimi:

Aunt Mimi: Darling, how are you? It´s been a couple of weeks since we spoke. I know you´re busy, but I just want to know if all it´s going right for you.

A: Hey, Aunty. I´m good, thanks. Many things are going on, but I´m alright, just working a lot and still trying to get used to this country, but how are you?

Aunt Mimi: Oh darling, it´s so good to hear about you. You know that I miss you already. I´m good, like always, with a lot of pain but cleaning the house all day, you know, my husband is a lazy bitch. It´s just getting messier in the house, so as soon as I get it clean, it´s dirty again, so it is driving me completely nuts.

A: Oh, sorry to hear that, Aunty. Why do you just not say to him? That could be helpful to him to understand and help you more.

Aunt Mimi: If you´d know… I did millions of times, and you know your cousin is still a child, but he's learning that from his father, and who is the bad one because I want to live in a clean environment? Yes, me. But apart from that, are you doing all right?

A: It´s not like you can do much more, right? Try to take it easy, Aunty. You know how straight men are. Yes, I have my days, but I guess I´m all right. It´s too soon to say something. It´s my first time living with a "partner", so I´m trying to get used to it.

Aunt Mimi: Well, darling, let me tell you. I´ve been married 2 times, and this is the 3rd one. It´s shit, but you didn´t sign any papers or anything. You do whatever you want, darling, and take the chance that you´re in there. You´re young and handsome.

A: I guess so. Thanks for the words, Aunty. Can we speak at another time? Was lovely to chat with you, though.

Aunt Mimi: Of course, I love you, my boy. I´m here for anything that you need.

A: Thank you, Aunty. I love you too.

Well, that was nice. At least I had some nice words in the day. I took the last puff of the spliff, and I binned it. I spent a few minutes contemplating the environment, feeling the cold in my numb body. I couldn´t describe how I was feeling then. Just a bit confused and spaced out. I thought that returning to the house and talking with Ernesto might be a good idea. Maybe the hangover affected him. I was back in the studio within 10 minutes, as I walked quickly, it was cold, and I started to feel a bit lazy because of the spliff. Ernesto was smoking a cigarette on the balcony and looked at me, very disappointed, as soon as I entered. ´Hey, can we talk?´ He finished the cigarette, entered, and closed the sliding door behind him. ´What do you want, Aiden?´ I sat on the sofa and invited him to join me with a gesture. ´Why did you react like that, Ernesto? Do you think I don´t love you?´ I said to him, looking for some understanding between us. ´I´m not having this conversation again. You´re just selfish and thinking of yourself and everything about yourself. How do you think I feel when you tell me that you want to fuck more people? Do you want to replace me?´ His leg was constantly moving. He was nervous, I could tell ´I´m selfish because I want to enjoy more my own sexuality? What if I don´t feel that satisfied? Is it selfish to just share my thoughts with you and be honest? I don´t want to replace you, Ernesto. I chose to change my life and live with you because I love you, don´t get things confused.´ I was desperately hoping he could understand my feelings. ´Well, Aiden, that´s not gonna happen, I´m not going to have an open relationship, and I don´t want to be with you. It´s just so rude and annoying, after all the things that I´ve done for you along the year that we´ve been together, and now it´s all about fucking someone else.´ He stood up and started to move around that small place that we called " home" ´Ernesto, I think you do not understand what I´m saying and honestly, can you just stop saying how much you've done for me? It´s not like I put a gun to your fucking head to force you. It´s pathetic this attitude, and I´m very disappointed.´ He turned around from the other side of the room. ´You´re the pathetic one here.´ Ernesto said without mincing his words. ´Are you happy to talk to me like that? I don´t deserve that and haven´t been rude to you. I just said that your attitude is pathetic, not you.´ Maybe my words were not the best ones. But when you get tired of explaining over and over the same thing, you get mentally exhausted. That´s what happened to me. ´I don´t give a fuck. Just leave me alone, don´t talk to me. Honestly, it´s just fucking annoying to even look at your face right now.´ There I was, myself again, in an argument that I didn´t want to be in, but to be fair, I was expecting it. It had been a while since our last one, and things had gotten too chill and calm. I wonder why he overacts in that way and doesn´t talk about his feelings. He never does. Why was it always my fault for the way that I felt and thought? Sometimes I just think that I didn´t know what I was doing there and why I decided to move there: don´t get me wrong, I liked Amsterdam, but maybe it was my opportunity to be alone and not again depending on someone else.

Why did I choose someone like him to be with?

Ernesto took his keys and decided to leave the studio. I didn´t know where he went, as he didn´t talk to me.

I needed to do something, so I started tidying up the house a bit, brushing the floor and washing the plates and cups in the sink. I checked the fridge but forgot I didn´t have anything prepared for dinner, so maybe I could prepare a nice risotto for lunch. I put some pop music on in the background and chopped onions, garlic and mushrooms and fried them in extra virgin olive oil. The key to a perfect risotto is a massive amount of parmesan cheese and white wine. After a couple of minutes, they were ready. I left them on the side and boiled the rice in slow heat. I went to the balcony, and I lit a cigarette. I was feeling exhausted, and I hadn´t done that many things. It was not even 2 p.m.. My head wouldn´t stop thinking. Maybe I was not being fair to him, as he said: I was carrying a heavy bag from my past, and I was overreacting. I was not sure anymore of anything. I just knew that I felt confused like I was there physically in the Netherlands, but my mind was somewhere else, being in different places simultaneously. It was a bizarre sensation. I finished the cigarette and stubbed it out in the ashtray. I checked the rice, and it was still cooking slowly, so I stirred it a bit and left it to finish.

I heard the sound of the keys inside the front door lock: Ernesto was back. He brought with him a couple of H&M and Primark bags. He still had a shit face, but not as bad as before. 'Looks like you've been shopping.' He took his shoes off and left the bags close to the drawer in the other room. 'Looks like you've been productive in the house.' He answered back. I could tell he was still upset. He entered the bathroom and looked at himself in the mirror to check if his hair still looked nice. 'Well, I cleaned a bit, and I prepared risotto. I know you love it.' He was looking at me through the mirror. 'That's good.' He was trying to hold his head up and pretend he was still angry at me. 'Nesto, can we talk?' Ernesto looked surprised but interested in those words, so he left the bathroom and came closer. 'What now, Aiden?' His voice sounded arrogant. 'I know it was intense before, and I want to apologise. It was my fault, and I think I'm wrong.' I surrendered myself to him, accepting all the bad things that were said. 'Wrong with what?' His eyes were analysing every movement of my face. 'Well, I didn't want to upset you. I just thought it was nice to have an open conversation about sex. But I guess I'm just asking for more than I should. And I love you and don't want to break up. Christmas is coming, and we just moved in together. We need to try to deal better with these things.' I didn't know if I really meant what I was saying. I felt a deep hole in my chest, swallowing all my emotions from myself. 'I guess you're right. I appreciate that you apologised because you were wrong.' Ernesto, summarising my own opinion with that short amount of words. 'I know, I'm a mess.' He smiled at me and kissed my lips. Ernesto looked happier then, and all the expressions on his face changed completely. He suddenly looked more relaxed and acted like nothing happened. I never understood how he could get away from those feelings so quickly and easily.

CHAPTER 17

It was December 18^{th,} and I was going to reunite with my Mum after almost 3 months. She was coming to stay for Christmas and to be with me on my birthday. I had to say the past weeks were a bit awkward, as Ernesto had been too nice to me, but I felt kind of spaced out with him. Yes, we had sex, slept together, and had our "normal" daily life, but there was something inside of my heart that didn´t feel quite right at all. I felt chained there like I just wanted to run away and leave it all behind. Still, for one reason or another, I was incapable of making any decision. 'Hey, baby!´ Ernesto had just arrived from Empari. It was 3 p.m.. He left his camel coat hanging on the white leather chair and came to kiss my cheek. ´Hi, how was your day?´ I asked him, feeling as if I had no blood running through my veins, just sadness and conformism. ´It was a mess. Now that Christmas is officially here, you can´t believe how many people are coming daily. But I´m finally here, and we can chill together.´ Ernesto took his shoes to the front door, removed his trousers, and folded his uniform, ready for the next day. ´Well, nothing strange in that. Christmas and working in sales is the perfect cocktail for being stressed, right? My Mum is arriving at the airport by 7 p.m. if her flight isn't delayed,´ I informed him, checking the screenshot my Mum sent me again. ´Cool, so we still have time to relax for a few hours. I´m going to take a shower. I stink of that fucking smell of a rich old woman.´ He took his t-shirt off, leaving his skinny torso visible. ´Ernesto, I don´t know if you realise it, but my Mum is arriving in 4 hours, and we didn´t go to buy the air mattress.´ He was taking new slips and a pair of clean black socks from the drawer. When he gets to the bathroom, he stops in the middle of the apartment and looks at me. ´You came home earlier than me. I just want to chill. I´m feeling tired.´ Ernesto was again passing me the responsibility. ´I was waiting for you because your family is coming and will also use it in a couple of days. I wanted to check it with you, and I won´t leave my Mum sleeping on the sofa.´ I was starting to feel annoyed. Maybe it was not a big deal to be angry about. But I couldn´t control it. It was like a massive power of emptiness towards him. ´Do you really need me to buy an air mattress? I think you´re mature enough to go to the shop, or do you need my approval for that as well?´ He left me speechless again, as I hadn´t finished the conversation when he slammed the door to the bathroom and locked the door. I didn´t get why he said that. Of course, I could go and buy it by myself, but maybe if I get an expensive one it will be a problem, or if it´s too cheap and nasty quality. Because everything was a problem with Ernesto.

I received a message from my Mum, she was waiting at Sevilla Airport to take the plane. But still, she had to wait a while. She needed to leave five hours earlier so she could feel that she had enough time for everything. Sometimes I was jealous of the way that she organised herself that well. I was pretty much more messy and bad at managing time. I lit a spliff to calm down while Ernesto was in the shower. I didn´t want my Mum to see us like that or see me sad. I felt the smoke getting inside my chest, passing through my throat. This was good. This was what I needed now. After a few minutes, Ernesto exited the bathroom and looked at me, annoyed. ´Smoking again, Aiden? Can you at least open the door? It´s not that difficult.´ I exhaled the smoke out my mouth while I turned my head slowly towards him. ´It´s not that difficult to at least not complain more and come with me to buy the fucking air mattress. I´m so done with the bullshit Ernesto.´ He opened his eyes, surprised by my answer, walking towards the balcony aggressively to open the door. ´What bullshit Aiden? Can you stop being fucking dramatic and act like an adult? Do you want to go to buy the shitty air mattress? Let`s go. I won´t rest at all after working all day to satisfy your need to buy that fucking shit.´ Dramatic? Acting like an adult? How should I act like an adult if I was still 19? Ernesto got dressed quickly in trackies and a grey hoodie. ´C´mon, Aiden, leave that shit and let´s go to the shop, don´t make me wait.´ I left my spliff on the ashtray and put my shoes on. I didn´t mention any words to him. I couldn´t be bothered, I just wanted to feel relaxed, but it looked like that was not gonna happen.

Our way to the shop was quiet, and in silence, you could feel the tension in the air. I was just not looking at him at all, and he was the same with me. We went into the shop and had a look around. Ernesto found a couple of air mattresses to choose from. ´Which one?´ He asked, with an arrogant voice. ´I don´t care, Ernesto, whatever you want, your mother and your sister will use it as well, you could also think of them. This one looks fine enough.´ He looked at me out of the corner of his eye and took the box, making our way to the till. ´You pay, I´ll transfer you half of the money now.´ So, that was it, it was something so easy to do. I didn´t know why it was that difficult to deal with him.

As soon as we returned to the house, I finished the spliff. Ernesto was watching some trash videos on YouTube: this kind of cis heterosexual guy trying to be funny. Still, he was just an asshole, but it was the kind of humour that Ernesto liked, pretty basic, if I was honest. I took a nap, feeling exhausted after that much drama, and woke up at 6:30 p.m.. ´Aiden, isn't your Mum arriving at 7 p.m.?´ Ernesto said loudly from the sofa. ´Yes, but the plane still needs to land, so I´m going to grab a quick shower, and I´ll go to pick her up.´ I went quickly into the shower to get the stinky smell of weed off me. I didn´t want my Mum to see me like that. After a quick irrational shower of unfulfilled dreams, I was just drying myself and looking at my face in the mirror. My eyes seemed sad. She was gonna notice it. I got out of the bathroom quickly looking to find anything to wear on the train. I was late, of course. ´I´m coming with you to the airport.´ Ernesto said as soon as I started to get dressed. ´It´s okay. You don´t need to.´ I didn´t want that to happen. ´I want to go to receive your Mum,´ he kept saying. ´Ernesto, seriously, it´s okay. I just need to go pick her up and bring her here. You don´t need to spend money on that.´ I was trying to go alone to save myself from seeing that disgusting cockroach face, at least for an hour. ´I want to, and I´m going to go, Aiden, whether you like it or not, she´s my mother-in-law, and I´m not going to stay here pretending that I´m not interested in picking her up.´ We got on the train at 7 p.m., 35 minutes from the airport. I hope my Mum didn´t need to wait long. There was a peaceful silence on the train until Ernesto started to send a voice message to his "lovely" friends out loud, laughing, saying how good things are going here. The vast amount of money he was getting. Feeling the vibration of that voice in my eardrum. It was dark outside, so I could barely see the few street lights. As soon as we got into the airport we looked around, it was busy with a lot of couples coming to visit the country. I felt pretty lost as I was not sure in which exact part she was, but after 5 minutes we found my Mum. ´Aiden!´ She said from the other side, a couple of meters away. She was wearing brown high boots with a black coat, a tied hoodie on her hips, and a backpack on her back.

She sprinted with her luggage towards me and hugged me. It was strange. She was finally there and hugging me like I really needed it. But I felt nothing. I felt like my body was not physically there. ´Darling, I missed you so much. I´m so happy to be here. Ernesto, C´mon here!´ She gave Ernesto another hug, but less intense than mine. We made our way to Almere Centrum again. Ernesto had changed his face completely, acting as if nothing had happened, as if we were happy and didn´t have any fights before. ´So, I guess you feel exhausted right Emma? How was the flight?´ Ernesto opened his mouth to behave like a role model boyfriend, caring about the mother-in-law. ´Yes, I´ve been awake all day, I worked at the office until the afternoon, and Ricardo picked me up with all the luggage and a sandwich so I could eat something. You know Ernesto, busy as always.´ She was holding my hands, and I felt a strange energetic heat coming from her hand. ´Now you´re here, Mum, finally. Are you hungry?´ She kept holding my hand, and looking at my eyes, trying to see deeper inside them, looking for answers to questions that she hadn't yet spoken aloud. ´Actually, yes, I´d love to eat something. Are there any restaurants open?´ my Mum asked, laying her head on my shoulder. ´I think so. There´s a pizza place close to our apartment that is very nice.´ The rest of the time, my Mum spoke with Ernesto about the flight and things of the day, but nothing too significant. I felt disconnected from the conversation. Maybe it was a bit selfish: I´d been all this time without seeing her, but I couldn´t be fake. I was just not feeling it. I knew I´d have time to spend just the two of us. As soon as we got back to the apartment to drop off the luggage, my Mum looked impressed and walked through it, looking in each corner. It didn't take very long, as it was minimal. ´This is very cosy. I love it! I´m so proud of you guys. Honestly, I think it´s the perfect place for both of you. Now if you excuse me, where is the toilet?´ She undid the button on her trousers, and Ernesto showed my Mum that the toilet was next to the main door, separate from the bathroom. ´Thank god, you know at my age I can´t hold it, it´s now or never, if not it could be a disaster if you know what I mean.´ Ernesto and my Mum laughed about the joke while I sat on the sofa, waiting until they were ready to go.

We made our way to the restaurant, it was 5 minutes away, so we arrived there very quickly. "Happy Italy": It was a 3-floor modern grey building with the main letters in shiny red, and there was a phrase at the bottom in white that said, "Everything to make you HAPPY"! Hah, happy? I was unsure if I knew what being happy was anymore, even though I didn´t have the answer. I was just analysing the stupid phrase of the restaurant. Ernesto opened the door and invited my Mum inside. She gently gestured to him, grateful for the "gentle" gesture. I asked the waiter if it was still open, and he said that we had an hour to have dinner as they were closing soon, so there was enough time. We took a seat, and my Mum sat in front of us. With his hand on my leg, Ernesto was next to me, smiling and looking very normal. We ordered one medium 5-cheese pizza and a Contadina with tomato and parmesan cheese. Also, rocket, but we decided to ask that it came without it. ´Tomorrow is your birthday! Are you excited?´ My Mum asked, smiling at me. ´I know, right? Yes, we will do something together, and I´m sure we'll have fun.´ I pretended to be excited when the reality was that I was not. ´It´s a shame that I´m working until late tomorrow. But at least you´re here, Emma, so he won´t be alone. Not any better company than yours, Emma.´ Oh, what a shame, right? Honestly, I felt quite relaxed and happy that he had to work the following day. I´d been all those months with him, barely having time for myself, and I think working didn´t count as time for myself. So having the chance to spend my 20th birthday with my Mum in Amsterdam sounded fantastic. And, of course, away from the lousy vibe of Ernesto. Maybe I was a terrible boyfriend for thinking like that, but honestly, I didn´t know the difference between right and wrong anymore. ´Ernesto! That´s a shame, I´m sorry that you have to work, but we will do something together another day, we have plenty of time.´ She added. My Mum looked at me most of the time. She seemed worried. Did she realise how I was feeling? Did I look sad? She tried to pretend to smile and act normal, but she knew me. She knew that something was going on.

CHAPTER 18

Happy birthday, my darling! Good morning my treasure. How did you sleep?´

I felt my Mum's hand pressing on my back. I had barely had the chance to open my eyes, and I still felt very sleepy, but I tried to wake up enough to talk to her. She kissed my cheek and touched my head. ´So so, I´m feeling a bit tired. But thank you, Mom. Where´s Ernesto?´ My Mum walked the short distance back to the kitchen and came back a few minutes later, bringing me a watery coffee, which she always prepared, but it didn´t matter. I knew it was made with love. ´Ernesto left half an hour ago. I spoke with him before he left. He was sorry for not being with us today.´ I took a sip of the coffee, trying to clear my eyes and soul to see if there was still something of that left. I stood up, and I moved to sit on the sofa with my Mum. ´Well, maybe it´s better like this Mummy, so we can have time for ourselves and chat more. Your company is more important than anything for me now.´ We had a big hug, and she gave me a couple of presents with light blue and red Christmas paper. ´Happy birthday, Aiden. This is for you, son.´ I peeled off the paper to discover the sweet surprises inside. The first was a picture of my Mum and me in Scotland; we took it in the fairytale pool It was made of dark grey stone and said on the back, 'For my son, now you can always bring me with you. I love you, Mum.' 'Mum! It´s beautiful. I love it, it´s very special.´ She couldn´t hide her smile and the emotions on her face. I bet she'd been waiting for that moment all month. 'It´s not the only thing, darling; open the other ones.´ I proceeded to open the next one, and it was a yellow and black jacket for the winter. It was not the kind of jacket I´d wear normally, but I appreciated her effort. And the other one was 1 kilo of Rosemary Spanish cheese. 'Mom, honestly, thank you so much. I´m very grateful.´ I said to her, contemplating the massive cheese in my hands. 'I couldn´t bring many more things, but there are a couple more for Christmas. Now get ready while I tidy up everything,´ she said, taking the discarded wrapping paper away. 'Wait, what time is it? What are we doing now?´ I was still sleepy, hoping the coffee would hit me harder than the depression. 'Darling, it´s 11:30 am, and you don´t expect your Mum to come to Amsterdam and not have fun with her only beautiful son on his birthday?´ My Mum looked pretty happy and excited about our day for us. 'You´re right, now I remember we spoke about it yesterday.´ I jumped into the shower and finished quickly, as I didn´t want to spend more time in the house. I had had enough at that moment.

I dried myself quickly and pulled my underwear on, then squeezed my legs into my super skinny black jeans; they were very tight, but at least my bum looked good. I decided to wear my black Puma Fenty trainers, the ones with the blue suede on them, a black hoodie and the new jacket my Mum gave me as a present. I looked at myself in the mirror, and I didn´t really feel comfortable with how my hair looked. It had grown a bit, but you could see that I was a bit bald. So I decided to put on my black alien cap. Both ready, we stepped into the train and got on our way to the city centre. My Mum looked excited: she had never been there before and I knew that for her to spend that time with me was very special. To be honest, I'm not really a fan of Christmas. I always had the memories of family reunions and everyone fighting with each other or any fucking drama that was not necessary. Or from the opposite side, when I was staying with my father, all the family went to an oversized humid garage where they placed a huge long table and many people that apparently they called 'family' were reunited and had fun. I remember myself being 14 years old, depressed and surrounded by strangers, feeling more alone than ever, so listening to music and not looking at anyone was the best choice. So yes. I hate Christmas. It´s the kind of thing that they sell you on the TV where you see everyone reunited and happy. All the problems are gone because 'it´s time to be together and family is everything' but I think it´s bullshit. Either way, my Mum always tried to give the best of herself and tried to make me enjoy myself with food, presents or whatever. One of my best memories is when my Aunty Mimi once bought so many presents that literally half of the living room was covered by boxes. I felt like the most special child in the world.

But I have to say that my teenage years weren´t easy, and I was a bit out of control of my mind, so sometimes I think I had been an awful son. On the other side, you had Ernesto, who loved these stupid holidays and always talked about everything. A couple of weeks previously, he'd wanted to buy silly decorations for the house. I wasn´t in the mood, so we had a dramatic argument. But I ended up buying the cheap plastic tree and the lights by myself. I went off and surprised him, so he looked happy and pleased when he saw it all. We built it together, and we had a nice picture for Instagram with Oreo cupcakes that I bought in Lidl, showing our 'followers' how beautiful it was being partnered and doing all that shit together: living the best Christmas together, right?

As soon as we left the station, we felt the slap of the strong smell of the weed. It didn´t matter what time of the day it was, it always smelled like that in the city centre. 'Wow, smells a bit strong, right? I hate it. But look, this is beautiful,´ she said, getting close to the canals and contemplating the small flats further from the stations. They looked very peculiar as the colours of the facade were dark and strangely twisted, so it looked like they were falling to the side. She was taking pictures everywhere and looking everywhere. 'Over here, Aiden! Take a picture of me here!´ Of course, she stepped into the enormous Dutch shoes that were outside one shop to have a picture. 'Smileeee!´ I took a couple of photos, and she looked pleased in her warm outfit with a blue scarf covering her neck. We kept carrying on a bit further up the street. It was already evening and dark already. But the streets were full of Christmas lights and decorations everywhere. 'Aiden, what´s that delicious smell?´ she asked, looking to both sides to see if she could guess where it was coming from. ´I think you´re smelling the fries truck over there. Do you fancy some?´ Her eyes went very bright as if she had been starving for a month. ´Please!´ We got a large portion of fries with chilli spices and mayo. I was so happy that my Mum loved spice like me, but she couldn´t deal with much. If she had too much... well, she quite quickly ended up in the toilet.

We ended up in Dam Square, where the Koninklijk Paleis was. The royal palace had beautiful classicist architecture: in front of the palace was a massive Christmas tree full of lights, at least 10 meters high. ´It´s beautiful, Aiden. I love it. I´m so happy to be with you here, my son.´ We both turned to each other in a big, powerful, energetic hug, one of those where you can feel a magical vibe passing through your body.

I took her to the Red Light District to show her around, and she looked a bit intimidated and confused. She didn't say any bad words about the prostitutes, but I guessed she was a bit shocked to see women showing themselves in a display as if they were part of a shop, a product that you could buy. Of course, I didn´t judge this, as I believe everyone is free to do whatever they want if it doesn´t hurt anyone: it's only if sex workers are forced into that work that I'm entirely against it. ´I think there's a bit of a strange vibe here, son. Shall we just go to have a drink somewhere?´ My Mum said to me after one strange guy offered her cocaine at the end of the street. ´Of course, Mum! I know the perfect place for that.´ After 10 minutes, we arrived, of course, in Bar Blend. That was my chance to take my Mum to a queer bar, and I didn´t want to miss it.

We ordered a couple of pints and took them to the end of the room, where the DJ area was, although there was a DJ on at that moment, just pop anthems playing in the background.

We took a selfie together. We looked very cute, but analyzing the pictures, my eyes looked sadly out into the unknown. My Mum took my hand and held it. ´Aiden, are you feeling okay?´ I was not surprised by the question, as I knew her and knew she would ask it at some point. ´Yes! I´m having a lovely time with you and enjoying it a lot. We've had a lovely evening together.´ She took a sip of the pint and inclined her head to the side, looking at me. ´Aiden, you know that

I´m not talking about today. I know you´re enjoying it and we´re having a lovely time. Do you remember that call when you got a bit angry at me? You told me that you were feeling strange here and that something was happening with Ernesto. I didn´t want to get into both of you because it is not my business, darling. I just feel like you´re a bit gone. There´s something in your eyes that is making me sad and worried.' I looked out into the room's busy environment. My right leg had the impulse to move up and down. 'Well, I just had a bad day, Mum. I think I was being dramatic, I guess. You shouldn´t be worried about it. I´m fine.´ Why was I lying to her? Was I trying to pretend that nothing happened when anyone with a bit of consciousness could see that something was going wrong? 'I don´t want to make you feel uncomfortable. I want to let you know that you can always trust me, son. Don´t feel like you don´t have anyone, alright?´ I kissed her on the cheek and jumped up from the table: 'Like A Prayer' by Madonna was playing on the huge loudspeakers, so I grabbed the moment to take my Mum and have a quick dance with her. She looked embarrassed, but in the end, she agreed and danced a bit. It was the first time in a while that I felt more relaxed. I received a message from my Dad: 'Happy birthday, son, 20 years already! You´re getting old like me, haha. I hope you have a lovely time and enjoy yourself with your Mum. Take care.'

I sent back a quick 'thanks, Dad. I guess I'm having a lovely time with her.' It was enough of an answer. We barely spoke to each other so it was not like I really wanted to develop a long deep conversation in that moment. 'Mum, I know you don´t like shots, but would you have a tequila with me? Just one for my birthday, please!´ She looked at me, making a disapproving face, but after seeing my intense blue eyes and sad face, she agreed. 'Just one, Aiden, you know that I don´t handle spirits very well.´ I ordered two shots of tequila from the handsome guy behind the bar. 'Okay Mum, first you lick the upper side of your hand, add some salt and take the lemon in the same hand. So you lick the salt, swallow the tequila and then bite the lemon.´ We clinked our shots together and put them on the wooden counter. You have to do that, or it's bad luck for your sex life. We did the shot and drank it straight. My Mum looked disgusted. She exaggerates wildly so it can be funny looking at her face: it looks like she was tasting bleach. 'No more, Aiden bloody hell.´

After that, we decided to return home. I felt a bit tired, and Ernesto was already there, waiting for us. He was wearing his pyjama and a grey T-shirt. Smoking a cigarette on the balcony. As soon as we opened the door, Ernesto dropped it and came quickly towards me. ´Happy birthday, my beautiful boy! I missed you so much today.´ His lips tasted like cigarettes, and he had freshly cleaned teeth. ´Thanks, Nesto. How was your day?´ I said, trying to think that there was no problem at all in our relationship. ´It was such a bloody long and tedious day, honestly. I really wanted to be there with both of you. Did you have fun?´ Ernesto asked while I undressed and got my soft and warm pyjamas on. ´Oh yes, we´ve been in the city centre and had delicious chips and excellent beers. It was lovely. Very stinky weed smell there, though!´ my Mum answered him, taking off her boots. ´I´m glad that you had a lovely time. Yes, every morning I get to Empari, and it´s the same. Even at 7 a.m., it smells the same. By the way, Aiden, can you come here for one moment? I have something for you.´ I sat on the sofa beside him while my Mum prepared some warm milk with honey. ´What is it?´ He showed me a pdf from his phone. ´This is your birthday present.´ It was tickets to see 'Mamma Mia!' the musical, the following day! ´Oh, darling! Thank you, that´s very exciting,´ I said excitedly to Ernesto, as 'Mamma Mia' is my favourite musical ever. ´I knew you loved it and wanted to see it so I couldn´t miss the chance to take you. We have to go to Utrecht, so I will organize everything with your Mum, and we'll pick you up tomorrow. Leave the rest to us.´

CHAPTER 19

The next day at work, it was slow, with just a few customers coming for cappuccinos and ginger tea. Some of them also had expensive lunches, based on the poor amount of food that they put on each plate for the prices they charged. But it didn't matter; I was just waiting to finish my shift at 2 p.m. Not many people besides my family sent me congratulations for my birthday. I didn't need much more. I was used to not being surrounded by many friends, so it was all right.

I picked up from the table in the corner, just next to the big window, a couple of dirty plates with some leftovers of garlic prawns and potatoes with bravas sauce. I went to the back area of the bar where the dishwasher was. I forgot to clean the other ones before, so it's better to get it done before my work colleagues who were coming to do the closing arrived and got upset with me. Surprisingly, Lucciano was there, with his light camel apron and his dark blue tight t-shirt and blue trousers. ´Ciao, Aiden! How are you doing?' He gave me a big smile with his bright eyes and a quick hug. ´I found out yesterday that it was your birthday, so here you have it. I tried to get as many as I could but happy birthday!´ I opened it up, and it was a big birthday card signed by everyone at the hotel. In the card there were messages from Fernanda, Ignacio, Vanesa and Jenna, and of course Lucciano, who drew a smiley face and a small heart. ´Oh, Lucciano! Thank you, this is so kind of you. I really appreciate it.´ I felt warm towards him, even if it was something silly. I was more used to not receiving much other than from my family. ´You're very welcome, you've been a good worker, and it's a pleasure to work with you.´ Lucciano shook my hand and entered the bar to start his shift. It was just a simple card but such a lovely gesture. It was adorable. He was charming. I thought I'd love to spend more time with him, but equally, we didn't have things in common other than working together, and he was straight: lovely, but straight. Couldn't change that. The time had finally come, and I went to change my clothes quickly, as my shift was done already. My Mum and Ernesto were waiting for me outside the restaurant entrance. I waved a quick bye to Lucciano, and I found them outside. They were both talking to each other and having a friendly conversation. I feel the cold Dutch weather against my cheeks. At least it wasn't raining. ´Hello, darling! How are you doing, my treasure?´ My Mum's eyes were bright, and she hugged me firmly. I could smell her wildflowers perfume, which I'd hated for years, but it was her and so it felt like home. Ernesto came to my lips straight away and kissed them. I didn't feel much. ´Bit boring, Mum, just waiting to finish. I'm excited about today! What's the plan, then?´ I said to her, moving side to side to keep my body warm. ´Well, we're going to have dinner in the place that you've wanted to go to for months, and after, we'll get to Utrecht to see "Mamma mia",´ Ernesto said as if instead of my boyfriend, he was my personal assistant. We were heading to the Amsterdam Zuid station. It was going to be a nice day. ´Sounds fantastic, darling. Did it take you long to get here?´ I asked them, not knowing it would cause that much drama. ´Actually, we needed help. We had a few rounds, and the maps took us a long way.´ My Mum said, looking at Ernesto. ´Really? I don't understand, it is so easy to get here. Don't you remember when you came with me to my interview Ernesto?´ He didn't seem interested in what I was saying, just replying to some text messages. ´Well, it's been a couple of months.´ We were holding hands, and I had my Mum's arm through mine, walking together. ´Well, it's pretty easy, darling. Next time you get out of the station, you just need to turn left, and then you walk for about three minutes straight on, and then you turn to the right. You can easily see the hotel building from there.´ Ernesto stopped looking at his phone and slowly turned his head to the right, looking at me, but this was not the kind of lovely way someone you love would look at you. This time, I felt a freezing cold judging look as he peered over his shoulder towards me. ´Why would I want to know the faster route to your work? I don't really need it.´ Surprised by that unexpected answer, I opened my eyes wider, not knowing how to react. I let go of his hand, still linked arm in arm with my Mum, walking together and feeling her energy and support. ´Maybe because you can pick me up? I don't know, Ernesto, it looks like you don't give a fuck.´ My Mum started to realise what was going on. ´I'm not very interested to know the information, that's it. If I want to meet you I will do it in the city centre, but I don't have the need to come here to pick you up, it's pointless.´ That simple answer just hurt my feelings. That was the thing about Ernesto. You never knew when he was unexpectedly going to stab you and make you feel like you were nothing. It was just the look on his face, his arrogant answer. My Mum looked at him and then at me. As soon as she saw my face, she tried to look elsewhere to escape the situation that was about to come because she knew me. She'd seen me at my worst and knew how easily I could lose it. It was something a bit silly, but with those words, instead of him saying, "Oh darling, yes, next time I'll ask you, or whatever", he decided to act like a fucking asshole as if he didn't really care about anything. What if he wanted to give me a surprise? Did he need to give me that cold answer? I just feel my chest in icy pain. ´I don't like that answer, Ernesto. You could try to be a bit nicer.´ I added, trying to be at least honest about my feelings with him to see if he can notice his attitude. ´I'm just honest, Aiden. Now leave the drama, and let's go for dinner. We're celebrating your birthday.´ I mute myself but with the voices in my head on replay, on and on, like being tortured by my own head.

We got into the station and boarded train number 5. 15 minutes passed until we finally got off at Amsterdam Leidseplein station. There was major tension in the air, it felt so thick that it can be cut with a knife. No one said a word until my Mum tried to break the silence saying how excited she was to see the musical, trying unsuccessfully to break through the tension. Walking towards the restaurant "The Avocado Show", I contemplated the beautiful views of the Street and the fresh air mixed with the background sounds of the bars and restaurants. The exciting and beautiful thing was that each building differed from the one next to it: different colours and structures. The street was full of life, with people hanging out with their friends, smiling and laughing. Having a wonderful time, and then there I was, not knowing anything about that. I wondered whether I would always have to feel like this. Crossing one small bridge lane, we got to the restaurant. It was in a corner, and as soon as we stepped in, we had our table prepared, as Ernesto had reserved a table. It was a small place, but I'd been waiting a long time to go there, even before we moved. Everything on the menu had avocado with it in some form or other. My Mum ordered smokey salmon that was served on top of the avocado with hollandaise sauce, flowers and poached eggs. Ernesto ordered for himself an Avoburger, which I think doesn't need much explanation. And I ordered a beautiful Avo Garden with hummus, spices, herbs and flowers. Honestly, it was so beautiful and well-presented. I still felt sad, and my face couldn't lie. I'm very expressive, and everyone can notice if something is not right with me. ´This place it's beautiful! I love it, guys.´ My Mum said while biting a piece of salmon with avocado. ´To be honest, Emma, it's a beautiful place. I mean, I miss the weather from Cádiz, but for now, we're having a good time.´ Ernesto tried to engage in an open conversation with my Mum, as he is the kind of person who knows what to say to be likeable. Still, you only needed to analyse him closely enough to understand that it was all a mouldy mask he puts on. ´You know Ernesto, that there was a moment when Aiden was a child. I wasn't working, and I almost came to live in the Netherlands, learn the language and start from the beginning, but it didn't happen.´ My Mum didn't stop looking at me carefully while trying to converse with Ernesto. ´I just can't fucking believe it, Ernesto. You're here conversing with my Mum like nothing else matters like my feelings are nothing.´ I couldn't resist it more. I exploded in the middle of my "Happy Birthday celebration dinner". He set his fork down on the left side of the plate and cleaned the right side of his mouth with the napkin, preparing his speach from the other side of the table. ´Aiden, you can't even make the effort for yourself so that you enjoy one day of your life? Look at us; your Mum is here, and we're in the place you wanted for your birthday, and the only thing you're doing now is having a repulsive face. You should enjoy at least one moment of your life.´ Ernesto said, making me realise that this food tastes like emptiness and sadness. ´It hurts, and I'm feeling upset. I can't change it.´ My Mum's face had changed, she was looking increasingly uncomfortable and tried to chill the tension. ´Well, let's relax, after this, we're going to Utrecht to see the musical, and we will have a lovely time together.´ I wished it was going to be like that, but unfortunately, the only beautiful thing I got that day was a picture of the avocado with flowers on the top and Lucciano's smile.

How can I describe what happened next?

Let me give it a try. Imagine that you're going to see your favourite musical ever with your Mum, who came from Spain to spend the holidays with you, and your boyfriend, who is supposed to give you love and balance. We should all have had a fantastic dinner in that fancy expensive avocado place and enjoyed the musical. Of course, nothing of the sort happened. And I know that this is not me exaggerating because of one stupid thing. I was not sure what it felt like to be loved. I was confused by the way that Ernesto treated me. It felt like sometimes everything worked perfectly, but equally, it could all go downhill really quickly. That simple "I don't care because I'm not coming here" meant he didn't care. It was disappointing, angry, and sad, and it may look like I'm dramatising, but I'm not. I would have loved to be living that situation in another way and to have felt differently about things. How do I really know if what I'm feeling is my own voice saying 'Aiden, something is wrong.´ The thing was, what was wrong? Was it me? Was it him? It was so depressing to sit in the theatre, next to my Mum with Ernesto next to her, as I didn't want to be with him. Watching Mamma Mia and feeling my heart in pain, like a thin knife penetrating the wound slowly. The fucking musical was in Dutch, even the songs, the fucking songs of ABBA in Dutch. What the fuck was going on? Honestly, just sat there for 2 hours dissociating, not enjoying myself, not smiling, just observing without any kind of conscience, not more than my thoughts repeating the same tapes that played in my mind over and over. 'You're nothing,' 'Look how dramatic you are'. I was punishing myself for feeling like that. I felt anger towards the world then, and the only thing that I wanted to fucking do was run away. On the way back, Ernesto and my Mum sat together on the train. The silence was so loud and uncomfortable that you could hear the 'tik-tak, tik-tak' of a bomb about to explode. ´Well, I hope you enjoyed today, Aiden, because I put so much effort and love into trying to show you a good time, but your face doesn't seem like you had it. What a shame. It's always like this with you, never enough,´ Ernesto said, putting his finger in my wound, knowing what he was doing. I couldn't hold it anymore: just seeing his face made me feel disgusted. ´Honestly, Ernesto, thank you for being such a fantastic boyfriend today. I was very grateful to enjoy your company, surrounded by really meaningful words.´ He lifted his right eyebrow and opened his eyes like an owl. ´Are you taking the piss out of me? After acting like you did all fucking day? I'm feeling disappointed with you, and honestly, if I'd have known this, I'd never have planned this fucking day.´ I felt my blood pressure rising, the thumping of the veins in my neck, and my face was full of redness. ´Are you talking about disappointment? When you can't even be nice to me, just being a fake bitch, just trying to pretend that nothing happened because you have nice words to say to my Mum? Ernesto, you're just awful.´ Our voices grew louder on the train, and the situation became even more tense. ´Fake bitch? That's what you have to say? Do I need to remind you who is the one here helping you when you don't have any friends? Maybe it was for a reason,´ he said with a Machiavellian face until my Mum couldn't hold it anymore. ´Please! Both of you! You stop now. This is really uncomfortable. I can't deal anymore with this. Just stop.´ She looked at me, begging me not to say anything more, without words, just with a simple look. She lay her head against the window and closed her eyes, trying to disappear from the awful situation that was unfolding. ´Either way, whatever, I mean it, Ernesto.´ He bit his tongue, showing me with his face that he would slap my face if he had the chance.

I fucking hated him.

CHAPTER 20

I took a sip of my espresso with some honey for my throat that I'd just prepared at the coffee machine. I needed it to get through my day. I was so pleased that I finished the dammed breakfast buffet upstairs. I needed to be by myself. Honestly, I couldn't sleep much more than an hour the previous night. It was a tense situation and even more so for my Mum. My head didn't stop, not even for a second. I started to believe that maybe I was at fault for everything that happened on my birthday, and if I just hadn't have reacted like that, nothing would happen. Yes: I couldn't just overreact like that. Ernesto did support me in moments when I was feeling alone. It had been very selfish of me.

The bar was completely dead, so instead of cleaning tables or glasses, I went looking under the counter for a piece of paper. I started to write a letter with a blue pencil. 20 minutes later and after a couple of interruptions because of customers ordering a fresh mint tea and a couple of lattes, I finished the letter. Signed with love, and I hoped this would help to chill the situation. I could see Vanesa coming from the other side of the room with her folder of duties for the day and a black pen on the side. She was sneaking to the bar quickly to have a small break and a chat. She was always smiling and friendly. 'Darling! How lovely to see you!' Vanesa had a seat on one of the high chairs that faced the bar. 'Likewise darling! Cappuccino?' I guessed for her, feeling more like myself and flashing a cheeky smile. While grinding the coffee and measuring out the exact amount of 4 grams, I inserted the portafilter in the group head of the coffee machine. And the milk started to get foamy. ´So, how was yesterday? Did you have a lovely time?´ Vanesa asked, trying to be friendly and breaking the ice to have a conversation, as everyone knew our plans. I tried to avoid eye contact, and instead, I focused on the cappuccino. ´Oh yes, we had fun and a lovely evening, the musical was in Dutch, so I quite hated it, but we are in The Netherlands, so I don't know why I didn't guess that would be the case before.´ I offered her the cappuccino in a takeaway cup while pretending to smile, lying, and saying that it was fun when it wasn't. Still, I didn't want anyone to know how I reacted or how bad the situation was. ´Thanks, handsome. Ernesto told me that it was a memorable day, and you all enjoyed it together, and that restaurant? Oh my god, I'm dying to go,´ she said, blowing on the cappuccino. ´Yes, the restaurant was incredible. By the way, I didn't know you had Ernesto's number.´ I said. That had been very subtle to get the information as I'd been with them most of the time and couldn't remember when it happened. ´Yes, he gave it to me last time we when to The Waterhole, and I spoke with him this morning. One of the girls in reception is leaving as her contract has finished, and she's way too lazy, so I think we just need to talk with HR about it.´ I just took a couple of seconds to process the information. I gave him the idea of looking for a better job for more money. Still, I didn't expect that to happen this quickly, and I was unsure how I felt about it. I guessed I should say happy. Right? As soon as Vanesa saw her manager coming from the edge of the room, she ran upstairs with the cappuccino.

The rest of the day wasn't busy, which didn't help with my overthinking all day. Honestly, the only thing that I wanted to do that day was to finish my shift and smoke a spliff.

It was 4 p.m. when I finally arrived in Almere, I realized. Fuck, it was the day that Ernesto's Mum and sister were coming. Oh, holy shit. I loved them, but that was the last thing I needed now. As soon as I opened the apartment's main door, I could smell the strong perfume that Carmen was wearing, which smelled like 'La Vie Est Belle' by Lancôme. Her dark bleached-blond head came rushing towards me, quick as a hurricane. ´Aideeeeeen! Come on here, my sweet son-in-law.´ Carmen squeezed me and gave me a big hug, swinging me around. Rosario gave me a hug as well, but not as big as Carmen did. ´It's so lovely to see you! How was the flight?´ I asked both of them, trying to be nice, the usual thing to ask. ´It was fine. I was terrified of the plane. I don't even remember the last time that I took a plane. But we're all finally together for Christmas! This is so special!´ Carmen said, quite excited and feeling like a child. My Mum helped them find a place for their luggage and organize the mess they had created in a second. ´Hey, darling. How was work today? Hope you are feeling better.´ Mum whispered and kissed my cheek. ´Boring, Mum. If I'm honest, I'm just exhausted. I barely slept last night.´ She quickly looked at Ernesto slightly and then at me. ´I bet no one did, darling.´ She said, joking and trying to smile, but I could perceive it. She was sad. I went to Ernesto and took his hand, guiding him towards the balcony. ´It's so nice that your Mum is here, right?´ I said while he took a Lucky Strike cigarette out of his trousers. ´Yes, I was missing them a lot. And I'm looking forward to spending Christmas together, but honestly, Aiden, yesterday was so out of control, and I don't deserve that treatment.´ Ernesto said, putting the cigarette in his mouth. I gave him the letter I wrote while I was working. My handwriting is completely awful, but you could understand what it said. I can't be good at everything. Ernesto took a couple of minutes to read the letter. When he finished, he smiled and hugged me, dropping the cigarette into the ashtray.´ Thank you, I forgive you and love you, Aiden.´ I felt insecure, but I said it back. ´I love you too.´ After chatting with my Mum and Carmen, we all went into the city centre of Amsterdam. Their first impression was as predictable as I thought. A shocking strong weed smell slapped them in the nostrils. It was already dark and cold, but even so, we took a couple of pictures together and had a walk around the area. There was this small souvenir shop 10 minutes away from the station where we spent 20 minutes. Rosario got a box with caramel waffles and a jumper for her new boyfriend. She was looking very in love and emotional and wanted to bring him with her. Still, the house was not like a clown's car. We had enough with five people in 20 square meters without a door on any of the rooms, smelling each other's shit as there was just one toilet. I couldn't be bothered. My Mum got a couple of souvenirs for my grandma. After several looks around the shop, I found the perfect gift for my aunty Mimi, a red cock magnet with the typical XXX. She was going to love it. We get ourselves (of course) a bunch of large chips with sauce and spices on the top. Walking around the busy streets full of Christmas lights and decorations, full of people spending lots of money. ´Guys, I have an idea.´ I said while Carmen gave me a quick look, knowing I was about to say something naughty. ´What is it?´ Rosario finally put her attention on me, even if just for that question. ´Well, you can't say you've been to Amsterdam without going to a coffee shop.´ I wanted them to have the experience, even if they didn't take anything, but it was part of the visit. ´Aiden, they don't smoke. They don't like that!´ Ernesto spoke for his family before they could even say a word for themselves. ´Indeed, we don't smoke, and I'm not going to, but why not go inside the shop? It is not going to hurt anyone.´ Carmen said, agreeing to my plan. Ernesto sighed and looked ahead. We made our way in the cold, wet evening. And then we were finally there, at Bulldog. One of the most famous coffee shops in the city centre. We all popped inside, and my Mum couldn't take it any longer. Her face was disgusted by the strong smell. You could get high just being in there and not smoking. It had a dark brown wooden floor and some leather animal prints sofas. The outside of the building had different paintings in colours and shapes, and it was in front of the canal. Beautiful and strange at the same time. I didn't miss the occasion, and I got a couple of special brownies and a gram of Black Widow weed for myself. After looking around, it was time to go home, so I got out the brownies. 'I know you don't smoke, but at least you must try this. It is so good. You will see.´ Carmen didn't hesitate much and took half of the brownie for herself and the other for Rosario. ´Actually, it tastes very nice.´ She swallowed it in a second. I offered it to my Mum as well. ´No way, Aiden. That's not happening.´ I made a sad cat face at her. ´C'mon, Mum! It's just one small bite. At least try it.´ She sighed and took a tiny bite. She spat it out as soon as the brownie made contact with her tongue. ´This is disgusting! taste like weed, Aiden!´ my Mum said loudly, more than usual, drawing the attention of an ancient couple walking around, probably thinking something offensive about us. She made a theatrical performance despite not liking the taste. It wasn't a stinky bumhole, it could always be worse. On the way back, on the train, I looked at Carmen. She seemed quiet but a bit smiley. ´Carmen, you look relaxed. Do you feel happy?´ I said, teasing her. ´Hahaha, I´m feeling all right. Doesn't the train move a lot?´ Carmen was very high. It was hilarious. In contrast, Rosario had gone very quiet and nervous suddenly. ´Rosario, what's going on?´ Ernesto went back to his possessive attitude with Rosario. ´I don't know. I just can't breathe. I want to get out of here.´ Rosario started to hyperventilate and have a panic attack. Thankfully we got home soon, and Carmen and my Mum took her to the balcony. ´I can't breathe. I'm going to die,´ were the only words that were coming out of her mouth. My Mum held her hand. ´Listen, you won't die. The brownie affected you. Now breathe with me.´ They stayed for 15 minutes outside doing breathing exercises. I mean, at least she wasn't asthmatic.

PEOPLE LIKE YOU

CHAPTER 21

It was the 24th of December, Christmas Eve. After the chaotic previous evening with Rosario's panic attack, I hoped that we can all enjoy ourselves for that day. It was not like I was very excited; for me, Christmas meant family arguments, drama and fights. Carmen and my Mum had just arrived back, having gone to the supermarket. They both came in many plastic bags with massive amounts of food and bottles of wine. They both organised everything and placed the groceries in the fridge. 'Was it busy? You took ages in there!' I said to them, looking at the time. 'Oh yes, that was why we took so long. Rosario, are you feeling better?' Carmen answered me and went to Rosario to give her a hug. 'Yes, I just have a headache. I don't know why that happened.' Rosario was having this kind of 'I'm a fragile bitch' moment, but of course, Carmen would be there to make her feel better or at least give her the attention she loved. 'I guess you had a whitey, and if you have anxiety as well, it's a bomb,' I added. 'I learned the lesson, that's for sure. Never again,' Rosario said, covering her face with her hands. 'When is Ernesto coming home?' my Mum asked while she was checking the stuff that they'd bought. 'I think around 8 p.m..' I started to get nervous. Honestly, I didn't like Christmas. 'Alright! Emma, shall we start preparing the dinner around 6 p.m.?'

Carmen said, looking towards my Mum and the whole mess of food in the kitchen. ´Of course, sounds good to me.´

The rest of the afternoon, I organised the house while Rosario was on her phone taking selfies for Instagram and talking with her new boyfriend. ´I think we could make everything festive with some decorations on the table and give Ernesto a nice surprise when he gets back,´ I suggested, trying not to be The Grinch, and have some empathy for Ernesto. He loved Christmas, and I thought that even if I didn't like it at all, I should be able to give a bit of myself to show him that I also wanted to make an effort for the sake of our relationship. ´Sounds lovely, Aiden,´ Carmen said, walking to the balcony to smoke another cigarette.

I realised that I didn't have any more decorations to use, so I quickly went to the shop for some silly Christmas stuff. I felt anxious, and being in a small place full of people made me sick as if every wall started to get closer to me, like a Jigsaw trap.

When I came back, I started to organise the table. I covered the dining table with cheap black paper. And while my Mum and Carmen were organising the dinner, I set out the decorations. I started with the napkins: they had a sweet print, although I thought Santa Claus looked a little creepy and like a pedophile. I folded them in half and made a "flag" pointing to the right. Then I got a couple of white candles and Christmas plates with silly logos. Five wine glasses, cutlery on top of the napkins and some lights to give presence to the table.

Our Moms prepared a very broad mix of things for the night: sliced Salami on one plate, then one with cheeses and bread sticks, Spanish ham, hummus with some crackers, Falafel with mustard curry dip and onion potato omelette. Everyone was in their pyjamas. No one cared about their outfit. We were staying home, so that was fair enough.

It was cold outside, and the fact that we had the heater on made it very cosy. Ernesto was about to arrive, so I locked the door and put the speaker on. I lit the candles quickly, and he knocked on the main door. ´One moment darling, wait just there.´ I quickly hit play on Spotify: 'All I Want for Christmas is You', of course, a classic from Mariah Carey. He knocked on the door again. ´Aiden! Can you open the door, please?´ We all stood up in the kitchen, facing the door with a glass of wine and waiting for the moment that the song breaks to open the door. Just 30 seconds later, when it was going to be the moment, I opened the door. Ernesto was looking at me really angrily and pushed me inside the house without even making any body contact with me. ´Why did it take you so long to open the fucking door? I needed to go to the toilet, and you kept me waiting.´ He closed the door and stomped into the toilet. Our faces were a poem, but honestly, I couldn't explain my feelings. Everyone was looking at each other, knowing that I'd been preparing for this moment all evening, and then that was the only thing he said as soon as he came in. I felt far from him and disconnected, like why was I even going to try to surprise him if he was going to give me that crap answer and look at me with that face like he'd smelled a piece of shit. He left the toilet and went to give his Mum and sister a hug, and then my Mum. ´I just wanted to give you a nice surprise, Ernesto. I didn't know that you needed to use the toilet that badly. I thought there were toilets on the train, so I didn't realise it would be a problem.´ He turned around and came straight to my lips to kiss them, and I felt his arms pulling me back towards him. ´Forget about it. Let's have a nice dinner, shall we?´ he said, trying to smile, but there was something in his eyes. Every time he smiled, you could tell the effort he was making in his eyes, which creased up way more than usual every time that happened. It was an empty smile, forced. ´All right,´ I said.

We all sat at the table while he was changing quickly and putting on his trousers and mustard jumper. ´Thank you for preparing all these. They look lovely and delicious,´ he said, looking at Carmen, who was sitting on his left side, and then at my Mum, who was in front of him. Rosario was at the end of the table, and so was I. My Mum gave him a short smile and looked straight away at me, trying to read my mind, looking to know how I felt. ´Oh, my beautiful boy! You're very welcome. We did this with all our pleasure, and Aiden prepared the table and decorations with so much love.´ Carmen tried to break the ice between us, knowing that her son had been an asshole. Ernesto held my hand. ´I know. Thank you, Aiden. It looks beautiful.´ Rosario took a couple of pictures for social media and tagged #Familytime #Christmaseve. Now we were all allowed to start to eat after that crucial influencer moment. ´I've been thinking we need to organise ourselves to go to Bruges because we need to rent a car,´ my Mum told Carmen: we hadn't made plans yet because we were waiting for them.

´What about the 26th?´ Carmen said, looking at Ernesto. ´I'm working
that day.´ Ernesto added. ´Maybe the 27th?´ My Mum was trying to
write an exact date and time in her mind. ´I'm working all these
following days until the 28th.´ My Mum looked at me, sipped her red
wine, and turned back to Ernesto. ´I'm leaving on the 28th, and if
you're working, I'm not sure how we can all go together then, Ernesto,´
my Mum added, being nice but starting to lose her patience inside.
´Emma, it will be so nice to go together. I'm sure we're going to have
a lot of fun,´ Carmen said to her while we were all eating. My Mum
just left a piece of cracker with hummus on the side. ´Carmen, you
need to understand that if my son has days off and yours doesn't, we
can't be waiting for something that is not going to be possible to
arrange. So I think it would be better if Aiden and I rented a car and
went by ourselves because there's not much time and we need to get it
organised, or we'll miss the chance,´ my Mum said, firmly and
resolutely, tired of waiting for everyone else to plan something.
Carmen looked at her and had a bite of cheese rolled up with the
Spanish ham. ´Well, if you think that's the best, it's alright,´ she said
and looked at Ernesto, wanting him to say something. Ernesto took a
look at both of them and then at me. ´Well, it's true that if Emma is
leaving soon and I'm working, the fairest thing would be for them to
go by themselves, and then we can go when I'm off.´ I think that was
the most reasonable thing that I heard from Ernesto. Ever. ´Sounds
fair to me, Mum. I'm very excited.´ She held my hand, looked at me
with a smile, and clinked her glass with mine in 'cheers'. There was a
bit of tension in the air until Carmen broke the silence. ´You know that
it was difficult for me to come here?´ she said to Ernesto and Rosario.
´Why, Mum?´ Rosario asked. ´I always wanted to come here with your
father, and you know. We couldn't do it in time.´ Her eyes filled with
tears and she covered them with a pedophile Santa napkin. ´But you're
doing it now, with them, and I'm sure he's here with you, Carmen. It's
so wonderful to have you here, thank you for sharing that with us,´ I
said, empathising with her. Even though I didn't have much experience
with death, it cost nothing to be kind. Ernesto looked out of the
conversation and said nothing about his father. He was just drinking
instead of speaking. Actually, he never talked about his Dad. In all this
time we'd been together, he just told me about it once. After eating
and feeling sated, we binned the dirty plates and kept the leftovers in

the fridge for the following day. ´Time for presents!´ Carmen was feeling better and wanted to distract herself with the gifts.

We sat around the green plastic tree that was strung with a couple of lights and decorations I bought to make Ernesto happy so he didn't think I was not getting involved with him. The presents were already under the tree, with the names of everyone on them. ´Mum, this is for you.´ She took out all the paper and discovered the fantastic soft black high boots we brought for her. ´Oh, this is so lovely. Thank you, Aiden! I really love them!´ She tried them on and didn't even hesitate to send a picture to her partner Ricardo to show how sexy she looked in them. Ernesto was very picky with presents, so we got some jewellery, make-up, and clothing for Carmen and Rosario. ´Now it's your turn! ´ I said to Ernesto, excited but distant. He opened the presents and saw the white trainers that I got for him. And then two tickets to see Dua Lipa in Amsterdam in May. ´Baby! This is so cool and exciting! Dua Lipa!´ He moved in close to me again and gave me a hug. Finally, I got my turn. Carmen and Rosario got me a Rick & Morty T-shirt, so cool and a very soft and warm hoodie to wear when I was stuck at home. ´Thank you, girls. I love it!´ I hugged both of them and took up the last present, which was a small box.

I opened it up. It was two boarding passes for Paris.

Ernesto looked at me. I could feel him analysing me, opening his eyes wider, waiting for an answer.

I was spaced out for a couple of seconds, trying to find an emotion. ´Paris? Oh, how cool! It's lovely, darling, thank you! You know it was on my list of places to visit.´ I went to him and kissed his lips, trying to pretend I was feeling happy. But Aiden, it's Paris! You always wanted to go there! Yes, I wanted to go to Paris, but there was something inside the deepest part of my heart that didn't feel connected to the emotion. It was a thought: 'Now you need to wait until February to go to Paris and not fight with Ernesto. It's now a responsibility, and I have to be with him.'

Some people would be jumping and reacting to this and making silly stories on Instagram saying #Paris #Truelove.

I didn't know if I really wanted to go with him.

CHAPTER 22

C'mon Aiden! We need to find the rent-a-car!´ said my Mum while we were making rounds at the airport for 15 minutes, like headless chickens. I needed to ask someone as we had booked the car for 8:30 a.m. Finally, I found the right way to get to the place, following the instructions and carefully looking at every sign to ensure we didn't waste more time. ´Look, Mum, it's that way!´ We took the lift to the level 1 parking, and the company's green logo was really bright and clever. As my Mum didn't speak English, I showed the documents to the person assisting us. And after signing all the documents and showing our driver's licenses, we got into the car. It was a dark grey Renault: it looked immaculate and smelled new. The seats were really comfortable. My Mum held my hand and looked at me, smiling. She removed her black coat and scarf and left them on the back seats. 'Are you ready? I need you to guide me with the GPS.´ She checked that all the mirrors were in the correct position. ´Yes, no worries, Mum, this is exciting.´ She started the car and began to drive. The weather looked cloudy and wet outside, but it wasn't raining. The only noise we heard was the GPS and the sound of the wheels on the road. I felt sad: happy for being on my way, on making this short trip to Bruges with my Mum, but that didn't change the fact that I knew it was just for a couple of hours. Some people may not understand that feeling when I had all I wanted: I was living abroad, I had a boyfriend, and we were living together. I had a job, and I was earning my own money. Some may call me selfish, others may think I was just uncomfortable because it was different, and maybe that was the case. I didn't know what was happening to me and why I felt that way about Ernesto. I was not brave enough to leave it all behind. I felt that I was just stuck in a situation, expecting him to be someone he wasn't. And the reality was that even though he had nice moments with me, I felt like a failure.

Why was I not capable of facing my emotions? I felt like I was letting the time pass, and the situation was getting bigger inside my head. Do you know the feeling of looking into someone's eyes and feeling all the love and energy of the connection, just with one simple, intimate look? Well, that was not the case for us. ´Aiden, darling. What are you thinking? You've gone quiet,´ my Mum interrupted my ritual of painful overthinking, looking concerned knowing exactly what was happening. ´Nothing, Mum, I'm just feeling a bit tired.´ I lied, although it was true that I was tired. But I knew that there was an emotional reason for that feeling. She turned to the right, where there was a petrol station and stopped the car. ´Okay, now we swap. You need to drive and disconnect your mind.´ My Mum touched my face and got out of the car, walking around to the side where I was sitting. ´Really? Are you sure, Mum?´ She smiled at me and held my hand. ´Of course, and I want you to enjoy today with me. We're going away, and it's just you and me.´ I got very excited. We swapped our seats, and I prepared myself for the drive after checking the mirrors and making the seat comfortable. ´But don't go fast,´ she added. I started to drive, following the directions and focusing on the road, observing the wet and green environment surrounding the highway.

It felt like freedom. Every kilometre away felt like a minor release of my pain. It felt like escaping, running away. I wished I could just have all my things in the car and drive somewhere and not go back and see that awful fake smile of his.

Freedom, sometimes I forget what it felt like because even living somewhere else didn't mean I could be free. There was one place I could never escape, and it was my mind.

All the same, I had to recognise that driving towards Bruges was helping. At one point, I started to get a bit nervous as the road narrowed, and the cars behind me were making a lot of noise with their horns, and I didn't know why. Maybe I was going too slow. But my Mum didn't get too worried about it. Finally, I turned to the right and found somewhere to park the car. As soon as we get out of the car, we felt the freezing cold in our bones. It was zero degrees. Mum came to me and gave me a hug. ´We're in Belgium! I'm so excited!´ She made some funny movements because of the cold and the excitement. We made our way to go to the centre, but it was impossible not to stop and look at the buildings on the way there. There was a canal in the middle, with a bridge that connected both streets. The colours were a mix of light brown and pale, nothing too bright: neo-gothic style, with a kind of triangular top ending in a square shape. I was impressed with it. I sat on the top of the stone bridge, and my Mum took a couple of pictures. In one of them, I was looking at the grey sky, and suddenly five birds were flying simultaneously as the picture was taken. Very spiritual, maybe?

We took a couple of selfies and kept carrying on to the city centre, but first, we stopped for a hot chocolate, as it was freezing outside. I took another selfie with my Mum as I found the simple message on the paper cup funny: "I'm hot". Of course, we were! We went inside 'The Old Chocolate House', a small shop that sold different kinds of chocolates from Belgium with delicious flavours. It was decorated in a rustic style and was very cosy. The smell was impacting my nose. It was pure chocolate, not like a commercial smell or flavour. I looked at the different shelves, and I found a box in the shape of one of the traditional style local houses. It was 40€, so I put it back where it was, and I went to the counter. I ended up buying chocolates flavoured with caramel, strawberry and ginger.

As soon as we finished buying a considerable amount of mixed-flavoured chocolates, we walked to Market Square. It was hard to take in just how beautiful it was and how impressed my Mum looked. The colours of the buildings were the same, but they were smaller and closer together. There were small stands in the middle of the Square, small shops and small tables to eat something. We took a couple of nice pictures together. Mum looked happy and smiley. I looked at myself, and even though I was smiling, I thought there was sadness in my eyes, and that you could see it. ´This is beautiful, Aiden. You look cold, do you want my scarf?´ she said, worrying about me getting sick, as I'm pretty sensitive to the cold like her. ´No, Mum, I'm fine, don't worry.' I didn't even have time to finish, and she was wrapping her red scarf around my neck because she preferred to get me warm. That's what small acts of love look like. Even if it meant that she might get sick herself, she always put me first. ´Look at that, Mum. Shall we get some mulled wine? I think it might help with this crazy freezing weather.´ I suggested, in the middle of that busy square, full of happy tourists. ´I'm always going to say yes to a wine darling, but just one, we have to drive back!´ Smells like a greasy hot dog and hot chocolate simultaneously at the square. I ordered two hot mulled wines; they tasted delicious, and of course, it was helping with the cold. Mum held my hand and looked into my eyes while she sipped. ´Treasure, you know I don't want to get involved in things I shouldn't. Still, since I came, I felt that you were not really here, like you're spaced out. I've been thinking about whether to say anything or not, but I'm your Mum, and I'm worried about you.´ I took another sip of the mulled wine tasting the strong cinnamon flavour. ´Why do you say that, Mum? What's going on?´ I said, trying to focus on the conversation and not fly away with my mind again. ´Are you really happy with Ernesto?´ At that moment, I felt myself go and froze for a couple of seconds. No one had really asked me that before. ´I'm not sure, Mum. Why are you asking me that?´ She hesitated with her head tilting from side to side. ´Those first days after I arrived, before Ernesto's family got here, I was very uncomfortable, Aiden. I didn't know how to deal with the situation, and you were entirely not yourself and very defensive.´ I looked down to the wet stoney floor. My white Adidas were getting yellow and black from my prolonged use of them. I thought that I might need to throw them away before too long. ´I know, Mum, and I'm very sorry for that. Honestly, I felt mistreated by Ernesto, and I don't know. I thought that coming to Amsterdam would help us start from the beginning and our relationship would get better, but it's just getting worse. And on the day of the musical, I felt wholly humiliated when he said that he didn't care about the address of where I was working, and instead of asking me if I felt bad or sad, he was just judging me. I know my behaviour wasn't the best, but I didn't know how to deal with the situation. Mum, I feel like sometimes I love him, and I want to be with him, but equally, I feel like I don't have anything in common with him,´ I said opening my heart to my Mum. She placed her hands on my leg, and I felt some energy coming from her. ´Darling, I know that you feel like that, and you know that I'm here for anything that you need. Relationships are complicated, and it's the work of the two of you. If the other one doesn't wanna make an effort, then it starts to fuck up. Smoking weed will not help you either, Aiden, I seen you since I've been here, and I think you're smoking quite a lot,´ she added, being very honest with me. ´I don't know how to deal with anything, Mum, it's difficult, and I'm not sure what I should do,´ I replied, realising that I felt like I was drowning. ´Well, I can't tell you what to do, darling, but you know that you can always count on my help and call me whenever you need it. You have your home in Spain, so if you feel like you need to come back at some point, you know what you have to do.´ We both hugged each other hard and powerfully. I felt my Mum's love in that cuddle, the worries and everything that we both felt simultaneously.

CHAPTER 23

I decided for that year that I wanted to be happy and make an effort for myself. I didn't know when and how I would do it, but it was the only thing I wanted. I looked at the time. It was 3:30 p.m.. I was hanging out that evening with Ernesto to have a couple of drinks, and who knows, maybe we would have some fun with someone else. I put the wet laundry on the hanger, as the heater was on and outside it would take ages to dry it. I hadn't really eaten anything all day, but I didn't feel that hungry. After that beautiful trip to Bruges with my Mum, we returned safe and sound. It was already 2020, Christmas was over, and I was going to miss my Mum. It completely broke my heart when I left her at the airport, and we both cried for a long time. She knew I wasn't feeling right, and I was feeling a bit guilty for her bad experience staying with us, as it was supposed to have been a lovely Christmas. Still, again the fucking drama was involved in everything. I locked myself in the shower, even though I was alone, but I like to know that I'm in control of the door and no one else can come in.

My reflection in the mirror was blurred. I could see that my skin was getting paler and my eye bags were more visible. I didn't like what I saw. When I was 18, I looked more handsome, and my body shape looked much better. Now it looked like I was a skeleton. I was just thinking about my time with my Mum; it was magical, and I needed it. I tried to use the 'stop' psychological skill, which basically means: When I had a thought that was staying more than usual, I accepted it, I didn't judge it, and I let it go. And I say 'tried' because my mind couldn't be still for more than 30 seconds without having a poisonous thought against me.

I stepped into the shower, feeling all the drops of hot water on my body, and I start to wash with the vanilla shower gel I got a few days ago at the supermarket. I thought it was funny that I never concentrated on the present – even when I was eating, showering or having sex. Most of the time, my head was somewhere else. I imagined that if I could add a filter to my life at that moment, I'd use the black and white one to give some sour sadness to the scene, recreating myself in all the drama and depression, like an Indie melancholic artist. When I finished and dried myself, I put some cream on my face to look healthy and not like someone who was very unhappy.

I was wearing trackies that day; I was not feeling in the mood to get stunning. I couldn't fake it. I checked that I hadn't forgotten anything and made my way to the train station. Every time I sat on the train, it got more challenging and repetitive, almost like being trapped in the same day.

Amsterdam central looked busy, as always. It was Saturday, and people continually spent money on weed, prostitutes, and caramel waffles.

I tried to walk fast, but my body couldn't deal with more speed, so I accepted it and went slowly, even if it meant that Ernesto had to wait. Sad music was the only company I had as I walked towards Empari on that busy street. I wondered how many people felt alone and surrounded by that many people. Maybe I was one of them. I finally arrived at Ernesto's work. He walked out, wearing his fancy posh uniform with those white leather shoes and the camel coat. ´Hey baby!´ He gave me a hug and kissed my lips. ´How was your day?´ I asked, even though I was not really interested in the answer. He got hold of my arm, and we walked simultaneously, close to each other. ´Not bad, but honestly, I'm starting to have enough here. I should change at some point, as I'd like more money.´ I could feel the cold breeze on my face, but unfortunately I knew it couldn't help with my Nosferatu eye-bags. ´Did you speak with Vanesa about the receptionist position? Maybe that would be great.´ He looked impressed by the question, making a quick movement with his eyebrows. ´I did indeed, and she told me they have a vacancy available to start in February.´ We walked inside 'Susie's Saloon' close to Dam Square, facing the canals, and it's on the corner of the street. There was background rock music and people of different ages everywhere, but it seemed friendly. I got two pints for us, and we went into the smoking room. All the decoration was made of rustic wood. There were football T-shirts on the ceiling, some shotguns and pictures hanging on the wall. We had a seat at a long wooden table with more people, but we had enough space. ´How's your family then? Did they arrive home safe?´ He sipped the pint, looking at me, his eyes wrinkling in the corners. ´Yes, they still feel a bit fatigued from the plane but had a lovely time. We all did, didn't we?' Ernesto said proudly. 'Now I can spend more time with you. Being together and sharing things is very important, Aiden.´ It felt warm inside the room, Ernesto took a cigarette out of his pocket, and I got my spliff out. I showed Ernesto some guys I spotted on Grindr close to the area. I want to have some fun. ´Are you going to smoke?' were the only words coming out of his mouth, ignoring my phone. ´Yes, this is a strong one.´ I said, laughing, and I took a long sip of the pint. The heat in the room was killing me.

I started to smoke and drink. ´I miss my Mum. I wish she had stayed longer.´ I added. ´I know, but at least my family were here the rest of the days,´ he said, forgetting that we had many fights and tension during those days. As soon as my Mum left, I only enjoyed going to work, as I didn't want to spend time with any of them. I almost couldn't visit Bruges because of them. Everything started to feel dizzy and blurry. All my body was boiling, and the music in the background was loud. Ernesto was taking my hand. ´To be honest, working in the same environment as you will be lovely for us, don't you think, baby?´ Ernesto said to me. I started to feel numb, and I couldn't hold it. Suddenly everything went dark. I couldn't hear or see anything. Like a painful and peaceful void, out in space. Just black. ´Aiden?! Aiden?! Wake up!´ I started to feel Ernesto's hand shaking me hard. I slowly made an effort to lift my head from the wet table. I'd poured the whole pint over myself, leaving me utterly soaked and smelling of beer. ´W..

wh.. what's going on?´ I said to Ernesto, confused as it was deafening and I didn't understand anything. ´Aiden, let's go out NOW!´ Ernesto shouted at me, and without hesitation, he took me by my arm. As soon as I stood up, I felt all my body weight headed towards the floor at the speed of light, almost as if it were a movie. It wasn't me. Still, it was. Indeed, I couldn't handle it, I needed to sit for a couple of minutes, but instead, I was being forced to stand up. Ernesto held me up, and I heard him apologizing to someone. I'd fainted on the legs of a man in a wheelchair. Thanks to him, I didn't break my nose or, even worse, smash my head. Still dizzy and confused, I felt some people lifting me up to help me out. They said to Ernesto to get me some water with sugar. While he went quickly to the bar, everyone was saying to me, ´don't worry, this sort of thing happens every day´. I felt the support and help from them. I sipped sugary water immediately, and before even a minute had gone passed, Ernesto pulled and pushed me violently out of the bar. ´What the fuck are you thinking about, Aiden? Did you see what you just did in there?´ He shouted in my ear. I was still confused, and my head hurt. My body was shaking and processing everything. ´Ernesto, what happened? I don't understand! His eyes bulged out of his head, looking red and blood-shot in a way I'd never seen before. He was looking at me angrily. ´What happened? You just fucking collapsed and started to convulse at the table.´ He was grabbing my arm forcefully. ´Convulsing?´ I suddenly felt my body bouncing; he was shaking me side to side with his abusive energy. ´Yes, Aiden. Fucking convulsing, do you know that we're alone here? I was terrified, and all because you decided not to eat anything today and make a scene inside. Do you know how embarrassing it is to see that my boyfriend just fainted on someone in a wheelchair?´ Ernesto kept shouting, pressing his finger hard into my chest, pointing at me. ´Ernesto, please can you relax? I didn't know that was gonna happen. If I had, I wouldn't have smoked. Please don't shout at me.´ People in the street were walking around us, and I could feel they were listening and hearing. ´Relax? You have to be kidding, you made me feel like shit and embarrassed me, and now you tell me to not shout at you? You deserve it.´ I felt completely disconnected from my mind and my body. I just felt dead inside. Why was it that a stranger treated me better than my own boyfriend? I just felt like a piece of shit, as if I was not fucking worthy. ´And now, because of your decisions, you ruined the night. We're going home, no drinks, no threesomes, nothing. Next time think better about it,´ he said, walking further ahead and quicker than me, leaving me behind. We were walking towards the station, and the only thing I could think in that moment was 'why does he treat me like this?', 'Is this love?'. Instead of shouting at me, why didn't he take care of me and give me the affection I needed. He didn't say anything on the way home, he didn't even look at me. I guessed that was my punishment.

And at that moment, I understood the reality of how alone I felt and the colossal mistake that it had been to move to Amsterdam with him.

CHAPTER 24

I took an order of two lattes and one mint tea from those one of those regular old customers who came around occasionally. It had been a hectic morning but a quiet afternoon. Not much to do apart from serving and restocking the drinks. While I left the mint tea-bag inside the cup, and put some honey on the left side, I warmed up the milk. While the cups received fresh espresso shots, I felt the jug was hot enough to stop steaming the milk. Sometimes I thought 'what would happen if I left my hand holding the bottom of the jug for longer?' It might be painful, but I was so used to it that it would just be a visible burn scar. Sometimes there are invisible scars. Some people feel them in their stomach, others in their head, but I always felt the pain in my heart.

As soon as I took the drinks to the table, I noticed Ernesto walking in from the other side of the room in a black blazer, white shirt with red lines and slim camel chinos.

He was dropping a bunch of papers in at the bar, with that kind of smile that I knew by the wrinkles of his eyes was a fake smile. 'Baby!' I was taken by surprise by his runway entrance. He left his blazer on the high chair at the bar and gave me a kiss that tasted empty. 'Ernesto! I didn't expect you. What are you doing here?' He sat on the chair and snapped his fingers together. 'I just signed the contract, I'm the new receptionist at the hotel, and I'm starting next week.' He looked at me, laying his head on his left shoulder with both eyes open, waiting for my reaction. 'Do you want anything to drink?' It was the only thing I could say back, almost like evading the information I'd just received. 'Cappuccino, please.' I got the ground coffee from the portafilter and place it on the group head. There I was again, heating more milk, more fucking milk. 'Are you not happy that we'll work in the same place?' I couldn't fake it. My face said everything. I couldn't hide my own truth. Now he was going to be working there as well, like I didn't have enough living with him. At what moment had I thought this was a good idea? Why did I even care if he earned less money than me? I thought I should cut off my empathy and just start looking out for myself. Now the only place I had where I didn't have see him was being invaded. 'Of course I'm happy, Ernesto. I'm just tired, but I'm glad you got the position. Did you tell your friends?' He blew on the cappuccino as it was hot. He looked surprised by my question. 'No, my friends think I'm still working in Empari, and that's how it will be.' Ernesto said, looking into my eyes, almost like forcing me to keep that secret, in case any of his friends texted me. 'Wait, I'm confused, but if you just got the...' I didn't even have time to finish the sentence when he interrupted me. 'They don't need to know, darling, all right? I'm a receptionist just for my family and the girls here, okay? What would they think of me if they knew I worked in the reception instead of Empari? This is just for the money, but I'm happy.' Again, he left me speechless. Jacobo walks towards us. He was in his blue suit with yellow socks and black leather office shoes, very confident and arrogant at the same time. 'Good afternoon! Aiden, can you make me ginger tea, please?' Another fucking drink, I couldn't be fucking bothered. 'Sure!' I said, smiling with my hospitality face. 'Ernesto, I heard that you're now part of the team. Congratulations.' They both shook hands. The situation looked too heterosexual for me to handle. 'Thanks, Jacobo.' He took out of his pocket a gold card and gave it to Ernesto. 'Tomorrow is my birthday, and I'd like you to come. It's nothing serious, it's going to be in my studio, with a couple of friends.' Jacobo looked at me then, as if trying to tell me something with his eyes with a quick two second look. 'That would be lovely, thanks for inviting us,´ I said to him, grateful for having something to do that was outside of the magnificent home that we lived in, even though again, Ernesto would be there. ´Thank you for the tea, Aiden, and you have my address and phone number on the card. See you tomorrow.´ I didn't know why, but I kinda fancied the idea of going to his studio. He was straight, and was not attractive, but he had something that turned me on.

On our way to Jacobo's studio the next day, we got a present for him. Ernesto didn't want to and complained about my ideas. I didn't know why people always find it inappropriate to buy underwear as a present. it's handy. But we got him a standard shirt from Primark, not his kind of thing, I guessed, as he could afford to get Gucci jackets, but at least we didn't go empty handed. We found the building quite quickly with Google maps. It was freezing outside. ´So it's building 10, but what was the number of the flat?´ I pressed the number 42 button, and it called straight away.

The see-through doors opened, and we went inside. Everything looked immaculate, and there were at least 200 mailboxes. We found the lift and pressed the button for the 4th floor.

There was even a sign with the number of the gym floor, bar, communal cinema, sauna, and swimming pool. How much money did this motherfucker have? After a couple of minutes of walking through an infinite number of hallways with hundreds of doors, all in the same colour, we finally found Jacobo's studio. ´Happy birthday!´ we both said and gave him a quick hug, literally one second. So the studio was relatively small but very cute. The kitchen was on the right side, and everything was open. There was a huge TV, like 40" and a long grey sofa. A wooden shelf gave a bit of 'privacy' with all his outfits, a double bed and a desk in the other corner of the room, with a new MacBook pro sat on it. Vanesa was there, drinking straight from a bottle of beer. Guys! You're here!´ She came straight away to us and gave us two proper kisses and a hug.

There was a table with some snacks to eat; I took a couple of pieces of edam cheese with some berry marmalade and a bottle of beer that Jacobo gave me.

Ernesto decided to go for the salami and all the meaty things on the table as if he wasn't allowed to eat them in our house. 'Ernesto, I'm pleased you got the contract! Finally, that lazy bitch was fired. Honestly it was so long waiting for that to happen,' Vanesa said, not having a fucking clue of how miserable Ernesto was. He was a good worker, yes. But an awful human being. 'Thanks, Vanesa. So do I, and more now, having the same work environment with Aiden and all of you girls will be very special, right, my love?' He grabbed me and pulled me closer, his hand on my hips. 'Yes, I guess,' I said, sounding like a robot. I didn't like the idea and regretted it. Still, I didn't have any other choice than to fake it because if not, there would be an argument about it. We got to dance to a bit of reggaeton and speak with a couple of Jacobo's friends, but nothing very interesting, apart from with his blond cousin, who also spoke Spanish and looked very glamorous and posh, but still like a nice girl. 'What happened with the girls Vane? I thought they were coming,' I asked her, missing them as they were funny and easy going to hang out with. 'Jenna was feeling sick, apparently, and Fernanda was fucking around with a girl and is not very close to Jacobo, so she didn't really care at all.' After 4 bottles of corona and one glass of wine, we sang happy birthday to Jacobo.

Some people were leaving as it was starting to get late. 'Aiden, we should go now,' Ernesto said, almost like an order. Jacobo came from the other side of the room and left his beer on the side. 'You could sleep-over here if you want, guys. If you still don't feel tired, there's enough room for everyone,' he said, like an indecent proposition that sounded perfect to me. 'That's very kind, Jacobo. But we're going to leave soon,' Ernesto said, without even asking me. 'Actually, I kinda fancy staying longer, Ernesto,'

I said, almost like daring him, to prove to him that I was still capable of doing whatever the fuck I wanted without his permission. 'Are you not coming with me? C'mon, don't be childish,' he said to me, placing a label on me again. No surprise, though, as I was used to that by then. 'Honestly, it's okay. He can stay. There's no problem.' Ernesto took the last sip of his bottle and left the studio with a shit face. 'See you tomorrow, Aiden.'

Half an hour later, after a gossipy conversation with Jacobo's friends about the other hotels and the Tea, they left, and it was just him and me. Actually, I wanted this moment to happen. I still remembered that small confession that Jacobo made to me at The Waterhole when I was ordering the drinks.

But I was glad Ernesto didn't stay, as I could chill out with him. I kinda felt nervous, as if the situation itself was erotic, even though nothing had happened. Jacobo took off all his clothes, and stood there just in red underwear. He was not fit, but I kinda fancied getting inside that bed, putting my hand in his underwear, and being his first guy. That would be so fucking hot. At the same time, I started thinking about being unfaithful to Ernesto like that, and I kinda felt bad. I didn't want to repeat the same old mistakes from the past. 'Well, here you have the blankets and the pillow, and the sofa is very comfortable.' In just one sentence, the whole fantasy disappeared into disappointment. I wasn't expecting to fuck him, but I wanted to sleep in the same bed with him and feel his body heat. But he made it very clear. 'Have a good night Aiden.' And in a few seconds, all the lights were off, and he was already in bed.

I slept a total of three hours all night. My head was full of shit, my thoughts were in a spiral, I was missing my joints, and Jacobo was snoring.

The alarm sounded; it was 6 am, and I got dressed quietly. I folded the blankets and left the studio as soon as I could, not before I took a look at Jacobo for a couple of seconds, thinking how much fun we could have had and how boring it was at the end.

I got on the train, and I called in sick to the hotel. I wasn't ill, but I wanted to chill at my house. As soon as I got to the place, after 40 minutes on the train listening to some sad music and feeling the cold in every part of my body, I quickly smoked a spliff on the balcony and stripped off. I climbed inside the warm bed. Ernesto was cuddling a soft toy that I bought him. He stirred, waking up a bit and kissed my lips. He smelled charming. It was kinda sweet with a bit of a sour wooden smell. 'I missed you last night,' he said. And we just snuggled until we went to sleep.

CHAPTER 25

I found it strange that Ernesto got on so well at the hotel. He always looked confident about what he was doing (even if he had never done it before) and he spoke with everyone. One part of me was happy as I could spend more time with him, and I found it cute to see him standing at the reception counter. Equally, there was another part of me that was feeling invaded: like a nest, you make it for yourself and for your firstlings, and you get defensive if you think the threat outside is getting close to you, slowly, not knowing if it's just a harmless animal or the most awful violent creature that is going to destroy every single part of you. The previous day, Vanesa came to the bar while I prepared some drinks and suggested a wild night out. 'There's a place called Melkweg, it's techno Tuesday, tomorrow and it's in the city centre so we can have a cheeky one.'

Ernesto and I agreed to go; honestly, I needed to go out. I wanted to go to another party in Amsterdam called Sweetie Darling. It was a queer party 'Why do you want to go to a party place that's full of gays? That kind of place is just for having a hookup and flirting with more people, and it is not what you want, right? Because we are together, Aiden and that place is not suitable for our relationship, you don't need that to have fun, and we go out a lot to Bar Blend and Taboo, so I think it's fair enough, right?´ That was Ernesto's permissive words. What else could I say? It looked like I didn't have another option. Sometimes it was frustrating: I was 20 years old and living in a very open-minded city. And I felt like I was chained to the expectations of monogamy: 'you're not going to go without me' and 'nothing else matters but us.'

I thought I'd love to go to many parties, even just for the experience, but Ernesto didn't want to. I had to respect that because I was 100% sure that if not, things were going to get very messy. We'd end up arguing shit, and I didn't have anyone else to go with. All the people in our group were straight, apart from Fernanda. She was bisexual, but she was doing her own thing, aside from everyone else. So yes, he agreed to go to this techno party, which I knew would be full of straight people, but at least we'd be going out. 'Darling?´ Suddenly, I returned to the present, as if my mind just went somewhere else, overthinking, like always. 'Sorry, I got distracted. What's up, darling?´ I said back to Ernesto. 'Where's my belt?´ I stood up and helped him find the black leather belt he liked to wear with those fancy posh trousers: they were from Empari and were quite large. 'Are you excited about tonight? All of our friends are going to be there!´ he said, tightening the belt on his hips. 'Yes, that sounds great darling, I'm just a bit worried because I have to work tomorrow at 7 am.´ I was being realistic. Equally, going out might be helpful for dealing with this massive hole of sadness in my heart. 'It will be fine, just don't be too naughty and you should be fine. Are you going straight away from there to work?´ Ernesto again reminded me that I needed to behave normally, not too naughty. Maybe a plastic doll was what he needed. 'I guess so, there's no sense that I take a train at 4 in the morning to then need to take another one at 6, so it's probably better if I stay awake all night.´ I didn't feel very comfortable with any of my outfits. It was weird because I had so many clothes. I didn't know what to wear, and my hair looked relatively thin, so the best option was to wear my black cap that had a funny alien at the front and the back said 'believe it'. I borrowed Ernesto's blue denim jacket and got a black T-shirt with long sleeves and white lines. I didn't feel attractive, but it didn't matter.

On the other hand, Ernesto put hundreds of layers of different creams on his face and looked for a single piece of messy hair in his eyebrows. He looked so confident.

I couldn't resist it. I walked up behind him and grabbed his bum. He turned around and kissed me, and suddenly he grabbed my neck with his hands. ´You know you've been behaving well these last weeks, right?´ Ernesto said, penetrating my eyes with possessiveness and control. ´Yes.´ I answered. ´That's what I like, when you're obedient and understand that I'm right, and when I tell you something it's for your own good, I just want to protect you.´ He was dominating me, and maybe he was right. I was being submissive, and I let him do it to me. I thought it was the best thing I could do: for me, for him. He gave me another kiss and grabbed my bum with both of his hands. Instantly, I felt like my body turn on, and I bit his neck. ´Aiden… we're going to be late.´ Ernesto said, ignoring the fact that he had started this. ´I don't give a shit. I want you to fuck my mouth.´ As soon as those words come out of my mouth, he raised his eyebrows. Our tongues were playing and dancing and the same time, I could feel his saliva inside my mouth, and he grabbed my neck again. ´You know you have to do it now, right? Make me proud of you,' he said with a dominant voice, taking his trousers off and putting his hard cock inside my mouth. He sat on the bath with his trousers at his feet. I knew what I was doing, so I started to find a rhythm, and all I feel was Ernesto's cock sliding to my throat. I undressed, and I was on my knees, doing one of the things that I'm most talented at, giving good oral. I opened my mouth, and he spat on my tongue slowly. I used that to lubricate his shaved cock. I loved to hold it hard and have it all for myself. He didn't touch me at all but then most of the time it was like that. So I get hard listening to him enjoying it. I felt myself while I choked on him until I was barely breathing. ´Do you want my milk?´ he said, grabbing my hair. ´Yes, please, I want all your milk in my mouth.´ With no hesitation, he choked me hard again and kept me going. I couldn't hold it anymore, and I felt my cum arriving and hitting the floor, moaning. As soon as Ernesto heard me, he exploded in my mouth, and I tasted the sour taste of his semen going down my throat.

He stood up, bouncing around, almost falling over because of my spunk on the floor. Quite funny if he had fallen over and hit his head,: I could imagine the news saying:

'A skinny faggot has died slipping on his boyfriend's spunk.' Getting back to reality, I checked the phone and I had three missed calls from Vanesa.

We finished getting ready quickly and went as quickly as birds to the station. While we were on the empty train on our way to Amsterdam Central, Ernesto held my hand and looked in my eyes. 'I love you, baby. I really enjoyed it before.' he said. 'I enjoyed it as well. You came a lot, I have to say.' We both laughed, and he sent a message to Vanesa, telling her we were on our way. It was pretty funny because I'd gotten used to not being that touchy. Sometimes, I think I enjoyed the fantasy of the situation more than the situation itself. For that reason, I liked it when he dominated me. Because the rest of the time, it was not like he really knew how to touch me.

Bloody hell, Amsterdam central was cold as fuck, and full of the smell of weed in the air. We had quite far to walk, so we held each other's arms and increase the speed.

I had to say it was quite busy considering it was a Tuesday. The Christmas lights were already gone. What a shame because it looked beautiful to walk around when they were up. 'Ernesto, I've been thinking.' He turned his head, getting intrigued about what I was thinking. 'What about?' I could hear a sigh before he even did it. 'Well, you know I'm very open minded and very naughty. There's one thing that I'd love to do with you.' I could feel his eyes full of judgement, but he tried to cover it by smiling, but the wrinkles round his eyes cannot lie. 'I want you to fuck someone, anyone you want, in front of me, but I won't be part of that. I just want to see you with someone else.' He moved his head to each side of his shoulders, thinking about my words. 'Do you want me to fuck someone else? But not a threesome? Just you watching me?' He asked. 'Yes, I think it's hot. I'd love to see you doing it.' I thought, for once, it would be easier to do something different with him. 'Well, it is not like it's something that I wouldn't do, so we could try it.' Ernesto thought for a couple of seconds about the idea. 'After that, I want you to do the same with me.' I said to have the same experience as him. 'What do you mean by the same?' Ernesto's voice sounded different. 'Fucking someone else while you watch.' I could tell now that he didn't like that. His face changed utterly as if he was disgusted. 'I don't think that's gonna happen. I don't want you to fuck with anyone else.´ He made his statement already, taking the suggestion that I'd made just for himself. ´But Ernesto, why did you agree for yourself, but when I want to do it, you don't want me to? It's not fair.´ We didn't have more time to speak because as soon as the situation became tense, Vanesa showed up by surprise with Ignacio. Saved for the bell, I guess. ´It's lovely to see you guys!´ Ignacio exclaims, getting closer and giving us a cuddle. He was a lovely guy. Same as Vanesa. ´Where's everyone else?´ Ernesto asked. ´Well, they just said they're not coming, so it is just us.´ Vanesa winked her eye at him. ´Let's go have some fun then, right?´ I said to get the fuck out of there, and finally, we all got into the club. I hate techno, but for one day, I was not going to die. After getting registered by security, we left our things in a small locker that needed a 1€ coin, and we went to the bar to buy a beer. The music was loud, and it was jam-packed. I tried to dance, but I didn't feel it. Just too heterosexual a place for me. ´I got something for you´ Vanesa said in my ear, placing something on my hand. ´What is…?´ I didn't even have time to finish the sentence when she interrupted me. ´Happy little pill. Take half and give the other half to Ernesto.´ I'd never done that kind of drug before, but honestly, all I needed was to get myself spaced out. We shared the pill, and I swallowed it with the beer. I didn't feel anything straight away, so Ernesto and I went to the upstairs smoking room while it took effect. It smelled like cigarettes and it was a bit cold. It was even difficult to see anything. ´Ernesto, about what I said before, forget about it. I don't want you to think that I don't love you. I thought it was a good idea.´ He put out his cigarette in the metal ashtray and looked at me. ´I'm glad that you're thinking with common sense, Aiden. You know that it is not easy talking to you.´ Wait, that sounded a bit…Whatever, he was being "nice", so let's leave it for now. We get downstairs, careful not to fall down the stairs as it was very dark and the lights changed every 3 seconds. It was crazy. ´OMG, have you seen that?´ Ernesto exclaimed, impressed. ´Seen what?´ He moved my head. Vanesa and Ignacio were kissing each other, very intensely. We get close to them, and they started to laugh. ´Guys, no one say anything about this,' she said. 'Sure, Vanesa, don't worry.´ Ernesto replied. Ignacio opened a small bag with white powder inside that looked like salt. ´There are 2 options, you can sniff it or take it on your tongue and suck it.´ Ignacio said to us. I didn't even think about it, and I stuck my wet finger in the bag and licked off the drug. Tasted awful, but I drank a big sip of the beer, and it went down.

Suddenly everything started to feel different. I felt like the middle of the dance floor was calling me. "Baby one more time" by Britney Spears started to play, and all the lights fell on me. Everything felt free, and everyone was dancing at the same time. I left Ernesto in the corner. Everyone joined me. It was like we all are connected and synchronised to a choreography. I was the star, dancing like the Britney in her excellent decade. While we were all dancing, I got one shot from the bar, and everyone lifted me up. I was the moment. I was a star. It was like being in heaven. I always wanted to be part of something like that. That feeling of moving simultaneously with others and being connected was just amazing and unbelievable, almost like being part of a video clip. Until I realised Ernesto, Vanesa, and Ignacio were looking at me. ´Is he okay?´ Ignacio asks to Ernesto. ´What did you give him?´ Ernesto answered with another question. ´It was Ecstasy,´ Ignacio said, looking at Vanesa. ´Oh my god.´ Ernesto came to pick me up from a corner. ´What are you doing? Let me dance! I'm fucking Britney BITCH!´

Ernesto's face was a poem. 'Aiden, you've been dancing weirdly in a corner for 15 minutes, and then you went to the bar and stole one shot from a Mexican girl. She was shouting at you, but you kept dancing, and she almost slapped your face. Not to mention the blonde wig you took off from that black girl. What are you thinking?´ He said, almost worried. ´What? But what about the people and the lights?´ I said, confused. ´Which people and what lights, Aiden? C'mon, let's have a sit down.´ The worst thing that I could do, sitting somewhere outside the noisy room full of shit techno music. I started to feel like shit, my stomach hurt, and I felt really strange. ´Ernesto... I need to be well. I have to go to the hotel in an hour.´ I said to him, looking for some reassurance. ´You better eat something, Aiden. Your eyes are like an owl.´ Time went slowly, and it was 5:30 a.m., so I left to go to the hotel. Ernesto left me in the station close to the club. Vanesa and Ignacio left to sleep together. ´Let me know when you get there, okay?´ I gave him a kiss and left all my body and soul on the train. It was freezing, and the only thing I could think of is that I had to work a shift until 3 p.m., and I was high on Ecstasy and MDMA. I took some pictures and videos of my eyes, and I moved my ass quickly to the hotel. I popped upstairs, and the old bitches I had to work with in the morning breakfast were surprised by my early presence. 'Good morning! How's everyone doing?' I said, quite energetic. Then I realised that I needed to fake it because I looked 'too happy' considering it was fucking 6 in the morning. 'What are you doing here?' they asked. I said that I needed a shower, and I came early so I could have one. I ran out of there, borrowed a robust coffee, and went into the kitchen. The Portuguese morning chef (who was a sweetheart) saw me and understood the situation. 'You, take this and prepare it downstairs, be careful that no one sees you.' He gave me a margarita pizza. Honestly, he was a lifesaver.

In about four minutes, I swallowed the pizza sitting on a chair in the small kitchen in the back of the bar. I went into the shower quickly and rushed to avoid being late. I tried to wash off the club sticker from my hand, but I couldn't, so I left it and dried myself. After a couple of hours working, I knew one thing going: never ever fucking again, ever. What awful shit. I was delighted about my fantasy of being Britney and everyone like me. But not being fucking hungover from drugs, with a horrible headache and vertigo. Honestly, I learned the fucking lesson.

CHAPTER 26

Vanesa was wearing comfortable trackies, and we were ready for a special moment. It was her birthday, and she'd arranged to go on a day trip to London. I was very excited as it had been three years since I last was there. We looked for the cheapest option and got Flixbus tickets: to go there and come back for 30€! It was a long journey, but we thought having a small adventure might be fun.

It was bloody freezing and raining. We were waiting for the bus at Sloterdijk Station until it finally arrived. Vanesa decided to sit upstairs on the bus with Ignacio as they were having a special moment. Ernesto and I were downstairs, close to the toilet. I was glad I didn't have to share the seat with anyone else. I still remember when we were travelling around Italy. I had to sit with a guy snoring and almost laying his bald head on my shoulder, and that's not even mentioning the awful smell of feet throughout the bus. This wasn't the case this time thankfully, but the travel was quite long. We slept a few hours, but I knew it wouldn't be enough. Still, we were going to have a lovely day.

We finally arrived at London Victora Station at 7 a.m., looking a bit dreadful but ready for the short trip day. ´Maricaaaaa!´ Fernanda appeared from the back of the queue. No one knew she was there, as she'd said she couldn't make it. ´Darling! What are you doing here?´ I exclaimed, quite excited to see her. ´It was a surprise! Vanesa, do you really think I was about to miss your birthday?´ Fernanda said in a sassy way. She didn't have her pink braids on, just her natural afro curly hair which I thought looked really cool, even though I was not used to seeing her like that. ´Fernanda! You bitch, come and give me a hug!´ said Vanesa, smiling and happy about the lovely surprise of her being there. We were meeting Jenna at the hostel, a few streets from Leicester Square, and it was very cheap. I was surprised that Ernesto didn't complain about sleeping in a room with 11 more people, but I guess he didn't have much choice as we'd all agreed that we were staying there. Jenna was waiting for us, seated on the grey sofa in front of the reception, with a big trolley bag. That bitch was insane. We were literally there for one day! Unless she brought naughty things to use in the middle of the night while we were listening to the snoring of a random fat bitch with a smelly bumhole. After getting the check-in done and leaving our things in the locker, we set off to Camden Town.

It was sunny, cold like an ordinary February day in London, but warm inside my heart. After three years, I was back in the place that had started it all, my first adventure alone. I still remember when I was 18. My heart was broken, as the summer before I broke up with Marcos. All the things that happened after that were very messy and chaotic. I finished the first year of my hospitality degree. I wanted to find myself, so my Mum gave me 800€, and with that, I took a flight, without a house or a job, just checking myself into a hostel. I had nothing to lose but money, and after two days, I had a job as a glass collector and a room in a shared house in Willesden Junction, zone 2. I have to say that just those months that I stayed there gave me all the experience and skills to know that I wasn't made to live in San Fernando: London had all the different cultures, the economy, readily available jobs – in short, it was nothing like Spain. Even though I had craziness and I had matured a lot since then, the experience strengthened me.

Walking down Camden with a chocolate, Nutella, and Oreo waffle (ready to kill a diabetic), I couldn't stop looking at my surroundings; sometimes, I was joining in the conversations that they were all having, but I couldn't focus, my mind was back in my 18th year, at the moment when I was single, healing my fragile broken heart and discovering that relationships were shit and very toxic. Still, that moment of freedom, of being just myself working, earning money and going out. I'd never been out before. One of my first times was in London. I'll never forget those nights out in Heaven, with pop music, an expensive Corona plastic bottle, and the foursomes kissing each other at 4 in the morning. I realised that I was not that person anymore. Even though I liked Amsterdam, there was an immense feeling of missing all of this, my youth, space, and liberty. Felt like it was not part of me anymore, and that brave and determined boy was being kidnapped.

'Guys! Look at that shop, shall we go in?' Jenna exclaimed. Hansel and Gretel's shop was full of candies and sweets, with a part where they sold ice cream with different flavours. It was full of childish fantasy decoration but charming. 'We should take a picture of us in there!' Ernesto said to everyone. He was pointing at a small table inside of a tree that was giving Alice in Wonderland vibes. We all sat in the tiny chairs, grabbed the cups for decoration, and had a silly picture with them. 'Guys, I know a really cool shop. It's literally 2 minutes from here!' They all followed me, and we went inside the shop. Cyberdog was one of the most popular and different shops in London. It had GoGo dancers and techno music with neon lights inside. The clothing was tacky, but the experience of visiting it was like getting into another world.

We went to the sex shop area downstairs after having a quick look around. Later, at lunchtime, after going to the M&M store and running away because Fernanda broke an expensive mug, we decided to eat at a Chinese buffet.

We all got really full, and even Jenna was puking in the toilet because she was a greedy bitch and ate more than she could handle. But something else happened that got into my head. The Chinese waiter immediately brought the bill to us without even asking if we were ready and picking up the plates. It was rude. But what really annoyed me was the way that everyone was acting. When he came, they were not even looking at the eyes of the waiter. Ernesto stood up and threw the coins and notes inside the bill basket, but in a haughty way, like he was better than the waiter, and because the waiter was rude, he now needed to be more so. As a waiter, that shocked me a bit, as it is true that I felt a bit rushed out to go by the place, but I'd never have acted like that, literally like a fucking cunt. Sometimes I forgot who I was living with, and it was not the first time he had a lordly reaction or said something rude to others.

Trying to forget about that uncomfortable moment, we went to where I really wanted to go, G.A.Y., that kind of pub where all the young queers of London go for a quick drinkie before going out. We ordered some beers with a Pride plastic cup, and I begged the barman to let me keep it. The handsome guy didn't have any problem at all. He said I just needed to hide it as soon as I finished and take it with me. We were all sitting on a sofa, and many pop anthems were on the hundreds of TVs spread across the room, followed by the pink light. I couldn't resist, and as soon as I heard, 'It's raining, men', I lift up Vanesa and started to jump around the room with her. It was a lovely moment.

Jenna was tired and wanted to go to the hostel, but we wanted to go somewhere else for a dance, and that's what we did. We found a straight pub with decent music but of course, full of straight people. We had a couple of tequila shots, and I was just dancing and trying to enjoy the moment, but something was wrong that didn't let me enjoy the moment at all. It was the kind of moment where you know you're supposed to be having a great time, but you can't fake it. The best part of the night was when we got kicked out because Fernanda felt asleep on the sofa, and the security guy wouldn't let her stay. ´Did you have fun, baby?´ Ernesto asked, holding my hand while we talked back together to the hostel. ´Well, yes.´ I answered, quite unsure. ´Yes, but...?´ Ernesto asked again, trying to get information about the situation. I looked down at the floor, to the dirty street full of beers and smashed vodka bottles. ´I don't know, I just had a feeling of missing living here, like when I was 18...´ He dropped my hand and looked at me with a disapproving face. ´Are you going to talk about this again, Aiden?´ he said to me, sharpening the knife of his tongue. ´Talking about what, Ernesto? You just asked a question, and I'm fucking answering.´ I saw the vein on his neck getting bigger. ´You're doing this again, talking about London. Do you know how many times

I've heard you talking about it? It's fantastic that you had that experience when you were 18, now get over it. We live in Amsterdam, end of the story,´ he said, with a nasty voice. I was as if he was jealous of me, and everything I'd done before being with him was annoying to hear, instead of feeling happy for me for having those emotions. It always felt like this with him, like six of one and half a dozen of the other. Being unable to be myself with the person I was sharing my life with, it felt wrong. I felt trapped but didn't know how to deal with the situation. ´I know Ernesto, but I don't think it's terrible to talk about it. I just missed living here. I feel like Amsterdam is a place for staying a specific amount of time, and I don't know, I would love to discover more parts of the world and travel, I don't know, maybe Australia. It's just how I feel.´ He laughed a hard, sarcastic laugh. ´Australia? I'm not going anywhere, Aiden. You should stop being so fanciful and get your fucking feet on the ground. Grow up. I'm not your father.´ 'Here we are again,' I thought. Me putting my head down and silencing my voice in the face of Ernesto's rules. I didn't understand this situation and why I didn't have enough strength to free myself all this time. ´You know what, Ernesto? I'm done with this shit. I deserve understanding and love. And you're just spitting shit and attacking me. I don't want to be with someone like you. I'm just so fucking done.´ I shouted, feeling the empowerment of breaking the chains. ´Are you breaking up with me? Today? At Vanesa's birthday? Do you want to humiliate me?´ he said desperately, stopping me in the middle of the blue carpeted stairs of the hostel. ´No one is humiliating you, you're just being shit, and I'm bored of this situation.´ His face looked confused by my determined words. ´What about Paris, Aiden? What the fuck are you doing?´ His eyes were opening wide as if they were to pop out of his head. ´You can go to Paris by yourself. I didn't even want to go with you.

CHAPTER 27

I was even impressed with myself; after all that fucking drama in London, I couldn't believe I'd confronted Ernesto and refused to tolerate more humiliation from him.

I wasn't expecting that as soon as we got back to Amsterdam, it was everywhere: the news, Twitter, YouTube, and TV. There was a virus that apparently was spreading from China; it was like a really dangerous flu that affected your breathing, and it was very contagious. Covid-19. I knew something was happening, but it wasn't really something I paid a lot of attention to until it got out of control. But now, it wasn't only in China: it was in the USA, Mexico, Latin America, Europe, and Africa.

People were dying at the hospital everywhere, so the government decided to shut down the country. ´Aiden, please don't say anything to the girls. ´Ernesto said, while we were in the lift going upstairs in the hotel, as we were working the same shift that day, him wearing his black uniform with his skinny arms bare. ´Tell them what, Ernesto?´ I said, pretending I was not paying attention to his face. I was getting tired of seeing him daily. ´About us, I don't want them to know that we broke up.´ I couldn't resist stopping looking at my phone and looking him fully in the face. ´Let me make it clear, we haven't broken up. I left you. It's the truth. Why do we need to hide it?´ He looked nervous, biting every single bit of skin left around his nails, almost about to bleed out. ´Because I don't trust them, they're not our friends, and if we say something they will talk about it. Everyone in the hotel will know.´ As soon as the lift stopped on our floor, the doors opened, releasing the awful smell of lies and fakeness. ´What are you saying, Ernesto? They are our friends.´ His eyes were looking to each corner of the hall, checking if anyone was around. ´We don't have friends here, Aiden. It's just you and me. I'm the only person that you can trust.´ As soon as he finished the sentence, almost whispering, Jenna and Vanesa came out of the cleaning area office, where they kept all the chemical products, towels, washing machine, and computers to prepare the rotas and the tasks for the day. ´Maricas! How are you doing today? I can't believe that they shut down the country!´ Jenna exclaimed, looking at Vanesa and leaning against the wall. I didn't even have time to open my mouth before Ernesto took the chance to jump over and give them both a hug. ´It's crazy, isn't it? I'm happy that at least I have Aiden. We both have each other to get through this situation.´ What a fake bitch. I couldn't believe he just said that shit. ´Yes, darling. You're lucky to have each other. Things are going to get worse in the hotel.´ Vanesa added, not knowing anything about Ernesto's bullshit. Finally, I found the chance to speak out. ´What's going on in the hotel?´ Vanesa and Jenna looked at each other with compassion and worry.

´As the country is shutting down, we don't have guests, just those living in the hotel. There will be less work to do, and who knows…´ Vanesa said to us, looking sad and disappointed. Fantastic news, apart from living with an asshole, and needing to lie to my friends because of him, now there was considerable uncertainty in each corner of my mind. They left to start working their shift together, and I went to the bar. Lucciano was on his knees doing FIFO (first in, first out) with the drinks. I could see he was wearing black underwear that was quite tight so that I could see a bit of the upper part of his hairy bum. ´Hey mate, how are you doing?´ I said to him, leaning on the bar and paying attention to his body. He didn't expect me and jumped, dropping a can of coke that went rolling through the long bar. ´Ciao, Aiden! I heard that you were in London for Vannesa's birthday. How was it?´ It was awful because I had lovely memories of my past time there, remembering my freedom. That fucking asshole Ernesto was annoyed because no one around him could be happy because he didn't live that experience himself. He needed to make everyone feel like they were annoying, blaming me. After all, I couldn't tolerate more; of course, it was my fault. Nothing new. 'Yeah. We had a lot of fun, it was too short, but enough for one day,' I lied to him. I didn't know why I was acting like this or why I couldn't just say how I felt. I thought you must get used to lying, pretending you're happy when you're not. When the other person tells you what is right and what isn't, you don't even know who you are or want to be. You're just trapped in the invisible chains of what some people would say is 'love': but love is free, love is caring, and love is being supportive, not having to silence your own voice. 'I'm glad! It's such a mess now, right?' He stood up and closed the fridge. 'I appreciate you, Aiden. Therefore, I must tell you something, but you can't say anything, right?' he said, looking at me with his honey eyes and beautiful lips. 'Sure, what's going on?' I couldn't deal with more bad news. I was feeling just simply tired of all the shit. 'As we're officially in a lockdown, we're going to be shut down for one month, just the managers will be doing a minimal job of providing service to the guest who are living in the rooms. Everyone else will have to stay at home, although we're still going to get paid.' All morning I was thinking about his words, also Ernesto ones. There was too much going on, and I didn't know how I felt.

I finished my shift before Ernesto, so I sprinted to the train so I didn't have to share the journey with him. I took a seat, and I called my Mum. 'Hey Mum, how are you?' I said. 'Aiden! My love, I'm a bit worried, to be honest; I didn't want to worry you, but I heard that the country is shut down as well. I saw on the TV that the Spanish government has made the same decision,' she gabbled. 'Really, Mum? And what now?' I replied. 'I don't know. You can't believe how bad things are here now, Aiden,' she replied, sounding sad and worried. 'But are you okay, is everyone in the family okay?' I had no idea what to do in the situation. 'They're okay, but we're in a lockdown. We can't go outside of the house unless we need to go shopping for groceries or go to work. You need to go to the closest supermarket. There are police everywhere, stopping everyone and asking for their address. If you don't have permission from your job, you can't go to work.' It sounded really drastic. 'But Mum, it's not like that here. Why are they reacting like that there? A work colleague told me they would just close the hotel here for a month. I'm just so confused, Mum. I don't want to be here,´ As I said it, I knew it was true. 'Listen, Aiden. I know this situation it's complex and strange, but we can't do much more. At least there you can go outside, but here… They're even selling face masks to protect you from the virus, but the prices are ridiculously high.' It was like a bad dream. ´I don't know, Mum, I'm confused. Are you with Ricardo now?´ I hoped she wasn't stuck in the house on her own. 'We'll speak about that another time, but please, Aiden, this is serious, don't get close to anyone and try not to go outside.' I couldn't believe this was happening. ´I'll try, Mum, take care, and speak soon. I love you.´ There wasn't much more I could say. 'I love you too, Aiden. Take care of yourself.'

After the call, I felt even worse. All the countries were closing, people were getting more and more paranoid, and the police were being cunts. When I got to Almere, I rolled a spliff, making it a strong one and feeling how every part of my body was disconnecting, floating, and going away. I felt like shit, and at the same time, I didn't feel it at all. It was strange. I got myself into the shower and left the water falling on my head. I stood under the water, thinking about everything, not knowing how to react. After spending 20 minutes under the hot water, and finally feeling relaxed, I realized Ernesto had just got back. I put the towel around my waist and prepared myself to leave the bathroom. ´Hey baby, how was today? I spoke with my Mum and..´ I didn't let him finish the sentence. ´I know, I also spoke with mine. Looks like we're stuck here.´ He analysed those words, getting closer. ´We're stuck here? This is not a prison, Aiden; we have each other. I don't know why you're saying that.´ He looked clean. I bet he had a shower in the hotel. He got undressed, just wearing his transparent white underwear. ´I don't know anymore, Ernesto. It's all very confusing, and I feel sad.´ He moved closer to me and put his hands on my face. ´Aiden, you're not alone. You have me. I'm always going to be here for you.´ I felt my blood running through every single vein of my body. I didn't judge the situation, and I hugged Ernesto. In the end, we lived together, and I needed to be there, I guessed.

I felt the pressure of our bulges rubbing against each other. We were both erect. We looked at each other, and we started to kiss. I dropped my towel to the floor and used it to get onto my knees. I felt Ernesto's erection straining to get out of his underwear, making a slight movement. I followed my natural instincts, and I started to lick him from the outside of his underwear, feeling his precum already. I pulled his underwear down, and I introduced his cock to my mouth, letting it slide slowly, making it lubricated, using all my saliva to cover every single centimetre of his penis. I could hear how he was moaning, and see he was looking at me, very concentrated, while I was submissive on my knees. 'Get to the sofa.' I said and slid my tongue over his anus, up to the bottom, side to side, and then in circles. He couldn't resist it: even though he never lets me penetrate him, he loves to be rimmed. I made an effort to push a bit harder with my tongue in his ass while, at the same time, I put pressure on his perineum with two of my right fingers. He was just moaning like a bitch, wanting more. 'Now it is my turn. Now you lay down on the bed.' He pushed me to the awful bed that we slept in and turned me so I was looking at the ground. 'Who is in charge now?' Ernesto said with a bossy voice, spanking my bum very hard. 'You.' I said, feeling my skin getting redder. 'Now, I'll fuck you, and you'll beg me for more. C'mon, say it.' Ernesto swapped his mood from a lamb about to be killed to a cheap version of Christian Grey. 'I want you to fuck me.' I said, accepting the situation, not even thinking about what a massive mistake this was. 'What did you say? I didn't hear you,' he said, spanking the same area harder, reaching the point where it was painful. 'I want you to rape me.' As soon as I pronounced that wrong term, he didn't think about it. With a spit of saliva onto my anus, he penetrated me hard without lubricating the area enough, moaning and sliding inside my painful self without any care. But I didn't feel anything, just something moving inside me, nothing pleasant. 'Open your fucking mouth. You're going to see who's in charge here.' I did what I was told to, and I felt how quickly he spat, but he didn't even try to get it in my mouth. The spit slid down my face, running over my beard. His eyes were as open as an owl, looking at me with empowerment, with mastery. He proceeded to strangle my neck so hard I could barely breathe. I just felt the tears in my eyes, holding them back, trying not to let them go. 'This is what

you deserve because you're a bitch, and I need to teach you a lesson.´
He looked like a psychopath; he wasn't even making an effort to try to
make the sex good, he was just empowering himself upon me, using
force and violent 'sex' to make himself feel better. Better than me,
better than anyone, because he needed to feel like everyone else was
less than him. As soon as he said that, I felt the power of his hand
slapping my face. At that moment, time stopped. I felt a massive pain
in my face, moving up to my head, feeling how my veins grew purple
and inflamed. I couldn't stand that. I'd had enough. I couldn't believe
he crossed that line. He didn't even ask me, he just took permission
from his desire to make me feel like crap. Without hesitating, I drew
all my anger together, and I slapped his face as hard as I could. He
looked up, shocked and stopped penetrating me for a second. ´Why
did you do that?' he said, surprised by my reaction ´It hurts, don't touch
my fucking face ever,´ I said, trying not to cry. ´Do you want me to
stop?´ I didn't know how to say no. I just surrendered myself,
humiliated, with my face irritated and with a colossal headache, waiting
for him to cum inside me and finish this awful shit. ´Keep going.´ The
only thing I could think of while a tear ran out of my eye was that there
was no escape: the country was closed, and I couldn't go anywhere. I
was trapped there with him.

CHAPTER 28

A couple of weeks later and time had passed, but every day looked the same. I woke up, had my coffee with a toast, lit up my spliff, lay on the sofa or played some video games, prepared lunch, smoked another spliff, napped, and watched some TV show on Netflix. Every single fucking day, it was the same, trapped in the time where the sadness was getting bigger, where there was not enough space in the apartment, just pain, darkness, depression and loneliness. Just hearing every day how bad things were going globally with that fucking pandemic and how many people were dying, forcing us to be prisoners in our own homes, in our own minds. ´Well, what brought you here, Aiden? asked the therapist. I spoke with my aunty Mimi about my situation, and she recommended a therapist she knew who would see me via Skype. That was helpful being as I was stuck in that fucking country. ´Looks like I'm not sure about anything anymore.´ I was just sitting in front of my Macbook Pro, in my pyjamas and having a cup of coffee. ´All right, let's start from the beginning. When did you start to feel like this?´ The cliché question had been asked, but I couldn't remember someone asking me that before. ´I've been feeling less worthy all my life, less than anyone. But since school, I have had problems with anxiety. I couldn't go, had few friends, and always felt different from the other kids.´ The therapist took notes in her notebook, paying attention to my words. ´Nice, this is a good start. Can you explain to me more about that time in your life?´ I took a sip of the coffee, and I breathed in. ´High School was a nightmare for me, and it wasn't just because some people called me a faggot in front of the main teacher, and he just laughed about it. My suffering was inside my mind. I felt terrified as if I were in the middle of the wild and didn't know what was hiding behind every tree. I never felt understood. I fought with my Mum and family because they didn't understand my depression and anxiety. The high school teachers said I needed a routine to follow the course at its own pace. But I never felt identified with that. I didn't fit in. I wasn't interested in maths or history lessons about rich people that I didn't give a shit about,´ I said, trying to organise the huge puzzle of the darkness of my childhood. ´So, when you say no one understood you, can you develop more about that?´ She was analysing my words from the other side of the screen. ´I didn't even understand what was happening to me. I felt petrified every time I heard the alarm at 7 a.m., like a stab in my chest, just a straight pain that went there as soon as I hear that fucking noise. I couldn't breathe and didn't want to get up from bed. It was my cave, my secure place. I just remembered my Mum dragging me out of bed every single day of the week for me to go to high school, but as much as she tried to do it (literally pulling off the duvets and everything), it didn't work. No one understood why a 14 year old boy didn't want to attend school. And as you know, going is mandatory until you're 16. So what I was doing was illegal, but my Mum couldn't do much more because she had to work at the office in the morning. She couldn't risk losing the position that she'd had to fight for as much as she wanted to stay. Either way, even if she didn't go to work, nothing could make me move from that single bed. It was the only place where I felt safe.´ I was starting to remember everything, opening the wounds again. ´I'm sorry to hear that. I understand you must have felt very upset and frustrated about it for many years. Unfortunately, the society that we're living in, and schools, are not really prepared to deal with these problems. They just send the police to do the work. Still, that doesn't get the best resolutions because the child's mental health is treated as unimportant. But it's courageous of you to seek help, so I'm here. Now tell me, how's your relationship with your father?´ The therapist went straight to the taboo point... ´Basically, I have a strange relationship with my dad, my parents divorced when I was a child, and I have always been with my Mum. But even though I have some good memories with him, some of his attitudes made me want to get some distance from him.´ The therapist kept listening and writing notes. ´When I started to have this problem of absence from school, and my Mum wanted to take me to therapy, my Dad was against it, saying that therapy was for insane people. I didn't need it, just needed some discipline. He thought everyone was putting him away, and you can imagine how it went. Being next to him made me uncomfortable because he thought it was just bullshit, I don't know. The thing is that I've had my comings and goings with him, it's been a couple of years without wanting to see him, but always I've ended up meeting with him again. He said or reacted in a way that made me feel uncomfortable, and it was just worse. But he's been in my life since a long time ago.´ All these months with my Dad out of my mind, most of the time, and now it looked like it was the main subject. ´I understand, and let me tell you, it happens more usually than you might think. Sometimes parents think their sons will be the same as them, but of course the reality is they're not. Also, seeing how you got distant from him at such a young age is interesting. We will speak more about this in another moment,´ she said, making a note to keep talking about it to the next session. ´I'd like to speak about something if it's alright.´ I needed to start bringing up all my emotions because being in The Netherlands was causing me pain right at that moment. ´What's about?´ she asked. ´Well, I moved to the Netherlands last year with my boyfriend. Ex-boyfriend, sorry. And I'm just so lost, so confused, I don't understand anything of my surroundings. I'm not with him anymore, but my life is meaningless now. I'm stuck in this fucking apartment with him. And I don't understand why one day he can be the most lovely person, and then the next he changes to treat me like shit and turns against me.´ I said, for once, honest about what was happening. ´OK, I need to stop you there. How long have you been together, and what happened to end the relationship?´ I took another deep breath, trying to concentrate and let the feelings talk. ´I met him around September 2018 on Grindr; he was lovely with me initially. I felt like he gave me everything and was there for me all the time. Still, as soon as I started dating him, I saw things I didn't like; he was saying disgusting, offensive things about random people as if someone was dressing awful or was just smaller or fatter. He needed to say something cruel. But I didn't listen to my head, and I kept dating him. Indeed, he was always there, and we went to many places together on holidays, and he came to stay with me when I was doing my internship in Poland for three months. But I always felt like I was slowly losing myself. I remember when we went to Oslo, and I wanted to have a threesome. I mean, I always wanted to do it. He said it would happen at some point, but I remembered we spoke about it when we were there. I don't remember exactly what he said, but it hurt me. I felt misunderstood, I needed to be in bed for an hour, almost crying, explaining why I didn't like it when he spoke to me that way, and we ended up having the threesome. But it was not just that, as everything has gotten worse since we came here to live together. We end up in a fight every day over everything, and there are not enough words to explain how I feel.´ The therapist kept writing and paid even more attention. ´The sex was awful, and I felt unsatisfied. Apart from a couple of threesomes, I wanted to discover more of my sexuality, and it was impossible with him. I felt like I was always giving but not receiving. Sex was just the same and boring. So I wanted to be with more people. Still, he's very jealous and controls everything, so every time that he agreed for me to be on Grindr, he was just making a lot of excuses for me not being allowed to meet the person, 'he's more than 29 years old' or 'too fit' and on and on. I remember I was talking once with one guy who did yoga and was very spiritual. Hence, I wanted to speak with someone about my feelings. Still, I couldn't because everything I thought was wrong. Going to the point, he told me, 'I don't know why you are talking about your fucking shit with a stranger when I'm here. You're fucking insane!' As I kept talking, I started to hear my own words, and all the fights, bad moments, and rudeness started to seem important, started to carry weight they actually had, that unfortunately I'd avoided by normalising them. ´I see. Look, Aiden, I don't know enough about him. Still, with what you told me, I'm afraid you might be living with someone with a narcissistic personality disorder. I might be wrong because I'm not treating him, but you said some things about his behaviour are clearly in the danger zone.´ I took a moment to think about what she just said. ´Narcissistic personality disorder? What is that?´ It was as if the gates of heaven were opening to help me, to give me the answers I'd been looking for all this time. ´It's a mental health condition in which people have an unreasonably high sense of their own importance. They need and seek too much attention and want people to admire them. They may lack the ability to understand or care about the feelings of others. But behind this mask of extreme confidence, they are unsure of their self-worth. They are easily upset by the slightest criticism. You can tell if he can be a narcissist with these points: grandiosity, attention seeking, troubled relationships, lack of empathy, sense of entitlement,´ she said, adjusting her square glasses. ´It's completely normal that you feel confused at the beginning. What I'd suggest you do is have a look at YouTube. There are plenty of videos on there about this kind of condition and how to spot it and take care of it.´ The more that she said to me, the stronger I felt. I wasn't crazy. It wasn't my imagination. ´Yesterday, I realised something, we were arguing about something, and the way he was acting, looking at me, brought me back to my past, to my first relationship, Marcos.´ I closed my eyes and opened the wounds of my heart, the ones that I thought were healed, but in reality, that was far from being the case. ´We had a very toxic relationship. We were just teenagers. Still, I felt like shit with myself, and I mistreated him. He wasn't perfect, but I was losing my shit with him in some moments, and I think it wasn't fair. Now, seeing Ernesto reacting like crazy and spitting shit from his mouth, I realise I was like that before. Something connected me again to that emotion with him.´ The law of the mirror, they call it. ´Have you spoken with Marcos about this discovery and the fact that you realised how you reacted in those moments?´ I took a moment to reflect on her words. ´Things ended up very messy, and I blocked him because we caused each other a lot of pain, but honestly since this happened with Ernesto, something wants me to speak with him. I had a distorted thought of him. I spoke a lot of shit about him. For one moment, I thought Ernesto was much better than him when actually he was doing what he wanted with me.´ I couldn't believe it, I realised the true face of my relationship with Ernesto. ´Maybe you should think about killing that ghost of the past, leaving it behind and trying to heal your wounds properly.´

The session had been very intense. I felt completely drained and tired. Ernesto was at work, and even though the hotel was shut down, someone needed to organise the documents on the reception computers and help the cleaners if they were needed.

I went on to Instagram, summoning up all the courage I could, and breathed out all the anxiety in my chest. *Unblock* "Direct Message to user Marxcoss."

Aiden99: Hey Marcos! I hope it doesn't bother you. It's been a long time…

CHAPTER 29

I couldn't believe that I'd just done it. The last time I spoke with Marcos was in 2018, two months after returning from London. I thought I had the situation under control, had gotten over the relationship, and was more assertive. None of this had been the case. In fact, as soon as I got to the corner of the street where I was living in San Fernando, and I saw him that evening, I was just feeling an awful pain in my chest, like needles in my heart. There was too much space in the room of my heart, so I was just allowing them to be. I didn't know how to make it better. In fact, I was still angry at him for cheating on me, and as soon as he told me in the shopping centre car park that he had a boyfriend, I couldn't handle it, and I had no other contact with him from that point.

My heartbeat was rushing to the edge. I did it. I'd opened the door to my past again.

@Marxcoss: Aiden! I didn't expect your message. It's been ages!

@Aiden99: I know, right? How are things going?

@Marxcoss: Well, apart from being stuck in the house all day? Pretty good, I finished my massage course, and I got a job as an assistant, so I get well paid.

@Aiden99: Of course, this situation is awful. I can't believe this is all happening. It feels like we're drowning in our own demons. I'm happy that you got a job! I guess now the shop is closed, right?

@Marxcoss: You're right, it's a bit crazy here, and I'm struggling, but it could always be worse. Yes, at the moment, it's closed. I hope my boss opens the place again soon because I will go crazy here! Hahaha.

@Aiden99: Is your family doing all right?

@Marxcoss: Same as always, nothing has changed at all. Apart from my dad being older and behaving like an old person, my sister is still stuck in the house without working or even cooking. She's like a parasite on society.

@Aiden99: Hahaha, you know how much I hated your sister. She was an asshole.

@Marxcoss: I don't want to remember when you argued in Barcelona.

For just one second, I went back to the past, to his sister and me, shouting at each other in the middle of Barcelona because she was a jealous bitch, who wanted to get all the attention until I couldn't take it more, and I exploded. In the past, I was with Marcos, the beautiful boy who I fell in love with when I was 15. Seeing myself there, with Ernesto, made me realise what I had then and what I had now. I had to recognise that our relationship wasn't perfect, but he was an extraordinary, caring boy with a big heart. But we were both pushing forwards across the enormous, deep, endless ground of depression. Sometimes, mixing that with not being mature caused a colossal collide in our hearts.

@Marxcoss: What about you? I've seen on your profile that you're living in The Netherlands.

@Aiden99: That's true. Here I am. Stuck in this fucking country and full of anxiety in every single pore of my oily face.

@Marxcoss: Are you still with that guy, the one that I saw you with that time in the funfair...

I'd forgotten that the last time I saw Marco's face was one night when I went to the funfair in San Fernando, and suddenly he was there in front of me. I wanted the ground to open and swallow me up. Still, I just smiled politely and avoided the situation as much as I was able to.

@Aiden99: I was. I'm living with him, but the lockdown came, and here we are. Need to be sharing this fucking apartment with him. I don't even have my own room. It's frustrating.

@Marxcoss: Oh my god, why? I can't believe you're stuck there, and in that situation, it must be difficult...

@Aiden99: It is, and it's driving me nuts. I thought we had a bad relationship, but this is just incomprehensible.

@Marxcoss: I'm sorry, to be honest, I've really been waiting a long time for this moment, Aiden.

@Aiden99: Why?

@Marxcoss: I respected your decision to not speak more with me and have your own life. But all this time, in one way or another, I've been looking through your profile with my other account just to see if you're doing alright. You know that I appreciate you a lot.

I can't believe it. This is so special and so wrong at the same time.

@Aiden99: Really? I thought you just had your life done and were happy.

@Marxcoss: Well, kind of, but I can't just forget my first love.

Neither could I, because, in the end, Ernesto was just a plaster in my life. I thought I really liked him and that we were in love, but no: I was just comforting myself, trying to fill the vast space of the void that Marco's left in my life.

@Aiden99: I know. I'm happy to speak with you, Marcos.

@Marxcoss: So, why did you drop me a message then? I'm pretty intrigued.

@Aiden99: Because I've been thinking about you today, and having this many arguments with Ernesto made me realise that I've done wrong with you.

@Marxcoss: Do you want to keep in contact? It would be lovely to see you.

It would be lovely to see you. Those words spun in my mind like a machine of toxic and painful emotions.

@Aiden99: Sure, I'd love to, Marcos.

Marxcoss has started to follow you

I followed him back, and I left the conversation there

I lay down on the sofa with a spliff in my mouth and sad music in the background. I tried to disconnect my mind, body, soul, and myself from this world. Just thinking about Marcos and Ernesto, how I got myself troubled by these relationships and the mess around them. I heard the front door opening quite hard. ´Aiden?´ I heard Ernesto calling my name, quite rough. ´Hey, what's going on?´ I opened my eyes, from the lovely nap I had been having, floating out of all my problems. ´Can you explain this?´ He pointed his fingers towards the kitchen and the apartment, making a round movement. ´What, Ernesto?´ I was still waking myself up, and I didn't know what he meant. ´Did you forget again? I told you to clean the house.´ I didn't even stand up from the sofa. I was still lying down there. ´I cleaned some things, but it wasn't a deep clean.´ He dropped his bag violently on the floor, making enough noise to show me his angriness. ´Do you think I'm fucking stupid? You've done nothing.´ He picked up a dirty napkin that was under the sofa. ´Can you see this? I left it there so I could see if you'd cleaned the house, and obviously you haven't.´ I was just hearing a blurry noise, like a dog barking. He took off his uniform and put it on the white leather chair. ´Ernesto, I told you. I haven't done a deep clean, just did the basic things.´ His face was getting worse with every single answer I gave him. ´What about the groceries? Have you got the groceries in?´ Surely, Ernesto was looking for anything and everything he could hold against me, to make me feel like I was a piece of shit. ´No, I didn't have time. I've been in therapy, and I was feeling tired.´ Ernesto couldn't resist making a loud, sarcastic laugh out of that Machiavellian face. ´You know what's your problem, Aiden?´ he said, standing in front of the sofa where I lay. I didn't have the energy to move my body. ´That you're a fucking liar, a drug addict who needs to smoke five joints a day to be enough because you can't even look at yourself in the mirror because you're disgusting, the only thing that you're doing is smoking and sleeping, you don't clean, you do nothing, it's just disgusting to see a fucking zombie next to me every single day.´ He puked all his abusive rude thoughts over me. ´Ernesto, you're being insulting. Stop.´ I was feeling uncomfortable. I hated this situation. I liked to talk about problems. I didn't believe in shouting and treating people like shit. ´And let me tell you, I don't understand why you're going to therapy. It is not going to work because people like you never change. You're just here to fuck up the people that are with you, that love you, like me,´ he said, feeling superior. ´You don't fucking love me.´ I stood up, and I faced him, both of us in our underwear, like if we were about to fuck, like in those kind of shit romantic toxic comedies. But not this time. I entered the kitchen, poured myself a tequila, and sliced some lemons. ´What did you just say?´ I licked the salt off my hand, swallowed the tequila and bit the lemon, the perfect combination. I sighed, making a noise placing the shot glass on the table. ´I said that you don't fucking love me because the only thing you're doing is fucking up my head, telling me how insane I am, or how pathetic it is to send a meme of me with a plastic cock to a WhatsApp group of our friends. After all, they're strangely looking at you at work.´ Ernesto opened his eyes wide as an owl from the other side of the room. He couldn't believe what I was just saying. ´Have you seen yourself? I'm worried about you, Aiden. You're acting insane!´ I served myself another shot, and I repeated the process. And I quickly found a joint I'd left in the ashtray for later. ´Maybe I am insane.´ I said, laughing at him. He was pathetic, awful, and trying to manipulate me. ´You don't know what you are saying. You look psycho Aiden. Why are you lying to me? Why did you say that you've cleaned and done the groceries and you haven't?´ I grabbed the speaker, and turning the volume up to maximum, I played 'Maniac', by Michael Sembello and started singing the song. At the same time, I inhaled all the spliff in my lungs, and downed another shot to cut my pain off. ´What the fuck are you doing, Aiden? You look pathetic! Look at yourself! You've completely lost your fucking mind!´ I'm done with the situation: I swung the brush stick against his head, making him bleed out. He looked scared. With all my strength, I kept going, hitting him repeatedly. I just wanted him to die. I wondered what could I do with the body. I could buy a proper butcher's knife and dismember every part of that cunt. Just seeing myself covered in his blood. There'd be too many questions, we lived in the centre, they would know, I'd go to jail.

All of this sounded very satisfying in my mind, very gory and visceral. He didn't deserve less, I was done with all this abuse against me, but unfortunately, instead of his head, I settled for hitting the fucking white leather chair so many times that I broke the stick.

Ernesto was just speechless on the other side of the room, in silence, in shock.

And while the song was still on, I couldn't control myself: I threw the stick hard on the floor and started to laugh while I was dancing. Ernesto looked scared, speechless.

´By the way Ernesto, I'm moving back to Spain.´

CHAPTER 30

Being stuck in The Netherlands with Ernesto, in a fucking studio with no doors made me even crazier. Someone who didn't live through it may not understand, but it was like being drowned in the breathless anxiety routine for me. I knew I was avoiding my emotions by smoking weed, but on one side I felt like it was helping me as it made the time go faster. On the other hand, I just saw a blurry body in the mirror, unknown to me, fragile, depressed, sad, and skinny. Why did I need to feel like this? As time passed, I was required to attend some shifts in the hotel again, just three days a week, and not for food and beverage work, for maintenance. Basically, they wanted me to clean the pipes of the sinks in every single room. It was fair because I was being paid even though the hotel had been closed. But I just felt out of it all the time. I felt like I didn't have the energy to even breathe, just to inhale the toxins of the weed. But I must confess that my motivation had been failing, and I didn't show up when I was supposed to be on my shift. Not professional, I know, but how could I explain this to someone? I didn't trust them anymore. I didn't feel capable of anything. I surrendered myself to whatever was going to happen.

I no longer cared about me, Ernesto, my job or anything. I received an email from Helen Muijen, the HR person for the hotel, the same woman who gave me the job. I needed to meet with them to discuss some things, which meant the company were going to finish my contract, as I was having regular absences. While they were talking to me, I was just gone, looking somewhere else. My head wasn't on this earth, maybe I'd gone to Venus, Pluto or more likely, fucking Hell. Smiling politely, trying to pretend that nothing was happening to me, that I was just tired when the truth was that I couldn't deal with anything anymore. As soon as I signed the document and left the office, I saw Ernesto with the hoover going to the elevator, but he didn't even look at me. He knew I was there, but he had just passed by, which was very strange of him.

I dropped him a message.

Aiden: Ernesto? I saw you passing by with the hoover, but you said nothing.

Ernesto: I don't want to talk to you.

Aiden: What's happening now? Where are you?

Ernesto: Do you want to talk? Come on, then. Room 206

I thought he was organising the reception. They didn't have much left to do, so housekeeping asked for help. I went to the the lift, and I felt the long space of the hall, with green walls and dark brown carpets. Looked as empty and lonely as my heart. I found room 206, and I knocked on the door. Not even a second later, it was opened quite hard. 'What's on now, Ernesto?' He went to the other side of the room, not saying a word, just looking at me with hate and disappointment. 'Hello? Are you listening to me?' The vein in his neck came up, and he opened his eyes, observing me as if he wanted to stab me right there. Kinda creepy. 'Do you think I'm fucking stupid, Aiden?' Out of nowhere, again, that question. 'Why stupid? I don´t get it Ernesto.´ He took his phone out of his blazer pocket and showed me a couple of screenshots. ´After all, I've done for you, being with you, supporting you, moving to another country for you. And now you're just speaking with Marcos?´ I froze for a couple of seconds, trying to understand the situation. Looking at my surrounding to double check where I was and what was in my environment. This looked like a trap, the kind where the fences shut down when you try to escape. Where you needed to fight the main boss, and then you get the key to open the door again, a classic from video games. 'What? Have you looked at my phone?' Ernesto started to move around the room quite quickly and shakily. 'Don't change the fucking subject! You're a fucking liar. Do you think I'm a fucking idiot? Do you think that you're better than me, Aiden? What the fuck are you doing talking with your fucking ex´boyfriend?' I stepped back. 'I didn't know I needed to ask my other ex-boyfriend (you) permission to talk to Marcos. We are not together, Ernesto. I can do whatever I want. The thing that you can't do is invade my privacy and look at my phone. It's mine,' I said, trying not to fall into his poison. 'You just talked shit about him all this time. I've done everything for you, and now you're paying me back like this? Do I have to remind you that we're still living together?' Ernesto spat those words at me like a threat. 'Unfortunately, Ernesto, I just need a couple of weeks to leave this fucking country and get you out of my fucking way. You're nothing but shit to me. Now you're spying on my phone.' I couldn't believe what I was saying. I was confronting his abusive attitude and owning my own power. 'Get me out of your fucking way? You're fucking nothing without me, Aiden, and let me tell you, NO ONE IS GOING TO LOVE YOU LIKE I DO!' Ernesto shouted all those words, grabbing the end of the white curtain and pulling it hard, aggressively, making it fall and hit the floor. 'You don't know what you're doing. You're going to end up alone, did you hear me? A-L-O-N-E!' As soon as he tried to get closer, in shock, I quickly left the room, ran to the stairs, getting away from that psycho as quickly as I could. I couldn't stop looking behind me, checking that he wasn't just about to reach me, hiding in a corner somewhere. I didn't feel safe in my own house, I didn't have enough money to go anywhere, Vanesa or Jenna ignored the fact that I tried to reach them, and I was just trapped in twenty five square meters with a narcissist.

Back to Almere, I was just thinking about all the things that had been happening, the slap in my face, the manipulation, the verbal abuse…

I got to the apartment, feeling cold down to my bones. I didn't wait long to roll a considerable spliff to take the pain away. I wanted to speak with the only person that I knew could help me, my Mum. She answered the phone straight away. 'Hello my darling, it's been a long time, how are you?' It was good to hear her voice. 'Hey Mum, I'm not well, to be honest,' I answered, not sure where to start. 'What happened? I'm here for anything that you need, right?' she replied. 'I can't deal with more of this, Mum. I'm drained. Living here is a nightmare.' As soon as I said it, I knew it was true. I was at the end of my tether. 'Did something happen with Ernesto?' she asked. I wanted to tell her all about the slap, now the curtains, but that would be too much, and I felt unable to talk about it. 'Kind of. It's just such an awful situation, Mum. I know I haven't contacted you, but there's a reason. I'm just so spaced out, so much that I don't even have the emotional energy to reply to your messages. And also, Ernesto's acting insane.' I didn't know how else to put it. 'Darling, I'm sorry to hear that. You should have told me that you were feeling like this! I'm your mother. I knew something was going on, please I want you to count on me. Tell me everything, Aiden. I'm here to help you with anything.' She sounded worried. 'I appreciate it Mum. I don't know how to start, and I'm tired, but do you remember when you were here for Christmas and all the drama with us?' Like she could forget it. 'Yes, did it get worse?' I laughed inwardly. 'Much worse, Mum, it's like being told every day that I'm incapable of anything or him telling me if I feel like this it's because of my past. He gets the medals for being my hero, being with me every day, and rescuing me from the darkness.' It was hard to say but it felt good to be honest about everything finally. 'Is he really saying those things?' I could hear she was shocked. 'Yes, calling me a liar because I didn't clean the house as he expected. I don't know, Mum, sometimes when I try to confront the situation, he makes such a long speech about everything, and I can't answer until he says I'm allowed to. I feel exhausted and drained and when I get my chance to say something, I've completely forgotten what I meant to say,' I sighed. 'Have you spoken about this with the therapist?' I took a second to inhale the smoke from my spliff. 'Yes, and she told me that it looks like he's a narcissist.' Even saying those words out loud felt strange. Could that really be the reason for all of this? Mum paused before answering. 'I know how you feel, Aiden.' It really sounded like she did. 'Why so, Mum?' I'd never heard her talk like this before. 'Because in some way or other, based on what we've been told in the movies and books, we end up in unhealthy relationships with that impossible love, which you think you must stay with, even if it hurts.' It sounded like she was having problems, too. 'You sound sad, Mum. Are you okay?' I asked carefully, not wanting to upset her. 'Ricardo broke with me. I didn't want to tell you anything because I wanted to feel better first.

He left the house as soon as the lockdown started. I've been alone daily, although not alone at all, as I have the dog. She's good company for me. But yes, Aiden. Love is not how society sells it.' She sounded older than I'd heard her sound before. 'Mum, I didn't know. I'm sorry to hear that.' I didn't know what else to say. 'You don't need to be sorry, Aiden. These things happen, and now I want to help you,' she replied, more briskly. 'But you're not here, Mum. How are you going to help me?' I appreciated the gesture but it seemed impossible that she could actually do anything to help when the country was locked down and we were so far apart. 'I've spent months alone, isolating myself in the house. I've had plenty of time to read and listen to a podcast. And now I'm going to share that with you.' I was intrigued. 'What is it, Mum?' I asked. 'There's one therapist who is very famous here in Spain. She's Silvia Congost. She has many books about toxic relationships; you might want to look. I'm going to send you the links. Honestly Aiden, this will help you understand and might be the tool you need to survive until you come here.' I felt a surge of hope. All I had to do was survive until I could go home. 'Honestly, Mum, I'd do anything to survive this situation.' She dropped me seven links to different videos and conferences featuring this therapist. 'I promise everything is going to be all right, Aiden. We are in this together. We may be heartbroken and far away from each other, but we were together.' I wanted to believe it, but it feel like I had a mountain to climb and no energy to do it with. 'And how can I deal with Ernesto? He's driving me crazy, and I don't know what's real.' It was true. I didn't know what to think about anything any more. 'You must stay focused on yourself now. It will be difficult, but you must follow this therapist and listen carefully to her. It is going to be crucial. Once you decide to leave, he will try in all the different ways to make you feel bad or guilty. It's just a trick. And I don't want you to think I'm against him or getting into your relationship. I'm your mother, and I feel your pain, and I'll do whatever it takes to help you, and if that bastard is making you feel like shit, then you're going to have your weapons ready to defend yourself.' She was right. 'I don't have enough words to thank you, Mum. I'm very grateful and feel a bit better after this conversation.' It was true, it had helped a lot. 'You're welcome, darling, and promise me, if you feel sad or poorly, don't wait until you reach this point, you just need to call me. I'll be here any time, 24 hours a day,' she finished. 'I love you, Mum,' I said. 'I love you, Aiden.'

I finished the spliff, and I dropped it in the ashtray. I put my headphones on, and I started to listen to Silvia Congost. Every minute I listened to, I began to understand the kind of relationship I'd been in and how narcissistic people had tried to manipulate me. I felt like all this time was a lie. He was hiding behind a mask of perfection, trying to embarrass me because of my personality and making me doubt my thoughts. I didn't wait for long, and I took the clothes angrily and placed them in the middle of the 'bedroom', making a kind of separation. I took out the air mattress and placed it in the corner of the room. Having my own corner, just for me felt good, even with no walls or doors at all, it didn't matter. I separated our clothes into different drawers. The left side was now mine, the right one his. I was incapable of sleeping one more night with the evil. It was time to make changes. I was not going to tolerate any more shit from him. I organised my space and put the bed sheets on. I changed the password of my laptop and phone.

Then one last thing, the one that I left and hadn't done before. Deleting all the pictures that we had together on Instagram and Facebook. I couldn't fake it anymore. This was the reality. He was an asshole and was treating me like shit. Why would I leave pictures of us smiling and him saying beautiful things on the post? I got rid of all of them. And then, I pressed the block button on his social media profiles. Not even two seconds after I blocked him, I received a message from him.

Ernesto: Aiden! Are you okay? I'm worried about you!

I didn't reply. Three minutes later, he kept going.

Ernesto: Aiden? Why did you block me on social media?

One minute and twenty five seconds after:

Ernesto: Aiden, I think we should talk. You seem poorly, and I'm worried about your mental health. I saw the things that you've been posting. It's the kind of thing that someone depressed posts. I want to help you.

I completely ignored the messages and kept listening to the fantastic therapist on YouTube, empowering myself and recovering my kidnapped self-esteem.

Having a glass of wine, and listening to those videos about toxic relationships for hours, was like a new drug, like the answers I'd been looking for all that time.

I heard the sound of the keys being inserted into the door lock.

Ernesto shows up, worried, with a sad face. ´Aiden darling! What's going on with you? I thought something had happened to you!´ I finished the delicious Rioja I was having and moved my head slowly towards him with a haughty face. ´Are you blind now? Can't you see that I have a glass of wine in my hand and I'm touching my balls on the sofa?´ He placed his uniform on the white leather chair, still showing the marks from where I smashed the stick days ago. ´I thought something happened to you because you've never ignored my messages before, Aiden. Why do you have this attitude toward me?´ I didn't even look at him. I keep drinking, pretending to ignore him. He realised that I moved the things in the room and that I'd made my space five meters away from him. ´What's this? Why have you done this?´ He looked desperate, biting his nails, looking for answers, seeing himself as a filthy piece of shit. ´I haven't done anything, Ernesto. For once in my life, I've been looking for myself.´

CHAPTER 31

The therapist told me that if I had the chance, I should do some outdoor exercise, and she was right. It sounds crazy, but in that hour and a half of running, I was getting further away from Ernesto and from the problems we were having. Listening to some reggaeton helped me to feel more empowered and energetic. Even though I repeated that Wilson Phillips song "Hold on", I felt like the lyric was holding my hand, helping me understand that I was not the only human being feeling trapped. It was easier to complain when I was like that, chained somewhere, in a dark room, with a moist, humid environment, waiting to die. But no: I was just chained in an abusive environment and stuck in my mind.

It felt like liberating myself whenever I stepped out of the house alone. Unfortunately, Ernesto needed to go running as well, at the same time, at the same pace. If I was running, he was just walking behind me, kinda creepy, looking like he was following me. Ernesto touched my arm to get my attention. ´Aiden, Can we talk?´ he asked. I took my headphones off, sighing. It was so annoying. I just wanted him to shut the fuck up. I even wished I was deaf, so I wouldn't have to listen to the voice of that repulsive faggot. ´What do you want, Ernesto?´ He looked to the ground and then at me with those kinds of innocent eyes that an abused dog has. ´I've talked with a therapist, a friend of my friend.´ Therapist? 'Stab me right now', I thought to myself. I bet I would not bleed if someone did. What the fuck was he doing in therapy after all the shit that he talked about it? ´You what?´ I couldn't believe those words. Every day he surprised me more, and not in a good way. ´I know this past months things were difficult between us, but I love you, Aiden. After my conversation with her, I thought I'd be up for having an open relationship with you.´ I stopped in the middle of the street, two minutes away from the house, processing the information from his mouth. ´Open relationship? What are you talking about, Ernesto?´ He stopped chewing on his nails, taking his fingers out of his mouth. ´She told me that she has an open relationship with her partner, and they're perfect together, they have some rules, and that's what I wanted to tell you, that we can be back together. You will be allowed to fuck one guy a month, no more than once, the same person, no one from the past, and of course, not bring them back here.´ I kept walking to get in the house, thinking about his words.´ What do you think, Aiden? Do you want to try it again?´ He asked, looking desperate to get back together. ´I appreciate your 'effort', Ernesto, but it's too late. I'm not interested, and I don't want to be with you.´ Did he think I was fucking insane? Going back to him again after all the shit that I'd had to swallow? One guy per month? Was this an Aliexpress parcel? ´But it's what you wanted, right? To have an open relationship with me.´ He kept digging, as Ernesto couldn't accept the reality of being rejected. ´You said it: that's what I wanted. Past tense. Not anymore.´ I kept thinking about the words of Silvia Congost in my mind, to not fall again into his arms. ´I don't understand why you're so cruel to me.´ He lit a Marlboro cigarette inside the house, leaving the awful smell of it everywhere. I went into the bathroom with my phone. I locked the door, and I checked if I had any messages on Grindr. I knew we were in a lockdown, with no close contact with anyone allowed. But at that point, I didn't give a fuck about anything else anymore. I just wanted to de-stress my mind and get that fucking disgusting narcissist out of my head. I started to have a conversation with a Dutch guy, Jake. He was 35 years old, good body and handsome. After a couple of sentences of discussion, I received a dick picture. I had to say, it was impressive. It was not like I was just seeing him because of that, but it was good to see all the same. I showered myself. I was going to meet this chap at his house. He lived in another town, so I needed to take a train. I left the bathroom with all the vapour expanding around the studio. I tried to be as fast as possible, so I didn't have to start any conversation with Ernesto. 'Do you want to come with me to do some shopping? There's a lot of sales on,' he suggested, trying all the ways he could think of to spend time with me. 'No, thanks. I'm going out alone, but you should go if you want to,' I said while pulling on my grey trackies and blue stamp thrasher hoodie. 'Somewhere? Where are you going?' He was starting to look desperate. 'There's the answer, Ernesto. Somewhere. You don't need to know every step that I take. I'm going for a walk by myself.' He stood up and approached me with his hairless torso. 'Are you going to leave me alone?' So now he swapped roles so he could play the victim. 'I'm not leaving you alone. You said you wanted to go to the shops, and I'm going for a walk.' Suddenly I could feel how his body language changed. He was trying to look confident. 'You know what? I don't need you. I'm going by myself to the shops, and I'm going to have a lot of fun by myself.' I couldn't fake it, and I let out a small laugh just because of how it sounded. 'I'm glad for you, Ernesto. It's excellent to spend quality time with ourselves.' I said, almost escaping from the house as if a murderer were about to kill me. I couldn't deal with more of his shit. I jumped on the train and breathed out, feeling the fabric of the seat as I sat down. The further I went from that house, the freer I felt.

Next stop: Hilversum. Yes, I'd had to travel a bit far, but it wasn't just that I was meeting this Dutch guy from Grindr. It was the experience of being somewhere unknown, far from that abusive bitch. I left the station, and there he was, wearing a grey coat and smiling at me. 'Hello, handsome,' Jake said, looking the same as his pictures. 'It's lovely to meet you,' I said while I gave him proper Spanish kisses – one on each cheek, but he gave me one more, as the Dutch like to give three. 'You too, come this way, my place is very close.' Instantly, he held my hand and pulled me close to him. 'So, how long have you been living here?' I took in the sights of the small town and the quieter neighbourhood, all silent, peaceful, with the good coffee shops surrounding it, but chilled. 'Since October. But my time here is about to finish,' I replied. 'How come?' How should I answer that simple question? Maybe by telling him that I'd been stuck in an abusive relationship with a narcissist who was blaming me for feeling a certain way, even making me forget about who I really was. Not recognising my own self, being lost in the smoke of all joints, as it was the only way that I had to survive it. ´Hahaha, well, let's say that my housemate and I are not having the best time, and I miss my family, so my time here is done,´ I said, decorating my traumatic experience quite well. ´Sharing a house is not the best plan. It can be a total mess. But if you're happy going to your country, you should follow your guts.´ We finally arrived at his house. We went inside through the garage. There was a lot of stuff and two bikes. I passed the door, and there was a toilet and a room on the right side. We went upstairs, and there was a huge living room. With a 60" TV and Dolby surround equipment. With a huge long sofa and a balcony. There was a kitchen on the other side of the room. ´Wow, is this all yours?´ I said, quite impressed. ´Yes,´ he said, smiling at me and winking one eye. ´I'll show you upstairs.´ Wait, there was more? How much money did this guy have? There was another floor with a desk and hundreds of books and picture albums. We went once more to the stairs and finally got there. ´So, this is the last floor, the bathroom, and my bedroom.´ We'd made it to the end of the stairs. ´I'm impressed. I've never seen a house like this.´ Now I thought it was too big for one person. Maybe he had a partner? Was he cheating? There were no pictures of him and another guy at all. I didn't care. I was not there to analyse whether he had a boyfriend. ´Do you want to lay on the sofa and watch something on Netflix?´ Jake suggested with that charming smile. ´Sure.´ We walked back down the hundreds of steps of Rapunzel's castle and found ourselves on the sofa, close to each other. We played a Spanish show on Netflix called "Locked Up" about a prison, women, and lesbians (what a cliché). But the main thing was that I was next to him, and he was cuddling me. I could feel his body heat on my back, touching my arms with the ends of his fingers, my head, and my face. Very tender. I couldn't resist anymore, and I went straight away to his big lips, making close contact with each other. I looked at him, and he looked at me back with his blue eyes and grey beard. I felt the movement of our tongues playing around, getting inside my mouth, making a fusion of our lips together. My underwear started to feel tighter. I took off my hoodie and my T-shirt. He rolled on top of me and let his tongue travel over my nipples. Feeling circling movements and then him licking my armpit. I shuddered. I felt desire, I felt present for once, I don't even remember how long. This was what I deserved. I felt his weight, quite heavy, his long, chubby body. It was perfect. I swapped, and I lay on him. Running my tongue down his neck and biting it, playing around with it while I moved my hand to his underwear. I felt how my penis was lubricating and pressing out of my undies. His cock felt like a massive monster, strong and soft. An indescribable size that was calling me to dry it out. I moved my hand up and down while I kept kissing his mouth. I just felt like my testicles were inflated and on fire. I went down, and I introduced his huge Dutch penis to my mouth. He kept looking at me with desire, but there were no bad intentions. It was like an angel looking at me, giving me protection. I got on top of him, feeling his cock against my perineum and a bit on my ass. I still had my underwear on, but I played with my bottom while feeling his warm tongue playing with mine. I couldn't hold it. My body, the room, and the sofa were getting wet. I felt his cock hitting my spot harder from the outside without even penetrating me. And suddenly, while I was feeling all the petting, I started to shake, exploding in my underwear. I felt how everything was wet, and I saw how my own semen escaped my underwear. I'd just come without even touching myself. It was the best feeling that I'd had in years. ´Sorry, oh my… I just, I don't know, I just got very excited.´ He put his finger on my lips. ´You don't need to. We're having a good time, right?´ Jake said with his lovely voice. Normalising the situation. ´Fuck yes, do you want me to..?´ He laughed and kissed me. ´Don't worry, it's okay. I'd prefer to spoon you.´ And that's what we did. Of course, I sprinted to the shower as I was covered in my own semen. After that quick shower, I went back to Jake, feeling his naked body heat this time on his bedroom, next to mine, embracing me. Made me feel like a home that I'd never had. I just wanted to be there forever, on that mattress like a cloud. ´I'd like to ask you something´ Jake said with curiosity. ´Sure! What would you like to know?´ After the intimacy that we'd had before, I felt more comfortable with him. ´You have sad eyes, Aiden. I know we don't know each other and probably won't see each other again. But if something is going on, you can tell me.´ Jake put his hand on my face, making me feel more protected and cared for than I'd been with Ernesto all those years. ´You're right.´ I add. ´My housemate is my ex-boyfriend. I've been dealing with a lot of shit with him. I didn't realise what kind of person he was until not very long ago. It's been hard. I feel mentally kidnapped by him. Ernesto just made me question everything I do, whether it's right, wrong, or questionable…´ I stopped as I was about to cry and couldn't show that to Jake. No one can ever see me crying. ´It's okay, Aiden. You don't need to tell me more.´ Jake put his lips closer to mine and stayed there a long time. ´We don't know how to deal with these things until we're so deep in it. Covered in shit and accepting abusive behaviours because we think that's love. And love, it's not about that. We accept the abuse because it's hiding behind the mask of love. When we let our guard down, it's the perfect opportunity to change ourselves and destroy ourselves.´ I felt completely understood, listened to and cared for by a guy I met a couple of hours ago. ´Don't worry, I know how you feel confused, but you're on your way, and soon you'll take that power back,´ he said, cuddling me, feeling his sweaty hairy chest touching me. ´Thank you, Jake,´ I said to him, snuggling and kissing him more. After hours and hours of laying in that bed, warm and cosy, I checked my phone.

Ernesto: Aiden, how are you?

Ernesto: Heeeeeey.

Ernesto: Where are you, Aiden?

Ernesto: If you don't reply to me, I'm going to call the police.

I didn't hesitate; I just sent him a selfie of me topless.

Aiden: I'm all right. I'll be there soon.

After 10 seconds, he replied.

Ernesto: Are you in a house? In someone else's fucking place?

Aiden: Yes, Ernesto. A friend's house.

After that, I didn't receive any more messages. It seemed very strange and made me feel worse as if something was going to happen.

´Jake, I need to go.´ I said, quite sad as that magical moment was ending. ´Sure! No worries, I'll take you to the station.´ I got dressed and went to the station with him, holding hands. ´Thank you for today, Jake, I really need it, and I'm not talking about the 'petting', just for being so tender and close with me. I don't remember someone who was that nice to me.´ I said open-hearted, almost sad to leave him.

'You're adorable, Aiden. I enjoyed your company, have a lovely trip back.' After a last kiss, I left that beautiful evening behind. Back to reality, to fucking Almere. I received an email confirming that I could fly back to Spain, and the company was not cancelling the flights. 26th of June. I felt happy and liberated for one moment, but the reality was that this wasn't over. I was still there and needed to wait until then.

After thirty-five minutes, I was back at the house. The street was entirely empty and cold. Ernesto was sitting on the edge of the sofa, smoking another cigarette. The ashtray was full of cigarettes, like a truck driver´s. ´Hey.´ I said, leaving the keys on the table. I felt the stabbing look on his face, looking at me with hate, with anger. ´Hey? You don't have any shame.´ Here we go. ´Because?´ I knew this would happen, so it didn't surprise me. ´You left me fucking alone on a Saturday, on an SAT-UR-D-A-Y. I wanted to go shopping and couldn't because you decided to go somewhere to have a cock. You left me alone. Alone. I couldn't go outside of the house. I've been crying all day because of you. It's your fault.´ The gaslight started to spread into each centimetre of the studio. ´You told me that you didn't need me to go anywhere and were very confident in your words; if you didn't go, it was because you didn't want to, not because of me. You're not disabled. You can walk on your own feet.´ Ernesto took a long slip from a glass of red wine and looked back at me. ´After all, I've done for you, you're disgraceful selfish, arrogant. All of this is because of you, because of your fucking mental health, because you have lost your mind!.´ Ernesto was starting to look like one of those crazy characters in the movies when in the end, they seemed to be the craziest ones. When everything finally makes sense, they act really mentally insane in the film's last fifteen minutes. ´Ernesto, you're crossing the line, stop.´ He stood up from the sofa. ´Now I understand why your Mum is so worried about you. She sends me every fucking day messages telling me how ill you're getting and how strange you're behaving.´ What? My Mum? But if I just talked to her a couple of days ago, what the fuck was this bitch talking about? ´Honestly, I can't wait to return to my fucking house. I can't take more shit from you.´ I could see how his eyes were almost about to pop out of his head. ´Are you going to be like that with me? Now you're going to deal with the real estate agency by yourself. I'm not going to help you with anything. Because apart from lying to me about cleaning the house, you're treating me like shit.´ Like shit? I thought he had completely lost his mind. ´Whatever, Ernesto, just leave me alone.´ I said, placing my spunky underwear in the washing machine and putting a spliff in my mouth. ´By the way, I resigned from the hotel,´ he said, with a Machiavellian face. ´What? Why have you done that?´ He looked at me, smiling. ´Because I'm coming to Spain with you.´

CHAPTER 32

Sometimes, I found it difficult to explain how I felt. How many times did I say, "Yeah, I'm good, thanks", smiling politely, when the truth was that I felt dead inside, like all I could feel was the rottenness of my own soul. Drowned in my anxiety. I even thought I was going crazy, as some days Ernesto looked like a different person. Acting politely, kind and even funny. And on the other days, throwing the abuse and gaslighting me again. All I could hear from him was 'because of you,' 'it's your fault,' 'you're feeling like this because of your past,' 'you're crazy,' 'you, you, you.' How funny it looks when you find yourself in the mouth of the wolf, thinking that it's a safe space where you can be yourself, attracted by the sweet honey and caramel smell and realising too late that you are trapped. Ernesto was going back to Spain as well. I couldn't understand it. He had a contract in the hotel until December, he could just move to a shared house, and that was it. Why was he going back to San Fernando? There were no jobs; if you found one, they paid you miserably; really shit money. Was he coming back thinking that he might have another chance with me? Whatever it was, I'd decided, and if I was leaving, it was to leave all that shit behind. I didn't realise how many clothes I had, as I needed to prepare my luggage, I needed to get everything in. To my 'surprise', it didn't fit. Why in the fucking hell had I thought that I was going to be good here: why had I brought all my stuff? 'It doesn't matter,' I thought to myself.

It's just material things, and thinking about Marie Kondo, I started to put all the things I didn't really need in a bin: shoes, T-shirts, hoodies. It was unbelievable how many things I put in that bag, including my emotions. Hopefully it might all be helpful for someone else. Ernesto was smoking a cigarette on the sofa, pretending we didn't have to leave the apartment in two days. I went downstairs to drop the bag of clothes and empty dreams close to the bin. ´Ernesto, can you help me, please? There are many things to do, and there's not much time.´ He finished the cigarette and put it out in the ashtray. ´Don't worry, Aiden, there's plenty of time, don't you see?´ he said calmly, with second thoughts behind those psycho eyes. ´Enough time? Have you forgotten that we need to have it all done in two days? You haven't even started to pack your luggage.´ I said, reaching the edge of my patience, as I wasn't sure if he was trying to make me lose my shit with that 'I don't give a shit' attitude. ´I heard you, and as I said, that's how it will be. When I feel like it, then I'll start to prepare things.´ I couldn't believe it, althought of course, yes, I could: he was inciting me to get angry and shout at him, he was too calm, and I knew behind all that calm, there was a Machiavellian game. ´Don't worry then. I'm going to do my part. You let me know when you want to prepare the rest together.´ Yes, together, as I was not going to clean the studio, paint the walls and everything else. But I wasn't in the mood to argue. It wasn't worth it. I didn't have much energy, and the limited amount I had I wanted to use to survive two more days with that motherfucker.

Later on that day, we went to Amstelpark to meet the girls and say goodbye to them. It was sunny, even hot enough to just wear a T-shirt.. Many families were having picnics with their perfect blonde, white children playing around. It was a massive park with plenty of trees that helped to shadow the hottest areas. We'd met in the park, next to the fountain, where the swans had the best life. Jacobo didn't come. In fact, since his birthday, everything had gone a bit weird, and he barely spoke to us.

As soon as we reached the girls and gave them a hug, we dropped our stuff on the grass, and I sat between Vanesa and Fernanda, taking a cold beer from the portable fridge. ´I really need to wee, guys. Anyone else want to come?´ I took my chance and went with the girls to have a wee. Vanesa, Jenna and Fernanda were squatting, watering the grass. ´Girls, I broke up with Ernesto three months ago.´ I finally said. ´I knew it!´ Vanesa said, jumping to pull her trousers up. ´But I'm confused. Ernesto said that you both were good and had a lovely time together.´ Poor Fernanda was so innocent that she believed Ernesto's words. ´He lied. I didn't tell you anything before because he didn't let me, he told me that you were not our friends, and I couldn't trust any of you,' I said because even if I don't see them ever again, I couldn't leave the country pretending that Ernesto was the best example of the perfect, caring boyfriend. ´I'm surprised, but then not at all,´ added Jenna. ´How come?´ Fernanda and Vanesa looked at Jenna. ´Because, first, Aiden deleted all the pictures from Instagram, and second, you just need to look at Ernesto's face and body language when Aiden asked questions about relationships. ´I don't even know what to say,´ Fernanda said, almost like when a child discovers that Santa doesn't exist. ´You don't need to say anything. You can be his friend but don't tell him anything about this.´ We went back out there, and Ernesto was talking with Ignacio about his next plan. Ignacio was going back to his country to disconnect his mind and be with his family. Suddenly Lucciano showed up with a pack of four Amstel beers. ´Lucciano!´ I said, standing up and running to hug him. ´Ciao, Aiden! It's lovely to see you,´ he said while we were hugging each other. Lucciano smells so lovely. He was wearing Molton Brown Tobacco Absolute fragrance. Ernesto fixed his eyes towards us, while he was talking to Ignacio. ´I hear that you're leaving for Spain.´ Lucciano said, kind of as if he were sorry about it. ´Yes, it's time to finish this fucking chapter.´ I said quite loudly while we sat on the wet grass. Everything went well until Ernesto swapped his place and sat beside me. ´Honestly, I don't understand. That girl just ghosted me. After all this time together, she disappeared from my life without saying anything.´ We were all paying attention to Fernanda until Ernesto started to lay on me, putting his hands on my legs and trying to look like the perfect (ex)boyfriend. My heart started to rush as if someone were strangling it so hard with thousand needles. I tried to get over it without any drama, but he kept pretending to be tender with me in front of the group. I could feel how Jenna, Vanesa and Fernanda were looking at us and then at each other, talking with their eyes, confused and waiting to talk about it later. ´You stop now!´ I said to Ernesto, whispering hard in his ear, moving away from his body and arm. His face changed completely, and suddenly he went to the portable freezer, and grabbed a beer, and started to laugh harder. What a fucking psycho bitch. I had a bit of dance with the girls, and then it was time to go.

We all said how soon we would meet and how much we loved each other and what amazing friends we were, and blah blah. Always the same shit. That was not true because I'd been alone all that time, I was suffering through that situation, and everyone was busy with their shit. We all have problems, but you can make a small space for a friend. ´Aiden, it was a pleasure to work with you. You're a lovely guy. I wish you all the best,´ Lucciano said, shaking my hand and smiling at me.

We left them all behind, knowing I would never see them again. But I didn't care because I knew my purpose, and now my focus was elsewhere. Ernesto went quiet for 20 minutes. ´I can't believe you did that, Aiden.´ I took a breath, exhaling deeply, like a balloon. ´Did what? Don't start again.´ Ernesto needed to say how he felt. Playing the victim and making me the villain. ´Did you see how bad you treated me in front of everyone? They're not stupid, Aiden. They're going to know,´ he said, expecting to keep that lie safe, to show everyone his perfect status. ´They know already. I told them about it when we went for a wee. I couldn't lie more for you.´ He started to shake his head, trying to find the proper answer. ´HOW COULD YOU DO THAT? I HAVE ANXIETY. LOOK HOW BAD ARE YOU TREATING ME!´ he shouted on the train. Some people turned around to have a look at what was happening. Being with people like Ernesto is like being inside American Horror story: Asylum. ´Honestly, Ernesto. You're full of shit, anxiety? my fucking ass.´ He kept complaining the whole way back, talking loudly and dramatically about how much pain he had inside his chest because of me.

As soon as we got back to the studio and while he was drank a glass of red wine the size of my head, I started cleaning with my headphones on in case he wanted to speak. Ignoring him was the best decision for my mental health.

While I was cleaning the wardrobe, I found a letter. It was the letter I wrote him after all the shit that had happened on my birthday. I snuck inside the bathroom, and I opened it to read it.

CHAPTER 33

Dear Ernesto

I´m writing you this letter to explain why I behaved so severely the other day. You deserve an explanation, and I want to be open about everything so you can understand how bad things have been and how I´ve been feeling.

I know I always act like I have it all together, but I realise now that I don´t. I´m starting to see that I have this dark side that stops me from appreciating the good things in my life and makes me lash out and hurt the people who love me the most. I misbehaved, and I wish I wasn´t such a toxic person. The other day I should have been enjoying myself with you and my Mum at the musical, but I made a drama of everything instead. I wish I had behaved better so that we could have done everything we planned together, like taking photos and having fun. I feel so ashamed about how cruel I was to you, and I can only hope you can forgive me in your heart.

Please know that you are the most patient person I´ve ever met. I´m so grateful for everything you´ve given me, for being so sweet and smiling, even when I make things complicated. You love me unconditionally, and I know I haven´t shown you the love you deserve.

You´ve given me so much happiness, and I can only hope you will give me another chance to make you happy too.

I love you.

Aiden

I dropped the letter to the floor in shock. My body started to shake, and suddenly I had a flashback of everything, of all those months, every single argument. The moment I fainted in the bar when, instead of helping me, he treated me like shit. I ultimately accepted a considerable amount of subtle abusive behaviour, and with that letter, I surrendered myself to his control. I was totally blinded by my low self-esteem. Everything he told me to do was for my own good because he loved me, but that was far from reality. As soon as I recognised that he was a god and I was a mess, I permitted him to do whatever he wanted with me and he treated me as if I was a piece of shit.

The day finally came. We woke up at 5:00 a.m. because he didn´t want to clean until the day of the flight. But I didn´t care. I was exhausted, but the only thing I could think of was taking that plane. Hour after hour, putting every single item of the house in the bin, cleaning the oven, each corner of the fridge, and the toilet. Everything. I just wanted to run away from that house, even though it meant that we lost that 1000€ from the deposit because we'd broken the contract. I didn´t care. When you're in that kind of situation, that drains every single piece of your dignity and own being, you don't care about the money or the material things. You just want to put your heart back together. ´Well, I think this is it,´ Ernesto said, dropping the plastic gloves he'd been wearing in the black bin bag. ´Let me take a video of everything, in case these motherfuckers want to get more money from us.´ I spent 10 minutes recording every single centimetre of that small place that had been my submissive cell, the own hell where I lost myself. 25 square meters, and all I could see was pain, suffering and abuse. I put the keys in the kitchen and didn´t look back. I dropped all the luggage in the lift wanting to run away as quickly as possible from this country. Usually, I´d say goodbye to a place, but not this time. I just wanted to be back there, in Spain. I didn´t felt any kind of sadness or attachment to that studio. Actually, I felt repulsed as all my memories there were absolutely disgusting.

On the way to the airport, I remembered how difficult it had been to deal with that situation. The amount of money I´d spent on weed, the tears that couldn´t free themself and got stuck in the wounds of my heart. All the fake 'I love you's' that actually meant 'I´m going to make you think that I love you, to fuck up your head and make you believe that you´re going crazy.'

The airport was full of security and health control, and people with face masks were everywhere.

It was funny how much I thought I loved Ernesto. Still, I depended emotionally on him, giving him the knife to stab my heart as many times as he wanted. I wondered if the thing was that sometimes you needed to be in a dark place so that you could find your way out: maybe that was what it took to finally build self-respect. And then you could slowly and carefully follow the tiny light back to freedom.

Ernesto tried to make conversation, but I ignored him. I wanted to close my eyes and arrive in Sevilla immediately. I dropped a message to Marcos, I didn´t have data, but he would receive it as soon as I arrived.

@Aiden99: Hey, handsome, good news. I´m home.

Waiting in the queue for people to be checked for COVID was annoying, but as soon as I got through that, I passed the doors, and there she was. My Mum waiting for me, with a face mask on. We ran into each other and started to cry, embracing as if we´d been apart for centuries. 'Mum, I´ve missed you so much.' I told her, about to cry out all the sadness I'd had to keep in my heart. 'Everything is going to be alright, Aiden. You´re home.' Carmen was with Ernesto. They were on their own family thing, I gave her a polite hug, as it wasn´t her fault for having a psychopath for her son, and we walked together to the airport parking. ´We have to go this way.´ Ernesto moved his body towards me and gave me a hug. ´I love you, Aiden. Never forget about it.´ I stepped back, feeling massively sick in my stomach hearing those words. ´Take care of yourself, Ernesto.´ And finally, we left each other, walking off in different directions.

I got into my Mum´s white Polo car, and as soon as she started to drive, I opened the window and felt it for the first time in ages. Breathing, I was home. I was finally free. Freedom was the only word that I had on my mind. I didn´t know that I was free from Ernesto, but not from my mind. Things were about to get even worse than I could imagine.

THE END…?

ABOUT THE AUTHOR

Yurell Benítez Borrego was born in Algeciras (Cádiz) back in December of 1999. Since he was a child Yurell was always interested in doing something different and unique. After he finished his hospitality studies, he decided to embark on new adventures throughout Europe. Life was full of surprises for him and after experiencing problems in his relationships, he wrote his very first book called "People Like You". This book was his way of telling a story about the problem of toxicity and selfishness in the world of relationships. He's very proud of writing such a compelling story without any previous experience

Printed in Great Britain
by Amazon